The Coconut Children by **Vivian Pham**

Life in the troubled neighbourhood of Cabramatta demands too much too young. But Sonny wouldn't really know.

Watching the world from her bedroom window, she exists only in second-hand romance novels and falls for any fast-food employee who happens to spare her a glance.

Everything changes with the return of Vince, a boy who became a legend after he was hauled away in handcuffs. Sonny and Vince used to be childhood friends. But with all that happened in-between, childhood seems so long ago. It will take two years of juvie, an inebriated grandmother and an unexpected discovery for them to meet again.

The Coconut Children is an urgent, moving and wise debut from a young and gifted storyteller.

T0363596

Praise for *The Coconut Children*

'Pham's non-judgmental portraits of parents living with trauma and children struggling to comprehend their parents' choices is nuanced and wise; work one would expect from a writer far beyond Pham's very young years. Each of us eagerly await the future development of this remarkable new voice and firework of a talent.' – Judges, Best Young Australian Novelist, *Sydney Morning Herald*

'*The Coconut Children* is rich and incredible, and unmistakeably wholly formed. Reading new author Vivian Pham's work is like discovering a pack of perfectly ripened strawberries and a bottle of beer at the back of the fridge. It's unlikely, it doesn't happen often, and when it does, you just have to embrace the whole experience. Reading Pham is like reading a young Salman Rushdie or a Zadie Smith. Her inventiveness with language and her keen read on the strata of society make *The Coconut Children* essential reading.' – *Overland*

'It's rare that a debut novel is so brazenly confident it swaggers but Vivian Pham's *The Coconut Children* is one such book. Set in Cabramatta in the late 1990s, it's an impressive synthesis of place and character, and the dialogue and set pieces between teenage sweethearts Sonny Vuong and Vincent Tran crackle with energy. In this pocket of western Sydney beset with poverty and its concomitant bedfellows, crime and violence, Pham draws deep from her own experiences, but the book is also adorned with poetic flourishes and irradiated with humour and warmth. Full of colour and detail and written with the bravura of adolescence that young Pham herself has barely left behind, *The Coconut Children* marks a new literary talent.' – Thuy On, *Australian*, Books of the Year

'You'd have to go back to Carson McCullers's debut to find such an accomplished and original voice in a writer so young. I've seen Vivian Pham stun an audience of 2000 with her oratory and original thinking on colonialism and the burden of history, and now she stuns on the page in this deeply felt and intimate coming-of-age novel. She shows a new Australia here, tied to her place and time but touching on universal themes of longing – and the alternately profound and ludicrous angst of youth. Vivian Pham is one of the indispensable voices of her generation.' – Dave Eggers

'This is an outstanding debut about love, memory, community and finding your place in a beautiful and heartbreaking world. Pham is a master at showing that all people are complex, contradictory and difficult to define. The characters in *The Coconut Children* will linger on in your mind like a great open-ended question.' – Felicity Castagna

'In lyric slivers as sharp as the "blade of water" refugees cross in the novel's preface, Pham maps the shape and grain of fierce and fragile resilience against intergenerational trauma, secrets and desire. The momentum of this novel, its originality, energy and verve, are extraordinary. Vivian Pham is, without doubt, a major new talent.' – Felicity Plunkett

'To read Vivian Pham is to read the future of Australian writing. What a brilliant, self-contained bolt of pure teenage genius. Be prepared to be awed over what Gen Z can deliver.' – Benjamin Law

'You can smell and taste this book – a vivid picture of Cabramatta in all its late millennium glory and grit. Vivian Pham goes straight to the important things in life – food, family, friendship, freedom, sex, love and death. The writing is full of grace and courage – fierce, frank and funny. And the tale keeps twisting 'til the end.' – Paul Kelly

'*The Coconut Children* is an incredible achievement. Pham writes with a poetic intensity and maturity that belies her young age. Pham delivers a frank insight into the complicated lives of these endearing characters and weaves plenty of humour throughout. An amazing debut!' – *Good Reading Magazine*

'An emotional, hilarious treasure, holding the wisdom and wicked humour of a gnarled old woman.' – Stephanie Wood, *Good Weekend*

'*The Coconut Children* is an all time, new favourite read for me. I was reminded of *Looking for Alibrandi,* but with more metaphors. Pham is a fabulous Vietnamese-Australian author who writes in an authentic voice that, quite honestly, you probably haven't heard before. That alone is reason enough to give it a go, but it's also well written, with a story that keeps you captivated the whole way through.' – Buzzfeed

'The novel sensitively depicts the impacts of drug use, domestic violence and sexual trauma – the aftershocks of surviving the American/Vietnam War. Pham conveys just enough detail to bear witness; the brutality surrounding and within these families is not spectacle but a cold fact of life. Lush and lyrical, irreverent yet poignant, Pham's prose crackles with energy. *The Coconut Children* is an effervescent debut filled with vivid characters, where a single gesture, a single look, encapsulates a world.' – Shu-Ling Chua, *Saturday Paper*

'For all its darkness and violence, the novel is graced with humour, vivid characterisation and an unerring sense of place and time. Pham juxtaposes surprisingly delicate moments amid the grit: bright respite, like the straggling flowers on the rail embankments that catch Sonny's eye, or the tender Vietnamese ballads of loss sung at karaoke by Vincent's rag-tag posse. *The Coconut Children* is about having second and third chances, about a defiance of hereditary malaise and a reminder, too, that "sometimes, having hope is as simple as letting yourself forget who you've been before".' – Thuy On, *Sydney Morning Herald*

'Brilliant, evocative and powerful, written with a distinctly new voice.' – *Sun Herald*

'A deeply affecting coming-of-age story. Pham adroitly evokes the emblems of suburban living, specifically Cabramatta. There is a meticulous level of detail in every sentence, elevating the ordinary into the sublime and imbuing the narrative with a magical quality. *The Coconut Children* is a book about what it is like to navigate a world that's not made for you, but it retains levity and a crucial sense of hope throughout.' – Sonia Nair, *Australian Book Review*

'While Pham's tale starts slowly and simply, it builds into a moving and emotionally gripping story that has the reader desperate for a happily ever after ending for Sonny and Vince.' – *Herald Sun*

'Along comes Vivian Pham, the 19-year-old daughter of a Vietnamese refugee, with a debut novel so searingly beautiful that any cynicism about the telling of trauma is forced to take a back seat. Her unlikely teenage love story, set on the hard-scrabble streets of 1990s Cabramatta, is so tightly embroidered with lyrical observations, I stopped marking passages that snagged my breath. Open the novel randomly and they fall into your lap. But a gift with words is only one tool in Pham's skill set. What gives this novel real power is her adept construction of her narrative; the exquisite descriptions captivate just long enough for the plot to sidle up and deliver a brutal gut punch.' – Christine Jackman, *Australian*

THE
COCONUT
CHILDREN

vivian pham

PENGUIN BOOKS

UK | USA | Canada | Ireland | Australia
India | New Zealand | South Africa | China

Penguin Books is part of the Penguin Random House group of companies whose
addresses can be found at global.penguinrandomhouse.com

First published by Vintage in 2020
This edition published by Penguin Books in 2021
Copyright © Vivian Pham, 2020

Cover illustration by Mikhail Bogdanov/Getty Images
Cover design by Alex Ross © Penguin Random House Australia Pty Ltd
Typeset in Minion Pro by Midland Typesetters, Australia

Printed and bound in Australia by Griffin Press, part of Ovato, an accredited
ISO AS/NZS 14001 Environmental Management Systems printer

A catalogue record for this
book is available from the
National Library of Australia

ISBN 978 1 76104 599 8

penguin.com.au

To Ba and Mẹ, the reasons I wrote this.

To Daniel, the editor of my thoughts.

To Na, my muse. I am who I am
because I want to be who you are.

Love,
Wii

'I certainly don't feel as if I am burning in hell.'
– IKYUU

'I simply wondered about the dead because their days had ended and I did not know how I would get through mine.'
– JAMES BALDWIN

Prologue

The Ripple Said to the Tsunami

The full moon floats in the night sky like a cataract. Heaven has turned a blind eye to the boat people. But you see everything, don't you? There, a tiny fishing boat carrying two hundred too many, bodies suspended over a blade of water. This is where myth and memory meet. Where history comes to daydream, immortalised in ink, mortalised in minds.

He is calling out to you, *ông bà tô tiên*. Ancestors. Here he sits, beneath entangled limbs and destinies. My father. Your son. You have watched him grow up from thumb-sucking infant to bullet-biting boy. You know him well; he does not disturb you from your resting place without good reason. He has only ever uttered your names in prayer to offer the harvest's first fruits, but he summons you now because a baby died last night, too young to know the taste of his mother's milk. Lowered over the side of the boat and all watched in a doomed silence, half-hoping the water would wrap itself around the newborn dead like a blanket, or that the infant would learn to swim in the last seconds.

Silence is another kind of drowning. There were the pirates, too, with cunning smiles that stretch whole horizons and machetes spoiled by saltwater rust, who stole generations of gold and all the pretty girls. Look at your son, the inheritor of your sun-soaked skin. The rest of the world may forget your death but he is the only evidence you ever lived.

Ancestors, I have heard stories about you. You and I are two kinds of spirits. My father has not even imagined my coming. I am two decades away. I am mist unborn, a gathering of dew drops, a thousand tricks of light not yet pricked with blood. Yours is an earthbound body that disobeys gravestones. Your disarrayed bones each have a mind of their own. You miss your missing limbs. Your hand writes love letters to you. Your spirit is steeped in enough suffering to last eternity. You are acquainted enough with death to keep it running other errands.

Won't you give him a blessing? Just enough to blow the boat on its way a little quicker. Perhaps some spare, to keep in his pocket for the next journey.

My father thinks about the bombs and baby blossoms dropping all around the world. That old poem comes to mind. The one written by a miserable leper who wanted someone to love but could never bear being seen.

Who wants to buy the moon? I'll sell it to you.

O, to be young and dirt poor, thinking that the world belongs to you. Turns out to be almost true.

Chapter 1

Morning Glory

On the day of Vince's release, you could hear his laughter thundering through the entire neighbourhood. It was February 1998. The centre of summer. The timbre of his voice shook the trees and rumbled through the streets, tearing through the delicate seams of silence. He was with his posse of old friends, the type of kids that carry knives in their back pockets. Maybe it was a trick of the light but it was almost as if he had never left – there was Vince, sipping on his sugarcane juice. There was Vince, with his gleaming gold necklace, the jade Buddha nestled contentedly between his newly defined pectorals. There was Vince, with his sunny smile and over-gelled hair, lying in the Woolworths trolley as somebody less important pushed him along. There was Vince, never less than vibrant, always pulsating, always looking as though he was about to break out of his own body.

He leant his head against the back of the trolley and looked up. As though the sky were an upside-down valley of fine powders, he sucked in a violent breath and closed his eyes to ecstasy.

'The air smell different?' his friends asked, amused. They watched how his face, once young and boyish, caught hold of the light, how it transformed again and again with every ripple of sunshine, as if to resist its own identity. What kind of secrets did the past two years hold?

Vince's body rocked to and fro against the rattling trolley cart which rushed into gusts of air. He smelled the cooking that seeped from the houses and the stench of soiled mattresses on the curb.

'Nah,' he said finally. 'Smells like home.'

Everybody was his friend. The stray cats with swollen eyes purred as he tossed them fried chicken. The Bible-swinging madman on the street corner, Vince smiled at him too. There was no pity in his eyes as he watched the man preach the Book of Revelation to a gathering of pigeons; he was so unlike the other passers-by who scowled and lowered their gaze. Even the sun reached down from its interstellar home to touch Vince's skin and beam into his eyes, saying, *Look at me, look at me.*

Cabramatta welcomed her son back with quiet rejoice. The sidewalk trees, which usually surrendered under the battlements of dusty brown apartment buildings, seemed to straighten their spines. Further up the street, front yards spilled with offerings to him. Those who lived in their own houses took advantage of every inch of property that bore their name. In their gardens, they planted massive lime, dragon fruit and mango trees. Families boasted bathtubs of fish mint, coriander and sawtooth herbs and draped luscious winter melons on hardwood arbours. While their neighbours were cultivating personal rainforests, the apartment dwellers chafed within the confines of old bricks and concrete slabs. Some were fortunate enough to enjoy garden views from their balconies, but those who lived in units which faced inwards could only stare miserably into each other's eyes as they hung their laundry out to dry.

The trolley-cart came to a halt and Vince jumped out. He crept into a garden and stared in awe under the dappled shade of a mango tree. He intended to only take the lone fruit that had fallen on the grass, but the others hung lowly on the branches blushed before him, draping the sunshine over their voluptuous figures, beckoning. He tore the two chubbiest mangoes from the tree, scooped the mushy one up from the ground and hopped back into the trolley. After prying apart the golden skin, he drank from its gently fermenting flesh. Then he whipped out his pocket knife and carved into the others. (He only ever used this blade for stolen homegrown fruits. In times of combat, he was imaginative with his choice of weaponry – he knew, for example, that the handle bar of the trolley cart he was riding in encased a usefully weighty pole.) Vince grinned as he offered slices to his friends, his mouth and fingers dripping with sap and syrup.

Mothers stood vigilantly, perched atop their apartment balconies like hawks. Across the neighbourhood, little boys set down their Pokémon cards and peered through the blinds, silently praying for a miracle: to grow up as big and strong as the neighbourhood menace. The glossy lips of prepubescent girls breathed life back into his name. Vince. The legend was alive and let loose on the street.

'He's gotten bigger, taller. I heard all he's been doing in there is training.'

'What got him in there in the first place?'

'Who's he coming for now?'

'Look at his arms!'

3

Sonny watched from her bedroom window. Held her breath and the windowsill for dear life. For her, Vince's return was something like a crack of light entering a prison cell. Since he had been taken away, it seemed a mist had settled over Cabramatta and their suburb had gone to sleep. The world was only awake when Vince was there to see it.

Now he was back. Wearing the same t-shirt he had left in, his back muscles rippling under the translucence of worn cotton, a few small holes revealing more intimate areas of skin, by courtesy of some peckish moths. And as Sonny watched him laugh with his mouth wide open and his neck craned as if in defiance of the sun, she tried to figure out what exactly this could mean for her. She hoped that maybe he would catch her eye and stop mucking around for one second, hold her gaze and make some kind of telepathic promise. Like: You look beautiful, I'm going to rescue you from your crazy mother. But of course, she wasn't in his line of sight and he was too concerned with pulverising glass bottles as he raced down the footpath to notice her anguish. Besides, she wasn't even sure if he remembered who she was. Sonny receded from the window, relieved she couldn't be seen like this. Framed by glass. Stuck in her bedroom. Soiled by the unspeakable.

The procession passed. He was gone. How careless he was, to leave a girl wanting to slow dance with his shadow and not even stopping to ask for her hand. Sonny had trouble falling asleep that night. She tossed and turned, conjured up all sorts of fantasies. See: Sonny walking along a crowded street, skipping and giggling with the incandescence of a little girl, Vince's arm easy over her shoulders. When she woke up, she thought to herself, *Shit, this isn't how I was raised – to aspire to be under the arm of a boy, and a street boy at that!* The kind that sold stolen car parts as a hobby and had developed a stomach for alcohol ever since he was twelve, the kind of street boy who, if you stripped him of his hair gel and booming voice, probably resembled some kind of mangled cat.

Was Vince the only one that had entered her heart? It was true that in the last couple of years, she had fallen in love with practically every male creature to have ventured within a five-metre radius of her. The KFC employee with bright green braces, who gave her a look of tender understanding when she had confessed to him her deepest desire: six Wicked Wings and a regular coleslaw. The curly-haired boy whom she'd witnessed help an elderly man with his groceries up a broken escalator. This one had a special place in her heart. She carefully memorised his facial features and body measurements, had kept the image of him in her mental depository for over a year now. Revisited him every so often to freshen him up and keep him from fading into a shadow. Whipped him out on a rainy day.

But by far Sonny's most serious commitment to date was to her Chemistry teacher. Mr Baker had a wispy tuft of hair left on his head, a protruding stomach and an odd nasal voice. In spite of these minor deformities, her nonexistent contact with boys her own age translated into acquiring a taste for older, wiser, physically unattractive men.

She pined for the 75 minutes of class with him three times a week, during which he called out *her name* for the roll. She would have to mentally prep herself, clear her throat and chant a mantra or two before the crucial moment. She never answered straight away, always waited for him to look up and scan the room before she said 'Here' and he found her. Ah yes, that little twinkle in his eyes, that slightly lifted brow, that look of bemusement, curiosity, perhaps even desire. Here was ample material to mull over when she was alone, making Mr Baker a convenient target for the violent ammunition of her love thoughts. In her mind, their affair was so artfully conspired that they had managed to keep it a secret even from reality.

As Sonny prepared breakfast, she listened to the eggs on the skillet, singing to her soul in spits and sputters. How did Vince like his eggs? Breakfast in juvenile detention centres couldn't have just been out of a can. The hospitality there must be Michelin-starred – after all, as far as she could tell, the two-year stay had worked wonders on Vince. It had nursed his metamorphosis. There, he'd grown out of his larval stage and taken the form of an ultramasculine butterfly, boasting a chiselled jaw, eyebrows blackened and as sharp as swords, and that same winning smile. He had grown much taller too, and he looked hard and firm all over. The topography of his body was so vast, you'd dream of hiking the famous Deltoid Highlands, Trapezius Valley and Abdominal Alps. Even the colour of his skin testified to his good health. The sun might have blasted you with freckles and turned you red, but Vince soaked up all that light and emitted it in shades of caramel candy. Of course, she'd only seen him ride past her house, caught a glimpse of him reclining in his chariot, his hair too stiff to catch the wind. Sonny needed much more time to study his subtleties, his finer details. But the mere thought of him made her head spin, and her heart feel like a simile – a psyche-delic experience that she'd felt only once before, when listening to the second verse of her favourite Backstreet Boys song and hearing *It seems like we're meant to be.*

Eventually getting a grip on reality, Sonny glanced at the clock and realised it was almost time for school. She rushed to the bedroom she shared with her little brother and grandmother. *Bà ngoại* was sleeping soundly in her separate bed. When she wasn't drunk, she looked like an off-duty guardian angel. Oscar

6

lay on the bottom bunk bed. He was so lost in his thoughts he didn't even notice her come in.

'Morning,' Sonny said brightly. 'Break any bones in your sleep?'

'Not this time,' he mumbled, rising slowly and easing his feet onto the ground.

'That's got to be a good sign for your first day. Come on, we're gonna be late.'

Oscar nodded and tugged the corners of his mouth into a quick smile. It took eight steps to reach the kitchen. He sat down and had his eggs, patiently waiting for Sonny to go and have her morning puff – of her asthma inhaler – so he could pour his glass of milk down the sink. He hated the way the heavy liquid slid down his throat, and, even more so, his sister's empty promises of its supposed magical bone-strengthening properties. He was convinced he'd been conned his whole life by dairy farmers.

To say that he was nervous about his first day of high school would be the world's biggest understatement. Unlike most loner kids, poor Oscar didn't even have the luxury of fantasising about who he could become in high school. Could he be the class clown? The sports star? The surly but sensitive poet that girls secretly swooned over? No, the label he'd be stuck with was the same one branded onto his forehead the very day he'd entered this world: the kid with that bone condition.

He had long before prophesied his high school experience, the images flashing through his mind with brutal clarity. See: a whole cohort of rowdy boys playing pranks on teachers, drawing penises on any surface with permanent marker, dangling each other's backpacks above the train rails, throwing footballs to one another across the corridor. Amidst this ruckus, cut to Oscar, staring into his locker until it no longer seemed sensible, surrounded by people but painfully alone, scraping his crackers in some cheese dip.

The doctors called it 'low bone density' but he called it a family curse. It meant his bones were so fragile a careless shove could cause fractures on impact, or that was what his mother said, anyway. Put him in the nearest public school with the roughest teenage boys to ever make it past Year 6 and you'd better have the ambulance on speed dial.

Forget broken homes, these boys were raised in the midst of hurricanes, moulded by chaos, breastfed by wild boars, it seemed. While other boys his age were worried about the pungency of their deodorant and making the cut for the basketball team, Oscar's mind was chiefly occupied by low-risk strategies of manoeuvring through crowds. With his entrance into high school, he tried to ditch the negative mindset and instead adopt a more practical methodology. The plan was simple: find a group of gentle-looking boys and stick to them like glue. Look for the kids with cowlicks and their lunches packed with neatly cut carrot sticks. Learning disability kids were the only ones with any humanity; this was a maxim that still rang true throughout the years.

After Sonny had finished preparing their sandwiches and Oscar had brushed his teeth, they both changed into their uniforms and began to make their way to school. They left their mother's sound snores and locked the front door, skipped down the two creaky wooden steps and concrete path. It was warmer outside. A sleeping cat on the other side of the road seemed to be in agreement with the weather. The sun was low and lustrous, casting morning glory on all of Cabramatta.

'Break a leg!' Sonny called. She stood at the gate of the Boys' School and waved.

He glanced back at her over his shoulder. Gave a half-hearted smile. Proceeded along his path. She stood for a short while to watch him walk into the school building. Every time a

8

bigger boy came close to her skeleton of a brother, her stomach lurched.

She started down the opposite side of the street towards the Girls' School and stopped to admire a bunch of freesias that bloomed from the embankment, on the other side of the fence. Year 11 was a milestone, the crucial time when the girls traded in their slouchy chequered dresses for skirts – skirts! It made a whole world of difference – you could customise the exact amount of leg you wanted to showcase and enjoy a complimentary breeze to air out your clammy thighs. More than anything, it was a clear signal to the rest of her school that Sonny was older, a senior, and therefore of a more respectable status, a critical detail that was often overlooked due to her short stature. With this skirt in hand, she thought, she'd no longer fear being mistaken for a Year 7 and being simply bypassed in the canteen line. With this skirt, she'd no longer have teachers asking her 'Are you lost?' in hallways. This was her ticket to maturity; she was convinced the immutable sovereignty of the school skirt would take her from where her half-assed growth spurt had left off.

Past the school gates, Sonny spotted her best friend, Najma, sitting on the silver seat that faced the basketball court. This was their first meeting since the beginning of the school holidays last year. The two embraced in a clumsy hug and settled into their usual routine. They sat side by side, absorbed in in-depth commentaries about the people that walked past them.

On Cheyanne, a volleyball player who never spoke to anyone and put her head down to sleep in every class: 'She's so pretty but . . . I mean there's nothing bad about her, but there's nothing good either. She doesn't *do* anything.'

'I don't know, I find her pretty *mysterious*.'

'Or just hungover.'

9

On a girl who insisted on being called Felix, with sharp, pixie features and the sides of her head shaved. She had recently become a drummer for a garage band: 'I see a lot of potential in her – the shaved hair is really doin' it for me.'

'Man, I just wish she was taller. Bigger.'

'Force her to take testosterone pills. Pay for her hormone therapy.'

'This is not what my parents expected when they put me in an all-girls school.'

On Mr Vongratsavai, a young geography teacher with weird ears that were trying to divorce themselves from the sides of his head, but broad shoulders and a self-assured fashion sense nonetheless: 'Oh my God, did you just see that?'

'Mr Vongratsavai?'

'Yes. He's so tall – when he walked past, his shadow was *all over* me.'

The Girls' School was humming its hysteria. Not only because everyone was eager to speculate about which teachers they would have for their subjects this year, or to state, for public record, that the belly-button piercing they'd gotten over the summer didn't hurt half as much as they thought it would. No, the headline of the day was Vince's return and it spread through the grapevine like a bacterial disease. A general consensus had been reached that the most likely candidate for Vince's girlfriend was Michelle Le, a would-be beauty queen – that is, if Cabramatta held pageants – with hair skimming her waist. She had a pretty face in the plainest sense; certainly no cause for a traffic jam, but it didn't need to be. Her popularity was undebatable, her confidence inextinguishable and her push-up bra heavy-duty. She'd even had a high-profile fling with Vince in the summer of Year 6 – legend has it that they were each other's first kiss! None of this, however, not even the image of the two prepubescent lovers, wet mouthed after their first saliva exchange on the monkey bars, sobered the rest of the girls. They still longed to witness Vince's rumoured post-juvie beauty with their own eyes.

During first period, the wailing of a fire truck could be heard: first in the distance, and then closer and closer until they were sure that the boys were starting some kind of trouble. From their classroom windows, they saw plumes of smoke rising from the school at the end of the road, dirtying the cloudless sky. A PA announcement had been made with the aim of tranquillising, but teachers still had to resort to shutting the blinds to keep the girls from staring out the window. You could feel the restless rhythm of gum-chewing and leg-shaking that rocked the Girls' School that day. When the bell finally rang at 2.50 pm, a swarm of the girls ran (read: walked briskly) to the front of the Boys' School, most under the pretence of picking up their nonexistent younger brothers.

'What could it be this time?' a Year 10 murmured coolly as she sped up and overtook another girl.

At the Boys' School, the annual wave of Year 7 students were viewed as utterly oblivious non-entities who breathed too much, and far too loudly, a detested vice redeemed only by their back-packs which jingled with the promise of lunch money. Luckily for Oscar, his appointment with the systemic abuse of the high-school hierarchy had been postponed; the older boys were too busy for bullying. The return of Vincent Tran left no room for sideshows.

As the bell rang for first period, the reigning boys gathered outside, at the front gate where the flagpole stood. Oscar watched tentatively, caught in the middle of a crowd he mistook for a morning assembly. Strangers stood so close he could smell the sweat on the back of their necks. Their ashy elbows poked against his ribs. His better instincts wore his sister's face and screamed at him to weave his way out, but he stood still.

He saw one of Vince's friends put a metal bin on the ground, and another climb a nearby tree to tear off a branch. Standing on the very tips of his toes, Oscar finally caught a glimpse of the famous Vince. He stood in all his glory, looking like Michelangelo's last word. Such origins might have explained his marbled musculature, the violent grace and violent liberty that marked his movements, as though he feared turning back into stone if he stayed still for too long. Vince's head jerked back wildly as he laughed with his eyes closed and his chin tilted towards the sun. Here was a man who had taught his sufferings to chisel him free.

Along with the gnarly branch, Vince struck a match and dropped both into the bin. While this was happening, another boy lowered the Australian flag, unclipped it from the mast, and threw it into the fire. Licks of flame quickly gathered along the edges of the fabric, then engulfed the entire flag until the white stars combusted into a blaze. Amused by the play of light, Vince smiled like a serial arsonist, or a troubled child. By the time he hoisted the bin up the flagpole, most of the school had flocked to the scene to watch. Meaning did not enter any of their minds. They were all intoxicated by the urgency of the moment, thrilled by the light and smoke of the fire, by the boy who had commanded everyone's attention with the striking of a match.

'Boys . . .' Vince was at a loss for words. The thirsting of the fire, its love of light, its desire for doom, spoke to him in ways that he could not yet articulate. 'This is *hectic*.'

This is how Vince made his first reappearance: standing

beneath a dying symbol, a sunrise scorching the edges of his evening eyes. By the time the girls had made it to the Boys' School, all that was left was the smell of something that had been burning. The object of their affection had been tackled down and dragged into the principal's office. The spectators themselves would later forget what the joke had been that caused Vince to laugh so riotously. They would twist and tangle each detail until no-one could agree on what really happened that day. But in the eye's dark room, images of the invincible smile, the gathered brow, the tensed neck, the riverbed veins of a free hand, and the eternally unbuttoned button-up, were already beginning to develop. Chemicals mixed with light. There, against the dark lining of their eyelids, backlit by their most golden memory, would live the real Vince. The boy, the flesh of legend, the breath of an oral tradition.

Chapter 2

The Story of Summer

Cabramatta clung to the light of the dwindling summer days. Although autumn had already found its way into surrounding regions, our beloved suburb had bargained with the seasons and won itself more sunlit hours. And so the sun was mighty that day. It beamed as though it had never lost a war, as though June was light years away, and the solstice, no matter how hard it tried, could never come close to fitting the sky in its closed fist.

It was under this sun that the sidewalks glittered with a fresh coat of bird droppings and homeless spit. Sonny could hold her breath and refuse the smell, but she could not close her eyes at the sight of the crumbling playground. Neither could she unlearn the sisterly impulse to cover Oscar's eyes as they passed it. She clenched her fists starkly by her side. It was not as if this image was anything new to him, yet still she wished these junkies would at least have the decency to overdose in their own homes.

Instead they sprawled their decaying bodies against the park benches for all the schoolkids to see. Some days she would wonder about the violence of the needle against the scarred vein, the physical act, and know it was wrong that someone should have to murder their senses in order to stay alive. But today she was capable only of contempt. She watched them go numb. The eyelid's last flutter. The left pinky twitching before the letting go. Their bodies might be bound by gravity, but the soul was hung from the edge of existence without a single thread to hold onto, and with impossible grace. What had happened to these people? What had happened to her?

When he was younger, Oscar had always begged for just one afternoon on the swings. He would scrunch up his face till it was a mass of crumpled skin with a bottom lip jutting out and hold onto her wrist with both of his hands. But their mother's warnings against the playground were final. To make it up to him, Sonny would reach into her pocket and fumble for coins – if she was lucky, she'd have enough spare change for them to share a lemonade ice block. But most days, her pockets were silent and she would have to sweet-talk him all the way home, doing her best to sell the suspiciously old fruit cup at the back of the fridge to him as his second-hand sneakers skidded against the pavement.

'So,' Sonny nudged Oscar with her elbow, 'how was your day?'

'It was okay,' Oscar answered, not looking up. He only realised the dullness of his tone – the one he was accustomed to using around his mother – once the words had already taken flight. He stole a quick glance to see if she noticed.

Sonny contemplated other questions – 'Did you finish your sandwich?', 'Are the other kids nice?' or 'Have you gotten bullied yet?' – but she decided not to badger him. If she couldn't let him play on the swings, and she couldn't control her mother's rage at home, the least she could do was give him a little peace while they walked. She contented herself with keeping him in the corner of her eye.

'Did you hear the fire truck come to our school?' Oscar asked after a short silence.

'Yeah, I did! What happened? Someone smash a fire alarm again?'

'No, it was an actual fire this time. This group of boys burned the flag and put it up the pole.'

'No way,' Sonny laughed, not so much at his answer but at the sound of his new school shoes, his first store-bought pair, the ones she had chosen. Rubber heels, double straps and squeaky black leather. She had made him promise to take good care of them. Sonny kept her eyes trained on the ground to see if he took notice of the sharp twigs on the path as he walked on.

'Yes, way. It was incredible,' Oscar said, transporting himself back to that death-defying moment. He thought about Vince. What was it like to be so heroic?

Sonny could already see a scratch beginning to form on the heel of her brother's shoe.

'Hold on, mister,' she said, watching him now, 'were you there when it happened?'

'Uh-huh,' he hummed. Abruptly, he turned to his sister and saw the anger in her face. 'I mean, no. No, I wasn't there.'

'Oscar! What did I tell you?'

'To stay away when I see people making trouble.'

'And what did you do?'

'The opposite,' he said with a huff, staring at a splintered syringe lying between the cracks of the footpath, at his shining black shoes. He wanted nothing more than to tear off his socks and take off barefoot. Running or skipping, hopping or limping, it did not matter; they were all ways of teaching your legs to hold up the burning sky.

'I know it's not your fault the boys at school are out of their

16

minds,' Sonny said, softly now. 'But you have to keep yourself safe for me, okay?'

Oscar nodded and mumbled a quick apology.

Both brother and sister began to drag their feet as they approached home. The windows and doors of the house had red and gold envelopes sticky-taped onto their surfaces. Such talismans would bring the family health, happiness and prosperity, or so their mother believed. Up the two creaky steps and straight through the door, Sonny and Oscar found themselves facing the crowded shrine in the hallway: a photograph of their grandfather in a scratched glass frame; a porcelain statuette of Quan Âm bô tát holding her branch of willow and a vase of pure water; a portrait of Buddha sitting beneath the heart-shaped leaves of the Bodhi tree; packets of unburnt incense and offerings of red apples to the spirits. The citrusy smell of disinfectant liquid infiltrated their senses; evidence of their mother's breathless labour, a precursor to her bad moods. Their mother's back was turned to them. She was on the phone with one of her friends whilst gutting a fish over the sink.

'*Chào mẹ*,' they said in unison. She seemed to have nodded at them, so they went into their bedroom to greet their grandmother.

'*Chào bà ngoại*.' Sonny and Oscar leapt into their grandmother's bed to rest their heads in the folds of her body. The scent of liquor still heavy on her breath, she smiled wide, revealing her toothless mouth, her face doing an impersonation of its own youth.

'My golden grandchildren are back from school?' she asked, smoothing her small palms over their hair and rubbing their ears. *Bà ngoại*'s eyes, which always looked wet as if made of glass, were focused on the small television set. In it, *Journey to the West* was playing. It was her favourite drama; the only one she ever

17

watched, with the same spurts of joy and sorrow as though each time were the first all over again.

'Yes, *bà ngoại*,' Sonny answered. 'Did you win the lottery today?'

'No.'

She did not hear the playfulness in her granddaughter's tone. Her face full of menace, she glared up at the Laughing Buddha sitting on the cupboard beside her bed. Every morning, she rubbed his belly, wet a cloth to clean his face and prayed for luck. This sweet old drunkard, dawdling through the streets of Cabramatta to the newsagency to purchase lottery tickets, kissing every scrap of paper like it was a ticket to her next life.

Each day, she would lose and curse the Buddha for wasting her money and knock his face against the corners of tables. When she was finished disciplining him, she'd saunter out of the bedroom and to the altar, where she would hide the food offerings to starve her dead husband.

Are you too busy up there, or down there, to help out your poor wife? You may be dead, but you still have a responsibility towards me. What kind of a man are you?

'If I knew Buddha just wanted to leech off me without giving me any good fortune in return, I wouldn't have given him such nice food every day, and a clean place to stay. But I taught that old fart a lesson,' she said, still stroking her grandchildren's heads. 'He knows what he did wrong now. Isn't that right?'

Sonny and Oscar giggled as they looked up at the Laughing Buddha, where their grandmother's eyes glared like two summer suns spitting furious light. Once glimmering in a coat of gold paint, the Buddha now looked as though his last six lives had been as an anvil. His face was chipped all over and paint peeled from every part of his body, bearing scratches from their grandmother's attacks.

Bà ngoại soon sailed back to her good-natured drunken self, cackling loudly at the drama. She was losing her mind, and yet she was such a joy to be around.

Heavy footsteps approached the bedroom. Lungs clamoured for air, but the breath stalked away to find a hiding place. The siblings had hardly any time to look to one another and exchange condolences before their mother burst through the door. The fury was hot on her tongue, the bedroom air already blistering.

'What did I do to deserve so much *phước*? My children come home and don't even bother to greet their mother,' she cried in her not-yet-shouting way. 'Why are you two on the bed? You haven't even changed out of your school uniform yet. Wearing those clothes the whole day outside and coming home to dirty the sheets – don't you care about your poor mother? God, these kids will only be satisfied the day I'm on my deathbed.'

'*Mẹ*, we did say hello to you.' Sonny tried to explain, but she was already faltering. 'I think you might not have heard us because you were on the –'

'You're always right, aren't you?' her mother bit back. 'I'm always wrong in this house! I'm just making all this up because I'm bored, is that what you're saying? I have nothing better to do, huh?'

Sonny sat in a quiet daze as she watched her mother become a stranger again. She tried to look for something in this woman that proved not only that she was her mother, but that she could be *anybody's* mother: warm and tender like dough, full of lullabies and a thousand hands that reached under your shirt to scratch your back as you drifted off to sleep.

Oscar simply glared. He had always been far too frail for conventional Vietnamese discipline, so he grew up listening to empty taunts that never materialised. It gave him courage.

'Look at the way he's staring at me! He thinks his mother is a crazy woman!' Her large eyes were framed by tattooed liner which had faded purple over the years, giving her anger a theatrical quality. 'Just wants to make noise and cause trouble for him! You think I don't *want* to be happy?'

Bà ngoại tried to narrow her eyes onto the small screen. '*Con nhỏ này*, let me watch my movie, will you?'

'Now that they're grown up, they think I'm useless. I don't go out and work like their father – I don't make any money for them,' she said bitterly. 'Maybe their father gave birth to them. Maybe he's the one that fed them every day and washed them when they couldn't wash themselves. When you woke up in the middle of the night, who rocked you back to sleep? Do you remember?'

How could they not, Sonny thought, when their mother never for a moment permitted them to forget it? She remembered, too, the fear that froze the world over when her mother brought out the bamboo stick, the way it whistled as it swung in the air, the explosiveness with which it met her flesh. Afterwards, the hours of kneeling in the corner of a dark room to repent; the bruised knees, the struggle to sit up straight, her spine disciplining itself even when she wasn't being watched.

'I just have so much *phước*!' she howled, storming out of the room and back into the kitchen. She prepared to cook with heavy hands, throwing down pots onto the counter; a sort of instrumental accompaniment to her screams. 'This family is so happy! *Vui quá!*'

The children followed her out of the room, digging their nails into their palms as they fought off the instinct to flinch. It was even worse now as their mother's eyes reddened and she blinked as though her tears burned her. Sonny and Oscar felt how, even in this state of rage, their mother begged for their sympathy.

20

'If you just said, "*mẹ*, we're sorry we didn't say it loud enough. Next time we will pay more attention." Is that so hard?! Then everything would be okay!'

The weather in their house was always impossible to prepare for. It had only been a few days since the last hot spell. Sonny and Oscar organised, colour co-ordinated and bundled up all their own emotions as if putting away winter clothes at the first whimper of heat. Unable to escape fate's clutches, the siblings dressed to swelter.

They hung their heads low before their mother and apologised. Sonny and Oscar repeated the mantra: *Xin lỗi mẹ, con không dám làm vay nữa.* But no gentle words would suffice. Talking to her was like talking to a wall that could throw bricks at you.

'We'll just leave her alone for a bit to cool down, come on,' Sonny whispered, opening the door into the backyard. 'Let's play.'

She walked barefoot on the ground, wiggling her toes with each step to feel the lush grass beneath her. She peered into the cardboard box at the corner of the garden and found Happy.

'Hi, Happy!' Sonny cooed, whisking the coffee-coloured dog into her arms.

It was the hottest time of the day and Happy still shivered before her – it was her way of saying hello. She peered at Sonny from beneath her lashes and licked helplessly at the air. Oscar scooped Happy into his own arms and ran his thumb along the edges of her floppy ears. Then he let her onto the ground and watched as she crept back into her dark cardboard home, tail tucked meekly between her hind legs. She'd suffered all day at home, alone with their mother, who screamed and punished her daily for peeing beside the lemon tree.

Sonny stood next to the trampoline and waited for Oscar to catch up. Their parents had never allowed him on the trampoline on his own, for fear that he'd injure himself; he could only play on the condition that his sister was with him. This was the way it had always been: him and Sonny, his mandated protector. In his memory, his older sister appeared more frequently, more vividly, than his own mother. It was Sonny who brushed his teeth every night, Sonny who filled the salad bowl with saltwater for him to bathe in when he got rashes, Sonny who taught him how to tie his shoelaces and how to use the tip of his tongue to catch nectar from the flowers that bees frequented. Those times had called for children to raise children not much younger than themselves.

Sonny propped a milk crate next to the trampoline and flung herself onto the springy mat. Smiling wide, she tied her hair and reached down to help Oscar up. Her little brother's weak knees meant their playing on the trampoline had always consisted of him standing still and holding her hands as she jumped, making gentle tremors in the earth beneath their feet. She watched Oscar close his eyes in delight and thought about how infinitely young he looked in the lemon-yellow light of the afternoon sun, with his head tilted back and his lips just forming a smile. Each breath told the story of summer air finding its way inside the dark; whenever it left his lungs, he looked like he longed to follow it. For a moment, the stiffness of his bones seemed to give way to the wind and he began to jump with her. Suspended in the air like a boy made of mist, he no longer held onto her.

Before Sonny could warn him to be careful, *crack*! A quiet noise, it could just as easily have been the snapping of a twig, but with it came Oscar's body falling down, down, down. He landed, luckily, on his bottom. Instinctively, he pulled his knees to his chest, folding himself in two.

Sonny crouched down beside him. 'Oscar, you okay? Are you hurt?' She tried to examine his legs but he shied away from her like the self-folding leaf of a touch-me-not.

'I'm okay. Just a little sore for some reason,' he answered. He was incapable of explaining his own body, why it never listened, and why it always insisted on going against him the moment things started to feel okay. 'I'm gonna go in and take a nap.'

He lifted himself up and staggered back into the house. Sonny stopped herself from running after him. From inside, she heard the home phone beeping, her mother waiting for a friend to pick up, and wondered why people were so frightened by their own silence. To Sonny, solitude was the sleep of dreamers, and she felt nothing but her dreams. Sometimes she could stand so still that it seemed the real world was passing her by, the way rain falls on taro leaves, or a drop of mercury spills off a human hand. That was the only way you could make life painless, by living it as though it was only an afterthought.

Spotting a pair of rainbow lorikeets in the grevillea hedge next door, she straightened her back and began to jump again. Sonny smiled a little as she remembered that, for her elders, the sight of birds was always cause for excitement. 'In Vietnam, you never see birds land like you do here,' her grandmother would say. 'If they did, they'd become dinner in seconds.'

Nestled in whorls of narrow leaves, the two birds drank from the pink flowers, their beaks dipping in and out of the pockets of nectar. After exhausting the syrup supply, they flew away and swooped across the sky, against the backdrop of beaming sunlight. The birds appeared so purposeful that they sometimes fooled her into thinking that sunsets relied on them; that they had to undo the hem of the horizon for evening to come. Sonny found herself jumping higher and higher until she felt like she too could unfasten the sky. When she looked down from up there, she could sometimes see people, and she imagined they saw her too. It was her way of calling for help.

'Aye! Be careful on there, you want to fall flat on your face?' her mother called from inside in that sickening voice, watching her from the window over the sink.

Startled, Sonny's body lost its affinity with the air. She stopped jumping. Her line of sight retreated from the mighty sky and landed back on the neighbour's backyard. Without the rainbow lorikeets gracing its garden, it was a sorry thing to look at; all cinder blocks, spreads of dimpled dirt, unruly grass, and tins of vegetable oil lying scattered around. No treehouse, no makeshift swing, only a deflated ball draped over a bush.

Bad neighbourhoods always had a way of forcing children to be more inventive but there was nothing to work with here; nothing a child could turn into a game, nothing to even suggest that *anybody* had ever grown up here. Yet Vince had. Well, he'd spent a great deal of his childhood at her home rather than his. Their mothers used to work at the same nail salon and would take the bus to work together. As a neighbourly gesture, Sonny's mother offered for Vince to be dropped off at their house to be taken care of by *bà ngoại*. This was the way it had been from two years old to eight, till Sonny's mother quit. He still came over to play regularly, until the trouble began.

From the corner of her eye, she saw a small figure dawdling around the garden. It was Emma, the tiny toddler. She had only recently begun to walk. She wobbled around and began to investigate the dirt in her small hands, using her finger to draw swirls. Emma was just about ready to dip her tongue in the dirt when Sonny called her over. Her feet on the edge of the trampoline frame, she hung herself over the fence to get the little girl's attention. Emma shimmied over to the side of the fence. She looked up at Sonny, astonished.

'You're so big!' Emma said, in her sweet muffled voice. Eyes wide, wisps of hair caught in her mouth as she spoke.

It was an odd accomplishment to appear to be big to anyone, even a child.

'You have to eat a whole lot to get as big as me,' Sonny laughed. She remembered the Kopiko coffee candy in her pocket and reached for it. Could children have coffee? It would have to do; a solid alternative to dirt, at least. She peeled off the wrapping and handed it to Emma.

'Here you go.'

The little girl's eyes flashed quickly with gratitude as she reached for the candy. She smacked her lips, cherishing the glassy sweetness.

Sonny surveyed the backyard again. When she was younger, she often saw Vince's mother, *cô Hạnh*, wander into the garden whenever she was free, wearing her conical hat to work under the sun. She would spend hours dividing daisies, walking barefoot on warm grass, sometimes even laying her cheek on the ground to check for four-leafed clovers. At work, she hacked her cleaver through bone and cartilage with the same indifference, but the flowers saw another side of her. Sonny loved to watch how gently the older woman handled every bloom, how she snipped them and put them in cups of water, let the light in to feed them.

Her own mother always scorned their neighbour for growing such impractical plants. 'Feast your eyes on them all you like but they won't fill your stomach!' she would say as she stuffed that season's bounty of winter melon with minced meat. The garden next door taught Sonny many more lessons, like how magnolias aren't much company when your husband is out drinking, and how a hundred red roses cannot sweeten his breath when he comes home. Maybe flowers were not friendly at all; maybe one of the peonies had mocked her when her husband walked through the door empty-handed, promising he'd win back the money he'd lost, every last cent. That time, they'd had to lend money to *cô Hạnh* to get through the week.

The flowers were no more. But the two mothers remained friends. They regularly spoke on the phone, discussing frivolous things which meant the world to them, like which grocer sold the cheapest spring onions. Whenever Sonny walked next door to give her mother's cooking or receive groceries, *cô Hạnh* would be already waiting at the porch, in front of her shut front door, as if to keep her home a secret. What was not a secret, though, was that wretched backyard. It horrified Sonny just how hostile it looked now, a cemetery of things that once bloomed, and the young girl who lived in the middle of it all.

Something did not feel right. Sonny looked to the house to find a man scowling at her through the window. He wore a white wife-beater, bearing stains of snot or vomit, or both. She yelped and fell down on the trampoline to avoid that gruesome face. Sonny wanted to wash herself just from being in his line of sight. How could someone as ugly as him have possibly contributed to Vince's genetics? Vince. She pictured Vince out of detention, rocking his little sister in his arms, mentally zooming in on the twitching of his biceps. Sonny lay there for a while, watching the sunset with the look of two lovers.

As the last glimpses of daylight began to disappear, *ba*'s beat-up Toyota rolled into the driveway. Sonny and Oscar rushed to greet their father.

'*Ba!*' the children crooned from the front door.

Their mother washed the rice roughly, gripping onto the grains in handfuls and throwing them down.

Dinner time. Boiled choko, caramelised pork and white rice.

'Oscar, I heard there was some trouble at your school today,' their

26

mother said. There was no doubt she'd gotten this information from the gossiping of her friends. 'That *thằng giang hồ* is back, isn't he? *Thằng giang hồ*,' she laughed to herself. 'That's what *cô Hạnh* calls her own son. I heard he tried to burn the whole school down.'

'It wasn't that big of a deal, *mẹ*, he just lit the flag on fire. Just for fun. He wasn't trying to hurt anyone.'

'Not trying to hurt anyone?' she scoffed, her mouth twisting in mock amazement. 'Tell that to the parents of the kid he butchered. *Tội nghiệp cô Hạnh dễ sợ.* She can never get any rest with that child on her mind all the time. Don't make your poor mother worry about you, understand, Oscar? I've got enough on my hands as it is, taking care of your sister.

'See what happens when a woman can't keep her house in order? Men go crazy, turn to alcohol and gambling, and boys get thrown into jail.'

Sonny excused herself from the table and brought *bà ngoại*'s bowl to the bedroom to feed her.

It was wrong what her mother was saying about Vince's mother, Sonny knew this. Whenever she walked past the butcher at Cabramatta, she would watch the older woman, how her eyes always seemed to be looking far into the distance, not seeing her customers even when she spoke to them or the red meat she handled – how flesh became pulp in the tenderiser, how the pink fluorescent light made her look like the kind of woman who wears blush.

The woman's face as her son was taken from her still haunted Sonny. She thought about Vince's arrest. A fateful day in the summer of 1996. This wasn't the first time he'd been in trouble with the police – everybody had seen him frisked before, pushed against the wall, his face bearing scratches from the bricks after-wards – but this time was the one that bit a two-year chunk from his life. The last she had seen of him, his wrists were held behind his back and locked in silver bracelets that glared when they caught the glint of the sun. His hair, wet from a shower. If it had been her mother whose child was being hauled out of her home, she would have pounded at her chest and screamed, publicly disowning her son before he was taken away.

But Vince's mother was a different kind of woman. A woman who did not need her pain to be seen in order to feel it. Her great eyes twinkled as she eased herself back into her home like a mouse. She closed the shutters on the watchful eyes of the neighbourhood and sat on her sofa before the tears could find a place to fall. She would not visit him for the two years he was in there. Ever since her belly began to swell, it aroused speculation by the neighbours, and as it grew, it was a wonder the phone lines in Cabramatta did not combust in sparks.

Nobody knew when her water broke, or why she had disappeared for a week, until the day she arrived home in a bus and stood on the front lawn with a baby napping earnestly in her arms. She stayed there for a while, looking at the house strangely, as if it were not her own. Her daughter's future in it flashed before her like lightning: the unfixable faucet, the shadow of a father passed out in the living-room, the always overgrown grass because the landlord didn't trust them with his lawnmower. Then, as if abruptly remembering there was no other option, she stuck the key into the door and sealed the fate of the sleeping child.

Sonny still remembered seeing Vince the final time. She had grown used to his absence but nothing spelt out 'loss' as clearly as the siren of the government's authorised kidnappers, the stunned onlookers of a suburb which had already lost too many sons. He didn't struggle when they walked him to the car and stuffed him in the back seat. He didn't keep his head down either. Looked everybody, all of his neighbours, all the people he'd grown up around, straight in the eye, without a smile or a scowl. *Don't forget me*, he seemed to say; to which the neighbourhood summoned all its sunshine to reply, *Never*. In her memory, Vince could never be reduced to an image. He was always in action; fighting or chasing ice-cream trucks, zooming up and down the streets in a stolen car, running around the neighbourhood as his father chased him with a butcher's knife.

Before the family turned off all the lights and went to bed, Sonny dragged Oscar to their parents' bedroom door.

'Come on, you know we have to apologise,' Sonny said. It was final. Her hand was already gripping onto the doorknob.

Oscar scowled and crossed his skinny arms over his chest. 'We already did in the afternoon.'

'She wasn't listening then.'

'What should we say this time?' he asked. 'I'm sorry you've got anger issues?'

Sonny smiled and touched his face gently. She turned the doorknob. Walking behind her brother to urge him past the doorway, she felt him flinch at the creaking of the floorboards.

And it happened the way it always had. Their father was already snoring and lying on his side and their mother sat with a pillow behind her back. Sonny held her arms before her in respect; Oscar stood with his hands hanging at his sides like a dying houseplant. Their mother had been expecting their entrance and greeted them with a severe look. She watched her mother's face with uncertainty and stood before her, trying her hardest to smile and resist the urge to smash her head repeatedly against the bedframe. Maybe then, lying in a hospital bed after a ten-hour brain surgery, her mother would finally ask her how *she* was feeling.

Her mother did not turn to face her. Her eyes red and downcast, she sat beneath the flickering light, silent. Sonny made a mental note to remind her father to change the bulb before her mother found the chance to complain about it. She tapped her mother's shoulder timidly. Behind her, Oscar lurked at the door, seeming to have forgotten his lines. Slowly, their mother's gaze began to thaw and she reprimanded them gently, the tenderness now clear in her voice, a final time, before calling them both over to kiss the tops of their heads.

'You children are the way you are because I've taught you well. If you had been raised by your dad, you would be just like the other kids. Every family needs one parent to play the bad guy. Your dad's got the easy job, do you understand? I love you. You're all I have. I live only for the two of you, do you understand?'

They both nodded weakly, blinking away their tears. Anything could be forgiven the moment their mother smiled. Sonny thought of all the words their mother had used against them since they were children, then one threat in particular. *Don't forget that I gave you your life. The heavens wouldn't dare raise a finger if I decided to take it away!* It made her wonder if your mother was meant to be both your god and your executioner.

Afterwards, the shattered children shimmied into their beds. Sonny tucked Oscar in, cocooning him in blankets like bubble wrap, as she had done since they were children. He was reminded once more of how he would always be fragile goods.

Sonny then climbed up to the top bunk and stared at the Backstreet Boys posters she had taped to the wall, as if beneath the crisp choreography and porcelain teeth they actually had souls. In some images, Kevin Richardson's irises glowed green, and in others they were indisputably grey. Most nights, she would try to figure out the colour of his eyes, and most nights she would only grow more confused. She touched the photo of Prince William, and recalled writing to him as soon as she heard of Princess Diana's death, urging him to not be afraid to cry, that she would donate her shoulder for him to rest upon if he would be so kind as to invite her to Buckingham Palace. His reply never came.

The walls of the house were thin. The dreary silence of the night was punctured by a series of violent (and certainly exaggerated) coughs from their mother.

'I wonder if it's cancer,' Oscar muttered humorously from the bottom bunk.

Normally, Sonny would reprimand her little brother for his careless way of speaking. But she was sleepy, and her head ached, so she said nothing. Just let those words loom like a prophecy.

Chapter 3

From the Fury

The fire stunt had accomplished two things: it had re-established Vince's reputation as the alpha of the school and gotten him suspended for the rest of the week. He smirked as the sentence was handed down, walked out of the principal's office triumphantly and strode towards his friends. They'd been waiting for him outside the front gate since they were released from their own interrogations.

'Well?' they asked.

'Well, how about a bowl of *phở*? I'm starving.'

In the streets, the boys paraded the return of the friend who'd been taken from them two years ago. They were street boys: they lied, fought, stole, and carried their youth the way homeless men flash missing-front-toothed smiles, glad to be foolish.

There was Alex Nguyen, Vince's best friend since primary school. Life had always been tough for him; his mother was still in Vietnam and relied on him to send money back for her and the younger children. Then there was Tâm, who the boys had christened Tim Tam. He walked with a limp from a fight with police officers. While Vince was in juvie, Tim Tam had gotten the words 'Only God Can Judge Me' tattooed across his chest. If there was a God, you'd think Tim Tam'd be the last person wanting judgement. Then there was Danny Mai: everybody's kid brother, with the bunny teeth and the perpetual smile, too polite to be feared but guilty by association. He walked on a pair of sculpted sprinter legs that were the other boys' pride and joy, legs that had won medals for them at regional athletic carnivals.

Cabramatta was flooded with teenagers in their school uniforms. As the boys made their way through the neighbourhood, they were greeted by the younger kids; kids who had probably never shown this much respect to their own parents, but who welcomed Vince back into their world with a sincere bow of the head.

The boys waltzed into an empty *phở* restaurant and, against Vince's expectations, did not make a show of sitting down. Why hadn't Alex grabbed hold of a chair, swung it out and sat the wrong way, crossed his arms around the back of the chair and stared at the owner? Why didn't Tim Tam and Danny put their feet on the table? Cautiously, Vince, with the sheer force of his presence, made every movement look like a form of protest. He propped his elbow on the table; he snapped his chin against his knuckles; he tapped his feet and made the startled ground a dancefloor; even his resolute blinking testified to his defiance. All in vain.

'Will it be four bowls of *phở* today, *đại ca*?' the lady asked. She looked not at all impressed by Vince's show of valour. Her hair, tightly pinned in pink rollers, stretched her face tautly, yet deep frown lines still creased her skin.

'Yes,' answered Tim Tam. No triumphant smirk, no nothing. Vince could only stare at the other boys, bewildered. Where had the good old days gone, when they could walk into a restaurant, kick a couple of chairs around, have bowls of noodle soup on the house and feel like they'd conquered the world? Surely, no other gangs had been crowned in his absence. At best, perhaps some jackals might have picked at carcasses he left.

The boys had evidently been regular customers. Vince unclenched his jaw and cleared his throat. His eyes darted around the room. It was strange to think that such a silly thing had wounded him: that the woman had not trembled before him, had not recognised him, had not even glanced at him.

Alex's face lit up.

'Oh, Vince!' he called out loudly. 'I've got to show you something.'

Vince pulled his chair closer and the boys huddled together. Alex reached into his back pocket. Then, with a torn envelope in his hand, he shook out its contents. A picture fell onto the table. His family in Vietnam. His mother wore sunshine on her face and held the youngest sister in her arms. The elder brother and sister were both in school uniform, standing on either side. Not as well fed as kids in Australia, but you could no longer see the hollows in their faces, and that was miracle enough.

'Look at them. My mum sent me this last month. That's the *thằng lớn*, he's in sixth grade this year. He's coming first in Maths – got a head on him, that kid.'

'Aw yeah?' Vince said, wide-eyed. 'Lucky he doesn't take after you, hey?'

'Fuck off. *Bé Vy*, she's still learning to talk. And this one right here' – he grinned and pointed to the infant with a toothless smile – 'that's my *khúc vàng*.'

'Wah! They're beautiful, Alex,' Vince said, in awe, in his normal way of speaking, which always verged on shouting. 'You been working real hard, hey? You're doin' well. Real well.'

He placed his hand on Alex's shoulder warmly. He thought about how far his friend had come: Alex's brief career at the grocery markets selling bruised fruit, his young face watching over cardboard boxes of bad stock; how his palms were etched with the thorns from leaky pineapples as he cut into the fruit, the sun glaring on the rusted steel of his knife, yelling, 'Sweet as sugar, only four dollars a kilo!'

The boys found other means of making money. Both Alex and Vince remembered the first time they walked behind people in the dark, their hands clenching and unclenching in their pockets; watched necks for the gleam of gold; how good it felt to hand over a necklace to the jeweller like you *earned* that shit.

Alex looked to Vince absentmindedly and nodded, his smile fading into something indiscernible. He gripped onto the cup of hot jasmine, dipping in his thumb and drawing circles. He knew that putting his fingers in burning tea wasn't good for him; he wished he wasn't so used to the throbbing.

Their food arrived. Vince had not used chopsticks in a long time and at first struggled to get a proper hold of the noodles; they slithered like serpents back into the broth, hissing at him. He used the spoon as a crutch. It tasted wrong from the very first sip. The *phở* lacked the earthiness and warmth of charred ginger. Worse than the flavour was the look on the woman's face when they left the restaurant without reaching for their wallets. It was the thoughtless glance one reserved for minor nuisances, like finding belly-button fluff or eating a fish with too many bones.

By 8 pm, the sky had dimmed and the boys began to walk back home. They passed the karaoke room they had sung and slept in the night before and laughed. Beneath pockets of light on lonely street corners, they recalled the times before Vince's arrest. Those were the Golden Days. Needle-infested playgrounds, men lying on park benches and frothing at the mouth, yes. The silhouette of a handgun in the pocket of a boy who reminds you of your little cousin, yes. The amputees who roam the streets like sleepwalkers in their military fatigues, yes.

But is that all you see? Try harder. You remember, even if you weren't there. The laughter in the streets, the sun warming you with your mother's love, at once distant and felt everywhere. Watch the way your friends dance in their sweat, limbs flailing and skin sizzling in the afternoon light, with enough mischief to escape their own shadows. Picture the thrones of cracked-leather chairs in restaurants where your name becomes currency. Keep your head up. Look everybody in the eye. Clear your throat. Your voice is the only thing that can save you.

Under faltering light, Vince knew they had arrived home when he spotted the old shirt dangling from the sweat-stained bench in the front yard, beside a stack of overly ambitious dumbbells. Ever since the death of Alex's father when they were thirteen, it had become a place the boys could run to in times of need. It had given them something resembling freedom, at the very least somewhere to revel in the stench of week-old clothes, somewhere to drink milk straight from the bottle, somewhere you didn't stay up at night waiting for parents who kept forgetting to come home. Everything looked exactly as it had before: the sofa on the front porch, still covered in clear plastic tablecloth – as if to seal the freshness of fake leather – the sparse tufts of grass growing amongst weeds, the pile of shoes outside the front door, a few pairs recently stolen from the piles of shoes outside a neighbour's front door. The window was boarded up with bolts and plywood. It had only recently been broken; shards of glass lay scattered in the moonlight. A break-in or a drive-by? Vince didn't bother to ask.

Danny unlocked the front door and left it ajar. Vince peered through the mesh of the screen and saw mattresses lying all over the living-room, clothes everywhere. It looked like a sleepover that had been dragged out for too long, a sleepover they'd all grown out of. Now, as he stood in front of the peeling fibro house, he realised he no longer had a home to run away from.

Vince walked up the porch and lay down on the sofa, wincing at the way the plastic stuck to his skin and shifting emphatically. A plump pigeon swooped down and pecked at the chips of glass on the ground. The boys grinned at each other knowingly. They used to set up traps for birds that wandered into their backyards, break their necks and roast them over a fire. Though they were poor, hunting was not a necessity to eat. It just took a while to get used to the supermarkets and grocery conglomerates here when their parents had laid awake in Vietnam so many nights to dream of the flesh of dead rats.

'Tim Tam, I can hear your stomach grumbling, bro,' Vince said, laughing.

'Remember that time we caught a cockatoo and this cunt made us let it go?' Alex accused with a jerk of the thumb towards Danny.

'That bird was too pretty to eat, bro,' Danny said. He thought about the bird with a broken wing, the colour of cotton candy. The others looked at him with silent scorn and tenderness.

'Have you thought about going to see your mum yet?' Tim Tam asked, lighting cigarettes for all of the boys.

Vince took a cigarette and squinted at its light, as though looking directly at the sun. 'She didn't worry about me when I was in there.' He sucked in deeply, the air around him smouldering. 'Makes no sense for this *con trai vô dụng* to come and ruin her new life.'

The boys sat quietly and watched the whispers of smoke pass between them. They flicked the ashes into what used to be a tin can of powdered strawberry milk.

'Have you heard anything from her?' Vince asked, careful not to let his voice betray too much. The boys noted how quickly his coldness had subsided. They had agreed ahead of Vince's return not to tell him about the birth of the baby girl. He already thought his mother had forgotten about him – a second child would only worsen the injury.

'No. We still see her sometimes, though, at the butcher,' Danny answered. 'Late shifts.'

'She look healthy?'

Alex looked at Vince gravely. 'Last time I saw *cô*, she was really skinny,' he said, shifting his gaze to the floor.

'Bruises?' Vince asked after a moment of hesitation. He held his breath while he waited for a reply.

'Some. Fading, though.'

There it came again. That feeling, like a black cloud passing over the perfect picnic spot of a child's brain. Darkness swallowing day. Dampness of rain. That sleeping suspicion that he had been born inside someone's subconscious, left stranded in a nightmare they were always just about to wake up from.

He was only twelve when every corner he turned began to urge him to start writing his will. The vomit that steals the asphalt, the decrepit playground he sits in, the swing that threatens to break loose beneath him, the eyes that flicker here and there the moment you enter a store, or the eyes that don't seem to see you at all. Too young to wonder why the world is already plotting to kill you. Most of the time he could survive death by paying it no attention. He only wanted to grow up quick, and grow up dangerous. Those days, sitting ironically in that sunforsaken playground of syringes and soulless bodies, he and his friends drank the cheap vodka that Tim Tam had stolen from his father's stash. The swaying bottle passed from hand to hand like a sacrament; it swilled their youth away and the fire in the belly turned them into men.

Why had Tâm's two sisters run away? Vince remembered being a little boy, always astonished by the older girls whose pockets always generated offerings of chocolate bars while they helped him learn his times tables. They walked, proudly, with heavy books in their arms and their schoolgirl skirts shimmying in the languid air. But bad neighbourhoods have a way of scratching at doors and luring children out on the street. He imagined the two girls, slipping into the night like smoke, leaving nothing behind but a few strands of sweet-smelling hair on their pillow case.

He wished for them the rest of the fairytale.

He was twelve when he crossed that dark alleyway. He told himself those girls could have been anyone but could not make himself believe it. It was them. Beside the dumpster, two sisters kneeled on the ground. Their hair was tangled, their eyes black and yet somehow see-through. Above them, a thirty-something-year-old thug, whose grimy hands grabbed and kneaded their flesh, moulding their schoolgirl bodies into something capable of sin. The spell had been broken. The clock struck twelve and then stayed still. It decreed midnight forever.

And when he would look at Danny, his heart dropped a little lower, until he could feel something thumping in his stomach. The star athlete, the boy who won all the races at carnivals. Danny Mai, a name that was cheered from the stands and carved in golden plaques. That bright boyish face, bruised by the wrath of his father. Where was there to run now, Danny, when all that was left between you and your father's fist was charged air?

He felt his jaw aching in memory, his left eye raw and throbbing, and remembered the grotesqueness of his own battered face. His father's pounding at the door, the rattling of wood in a frame, the faith that gathered each time it held out and the *crack!* of its inexorable surrender, how Vince would try to cover the expanse of his mother's body with his own. But she was too much, and he was too little, and he would be tossed aside with ease. Sometimes his father came home after gambling away all his wages. Sometimes he came home with the sad stench of alcohol in his clothes. Sometimes he came home with flowers, and held his wife from behind, slopping kisses across her nape and sighing his sorrows into sweet nothingness, threw furniture around when she trembled at his touch ('Even my own wife thinks of me as a monster!'). Sometimes he didn't come home at all, not for days, but even this did not give Vince any peace. So long as his father had a heartbeat, it could be heard inside that house.

They went to bed early that night. With the lights turned out, Vince lay sleepless on his mattress and stared at the ceiling. It had been a long day, yet his body showed no inclination for rest. His mother's face was on the inside of his eyelids, always within splashing distance. He thought of his nights in juvie, when he would slip his hand under the frozen pillow and think of knotting his fingers in his mother's cold hair again. He fished out his old wallet from his pocket, and was careful not to wake up the other boys with the tear of Velcro. Vince slid out the crumpled photo of his mother and propped it against his pillow. With no incense on hand, he grabbed a packet of cigarettes lying on the floor and an ashtray from the coffee table. He lit a cigarette, took a single drag, and fanned it where it glowed. Kneeling on the ground, Vince held the cigarette between his fingertips and pressed his palms together. He reached out from his irrelevant hell with his hands locked in prayer, and felt he was holding the heart of a heartless world, hoping for a hum, a shock, anything.

Letting go of the smoke in his mouth, he finally took in a breath. The night weighed down on him, on his heavy hands which were not used to begging for things. He thought of his mother and asked for her safety, her health, maybe even her happiness if there were blessings to spare. He had only the dimmest idea of who might be listening. But he knew that, however holy he felt at this moment, his prayer was not worship. It was desire in its most manic form, a wish caught on fire, an irrational flame somehow holding up against a darkness everlasting. He wedged the cigarette into the tray and lay his head back on his droopy pillow, watching all of his hopes stand still, before sinking into a sea of ashes.

So the next few days passed like this: going to Cabramatta to have sugarcane juice and Red Lea hot chips, hanging out at the billiard halls, playing at gambling dens, smoking on the streets, playing *tiến lên* and Texas hold 'em in some gangster's garden. Alex, Danny and Tim Tam would head out at times by themselves to work. Vince asked often about what they did and made it clear that he wanted to help out too, but he was told to rest for the time being. He had always been in the habit of taking multiple showers a day, a habit which had been strained in juvie, so when he was left alone he could spend hours standing under the showerhead.

With the week coming to a close, Vince's friends prepared a big house party to celebrate his return. Two years without any inter-action with the opposite sex left him delirious. In preparation for the party, the boys set a lawn chair in the middle of the backyard and gave him a haircut. He sat in the warmth of the morning sun, eyes closed and smiling as the steady whirling of the mechanical razor zoomed up and down the nape of his neck.

The boys had crashed the Ford Laser they'd stolen, so they had to take a train to the city. The plan was to shop around the department stores and restock Vince's wardrobe, which up until then consisted of white t-shirts and the same pleated microfibre pants. The boys each did a set of pull-ups on the overhanging metal handrails as a few elderly Vietnamese women, dutifully wearing their sun visors even as the train entered a dark tunnel, watched on. Only after breaking a sweat could the boys sit down. Alex lifted a glossy brochure off their seat and scrunched his face up.

'Check this out,' he said. 'It's a newsletter from one of those rich private schools.'

'Oh, this is gold,' Danny muttered. He cleared his throat quickly before putting on a ridiculous British Lord's accent. 'Last term, our student body's orchestra had the privilege of being visited by the eminent Russian composer, Sergei Kalivikinovska.'

Tim Tam took the paper from him and squinted. 'Mr Kalivikinovska has achieved international acclaim for his cutting-edge teaching strategies, which include ramming a violin bow into the students' anal cavity.'

As the train exited the tunnel and a single pane of sunlight fell in through the foggy windows, the carriage rumbled with their violent laughter.

'That explains why those posh kids always look like they've got something stuck up their ass,' Tim Tam said.

'Compare this to our newsletters,' Alex sneered. "'Boys, we found a mandarin peel in the compost bin – you know that's not where it goes."'

"'It'll kill the worms, kids! Don't you care about the worms?!"' Tim Tam called out in a shrill voice.

'And "If you don't collect your lost property then we'll donate it to disadvantaged people", Danny added. 'Man, we're as disadvantaged as it gets. What kind of dickhead steals from the poor to give to the poor?'

They walked from the train station to the department store. Vince was hesitant to enter its vast revolving doors. Under the unrelenting lights that turned his skin into ash and dust, he walked with the alertness of a trespasser.

'Tell me what we're even doing here again?' Vince said in a low voice, acutely aware of the wary looks they were getting from the workers. The other boys made a point of pretending not to notice, but Vince couldn't shake his discomfort. The girl at the cash register stared at him like he was an exotic fruit responsible for the nationwide rise in knife crime.

'You know how much this costs? A hundred-fifty. For a belt, bro.'

'Can't you just whore yourself out to Danny's mum for some spare change?' Alex grinned, placing his palm on the side of Vince's neck and pulling him playfully. 'Should get you close.'

Vince sucked his teeth. 'Nah, last time she didn't pay. Gave her the full premium package and she duped me, man,' he replied matter-of-factly. 'She even said let's do it on Danny's bed, 'cause he's a gigantic faggot and that ought to set him straight.'

The other boys walked around, careless and loose-limbed, but Vince couldn't force himself to act natural, nor could he forget whose body he was in. The things sold here did not want to be possessed by him. Neckties looked like nooses. Fine fabrics and shimmery things shouted their taunts at him. Porcelain, wool, cashmere. Even the words repulsed him. He did not like his syllables made of silk.

Against Vince's constant protests, the boys managed to pick out a few things they thought matched his persona. For encouragement, but also because he was an avid shopper of all things luxurious, Tim Tam chose clothes for himself. He looped a scarf around his neck and tried on a crisp, velvet-lined jacket.

'How do I look?' he asked, eyeing himself in the mirror. He turned to Vince and twirled in a circle to showcase his stardom.

'Don't ask me, bro,' Vince said. He had caught sight of that ridiculous tattoo and chuckled to himself. 'I can't fuckin' judge you.'

They congregated at the cash register. Each boy had a thick stack of cash in his pocket, which they had taken to tying with rubber bands rather than carrying around in a wallet. They enjoyed pulling out their money, licking a finger and flicking through to count the notes whenever they paid for something. The boys all cut a generous fraction of their stacks and slipped it into Vince's pocket.

'Where's all this money coming from?'

'Your boys got steady jobs now,' Alex said with a lazy grin. 'Too much money comin' in we got to find a way to spend somehow.'

As he strolled out of the store, Vince caught sight of himself wearing his freshly bought outfit in the gleaming shop window. His father had said he saw the spirit of Satan inside his little boy, whenever he was drunk enough to see things. His mother explained it away as merely being memories of the refugee camp, of the missionaries who'd only feed those who said enough Hail Marys. But Vince now saw that there might be some truth in what his father said. If he was, in fact, a devil, then he thought himself a handsome one, too.

At home, the boys began preparing for the party. The mattresses were taken into the garden and stacked on top of one another. An endless supply of VB sat in the corner of the living-room, pizza had arrived, and a revolving disco light was plugged into the power point. Teenage boys that Vince recognised began to walk through the door, their backpacks heavy with their parents' alcohol, already tipsy from mixing the drinks in large empty Coke bottles and taking swigs as they walked to the house.

The boys greeted Vince, called him *đại ca* and told him they were glad he was back. He was surrounded by familiar faces and eager to relearn what ties he had with these people, curious about who they had become over the years he'd been away. Juvie hadn't knocked him out of the orbit of himself. He received everybody in his usual way; with courtesy, in the most honest sense of the word. He shook their hands, pulled them in for hugs, grinned and looked people in the eye. He let himself be seen and saw people for who they were, beneath the compulsive smiles and loud mannerisms, the parts of themselves sulking at the bottom of their gaze.

The girls wafted into the house like apparitions. Faces powder-pressed and eyebrows plucked with an unshakeable finality. They reminded Vince of a funeral he had attended as a child, and the grieving woman who had bent over the casket to paint her dead daughter's lips blood-red. He watched their mascara-laden eyes, the way they moved about the room with as much dark magic and magnetism as a *ma cà rồng*.

When the music began, they came alive again, if only for one night. Each girl danced away, hips whirling and hair twirling in ways he had never before witnessed, either using their ruinous looks to cast spells or unaware of themselves altogether. Each girl was corrupt and coming to collapse; a crisis in feminine form. Each girl, hips whirling and hair twirling, a banana republic of mouths in the dark, everywhere.

Alex, Danny and Tim Tam brought out dessert to the fervent claps of the crowd. It was a cake typical of Cabramatta's homely bakeries: covered in white whipped cream, the edges decorated with a ring of honeydew and rockmelon carved balls, and a message written in bright red cursive: 'Welcome Home Vince'. The candles' meek flames struggled to hold up in the room of sweeping northern lights. Vince had the first slice of cake and bit into it eagerly. A deep, custardy musk filled his nostrils. Wrinkling his nose in disgust, he wondered how long the cake had been sitting at the back of the bakery before their purchase. He spat it out and lunged for the box of tissues on the table to clean the taste off his tongue. But the traces of sulphuric sweetness left over in his mouth were warm and familiar to him.

'Durian?' Vince mumbled to himself, contemplating the flavour that had grabbed hold of his tastebuds and refused to part. He looked between the three cheeky boys who had for all this time been containing their laughter. Their expressions gave enough evidence to name the sole perpetrator.

Vince roughly grabbed a handful of the cake and rushed towards Alex, whose grin turned into delighted fear as he careened through the crowd and out the back door. Even as he taunted Vince while he ran in circles around the garden, he counted the seconds before his inevitable capture. The sun was just dipping below the backyard fence when Vince finally tackled Alex and the two fell onto the yellowed grass. Shoving a fist of durian cake into Alex's mouth and smearing it all around his face, he laughed triumphantly to the crowd that had rushed to witness the action. In spite of their reputations, these were two children, wrestling on the grass, each feeling they'd been discovered again.

The night went on. Beautiful people always find each other, even in the dark. The symmetry of a face or the glimmer of eyes must be hard to spot in a house party that feels like being stuck inside of a headache; yet, Vince and Michelle saw each other. Was it love at first sight, or did they just stare secretly across a crowded room and wait for the years in between to pass? Each noted how the other had changed. Him: wondering what she smelt like, what she felt like, what surprises puberty had sculpted into her figure, and if there was any chance of him getting to spoil them. Her: planning how she'd change his hairstyle once they became official, imagining the envy of all the other girls, assuring herself that he remembered the nights they'd spent at the bottom of stairwells with their bodies catching every possible shade of moonlight.

Michelle sat dreamily by the drinks. She spoke to no-one. The heat of the summer night, trapping and being trapped by all those wasted dancers, began to press against her like a chloroform towel. Michelle sat drowsily by the drinks. Boys made eyes at her and tried to break in through the windows of her soul. But she looked at no-one.

Michelle strutted into the kitchen, leaving the door unhinged behind her. The refrigerator was decorated with the signs and symbols of childhood. Danny's cross-country ribbons, a photo of a naked baby Alex in a bubble bath, a picture of Tim Tam as a toddler sitting on a part-time Santa's lap, and Vince's last school photo, brutally handsome, hair combed back cruelly with much too much gel. The innocence which shone through their faces was almost laughable; Michelle could hardly look at the photos without feeling as if she'd broken into some stranger's happy home. She half-expected to see finger paintings and macaroni art on the walls if she were to walk through the hallways.

She opened both refrigerator and freezer and stood before the icy compartments of condiments and rotten leftovers. She held herself confidently, convincingly, the way a con man holds the cards, knowing every sleight of his own hand, and turned towards the door as it creaked open. Glowing against artificial light, she stared at Vince.

'What you doing in here?' he asked, rummaging through the cupboards for a snack. Even in this tiny room with only the two of them, Vince's voice was as big as ever. He found a packet of Mamee noodles and crushed it against the kitchen counter. 'Hungry?'

'No, just wanted to get away from the noise for a bit. Cool down.' She turned towards the fridge again and let the chilled air settle on her face. 'Think I might be coming down with a fever,' Michelle said, her voice only a little louder than a whisper. She did not face him. It looked as though she were speaking to the lonely family-sized bottle of ketchup.

In three strides, Vince closed the distance between them. With one hand, he held onto the corner of the freezer and, with the other, he reached into the cold. His arm brushed against her shoulder as he pulled out a Golden Gaytime. Michelle turned to face him and gave a half-smile as he pressed the cold wrapper against her forehead. Time ached past. Her eyes were full of him. Each blink begged the question: truth or dare? Her lips parted a fraction of a millimetre, yet it was a certain invitation. Vince's heavy breath hovered in the air. He leaned down, inching closer and closer.

The air between them was thunder-charged; it became difficult to breathe through all the electrons. They had been alone the very moment he entered the room, and yet it had only just dawned on him what that could mean. He watched helplessly as her chest rose and fell, as her eyelids dropped and her lashes cast shadows all over her face. He wanted to claim water from the hollow between her slender neck and collarbones. Was she safe to drink from? If he touched her, would she slip right through his fingers? Now was not the time for dipping toes, but for skinny dipping in the dark. Michelle put her palms on his neck and pulled him into the deep end. She gave his lips someone to forget. His fantasies something to dream about.

The magic of the moment had arrived years too late, in a less than sparkling state. Before juvie, he and Michelle were just two children looking for imaginative ways to misbehave. It always happened after dark, when his father was snoring and his mother was pretending to be asleep, and he could finally haggle with the moon for some time alone. Some nights, he would steal out of the house just to see his breath condense into clouds. He walked out into the cold, and the cold walked back into him. The silence of the streets sang to him. With his hands stuffed in his pockets, he'd storm through mist and gloom and the spirits of those who had overdosed on the side of the road. He knew Michelle would be awake at this hour. Even on schooldays, she could be found sitting on her apartment balcony, warming herself with a midnight smoke she'd pocketed from her mother's purse. Her mother always had visitors this time of night; strangers that remained strangers no matter how frequent their visits, who handed her father cash to stand outside the bedroom.

Never one for much conversation, Vince would strike a match instead, a silent request for a cigarette, whatever stolen warmth she had to offer him. The dark of night made his flame easy to find. When she saw the light, she would stub her smoke against a brick and meet him at the bottom of the stairwell. In that wretched housing commission of rats and cockroaches who couldn't afford the rent elsewhere, where blades flashed and men pissed daily, and the dust was so thick you felt it in your throat,

Vince's body would burst with colour. Deep purples, yellows, greens and blues melding in swirls, covering his face, his ribs, his back and his shoulders, either evidence of his own fights or from his father's drunken beatings; so much pain packed into one boy. His skin reminded him of how he could never separate himself from that man, could never run away from the fury that was already beginning to become his. And yet, Michelle was always magnificently unimpressed by it all. Even when his lips stung, or when she pressed down on a sore spot, she never trembled, never said sorry for what had happened to him. The sibilance of his hisses only added to her thirst. She would spill herself in his hands and take a sip of his secret to make up for the liquid lost.

As Vince stood before her now, the unholy refrigerator light glaring on his face, he felt too close, and he feared that if anything were to become of this closeness, he would be found out. Michelle reminded him of a version of himself that had died years ago. Her eyes promised reincarnation, and he only wanted to linger as a ghost for a little while longer.

He felt the moment begin to gather, felt her pull him in closer, and tore himself from her lips.

'Go home if you're not feeling well,' he said, walking towards the door. Then, 'You're hiking up the power bill.'

Chapter 4

Caught in Guerrilla Warfare on the Way to the Loo

Monday morning. Michelle, still drowsy and dreamlike from the night before, flaunted her hangover like a heavy, jewel encrusted crown. Michelle with her fluttery, Herbal Essences hair, strands of midnight marigold picked up and kissed by the wind. Michelle with her long, golden legs; the summer day, an oven for the buttery shortbreads she walked on.

Sonny and Najma watched from the periphery of their silver seat as she passed. Michelle's nose piercing fiddled with the light; it shimmered for a moment, then got shy when her face turned to the side. She had practised first on both ear cartilages before attempting her nostril, the tip of her mother's sewing needle hot from the stove, the ice cube numbing the patch of skin that was to be punctured. She strolled around the courtyard with her group of friends and visited the Year 11 groups, discussing last night's party under the guise of giving out permission notes to SRC members.

As usual, Sonny and Najma only heard of such seminal events after they'd already occurred, by the grace of girls like Michelle.

Najma cleared her throat to demand silence over the already existing silence. 'You know, last period when I went to the toilets, Michelle was in the cubicle right next to me. Even her piss smells like Victoria's Secret fragrance mist.'

'*Pear Glacé*?' Sonny asked, wincing a little as she took a bite of her apple slice. To keep them from browning throughout the day, she had accidentally soaked the Granny Smiths in saltwater for too long that morning and hoped Oscar wouldn't notice.

'No, that's way too fruity. I'm getting more of a floral aroma from her.' Najma tapped on her nose as she held the odour in her memory.

'What kind of floral?'

'Sweet, but not overpowering. It doesn't force its way into your throat – it kind of just wraps itself around you, and then disappears.'

'Jasmine . . . or honeysuckle?' suggested Sonny as her pickled tastebuds fought against the imagined floral scents. 'Maybe chamomile?'

'Yes! A mature chamomile top note,' said Najma, clapping Sonny on the back with a grin. 'With just a hint of vanilla.'

'No citrus?'

'No citrus.'

Sonny tilted her head and squinted at Michelle, who was talking and laughing under the courtyard's blossom-heavy jacaranda tree. As if sensing someone's stare, Michelle reached up and shook a branch, letting lavender petals land on the crown of her head, before falling to pepper kisses at her feet.

Sonny looked away, feeling suddenly nervous and unworthy. True beauty stares back at you and spits in your face.

'That's strange,' she said vaguely, a little spooked at the idea of Michelle appearing in her dreams later that night. 'You're sure there wasn't even a whiff of mandarin?'

'Let me try again.' Najma fanned some air towards her nostrils to lend greater weight to her almost baseless opinion. 'No, no mandarin reading here. But there is something missing still. Something warm. Balsamic, even.'

'Ambergris?'

'Yes, ambergris!'

'Well, it has to be *Amber Romance* then!'

'That's what I was thinking!'

The truth? Michelle never wore perfume, and neither Sonny nor Najma had ever stepped foot into a Victoria's Secret store, let alone known what *Amber Romance* actually smelt like. They could only ever wonder about *Pear Glacé*, *Love Spell*, *Pure Seduction*, *Vanilla Lace* and all the rest. But the vintage books Najma's mother collected on the attar of different flowers, the work of Persian polymath Abu Ali al-Hussein Ibn Abdullah Ibn Sina on the alchemy of distillation, and the fragrance catalogues she had mailed to their house every week taught her the romance language of the olfactory system. And Sonny was always a willing learner, a collector of words sensual, ancient and yet cosmopolitan-cool. Damask rose. Moss. Lavender. Frankincense. Resin. On several occasions, she and Najma had used the word 'ambergris' to convey the slow viscosity of honey scented with orange blossom, without knowing it referred to the excrement of a sperm whale.

Again, Najma cleared her throat. 'I never really liked Michelle, to be honest.'

Sonny tried to find a hint of humour in the unexpected statement. Because of her friend's sincerely held religious beliefs, it had always been an unwritten clause of their friendship that any gossiping must be comically motivated. It would be immoral otherwise.

'Really?' Sonny said, hesitantly. 'How come?'

She took another bite of apple, this time noticing the crisp, after-rain sweetness that the salt imparted. She had never found a reason to dislike Michelle; she certainly wasn't modest but Sonny liked her confidence, had thought often about the way Michelle stared back when boys looked at her, how she had charmed everyone into believing her lips were just naturally shiny, though it was no secret that she always kept watermelon-flavoured gloss in her pencil case.

It is a well-documented truth that popular girls like to talk about themselves, but it is just as true that loners like to listen. Sonny and Michelle had been Hospitality partners since Year 8. While they rolled out expired pastry sheets, whisked lumpy cake batter and diced bruised tomatoes together, she would listen intently to Michelle's monologues. *If a boy modifies his car for you, that's how you know he's really in love. Kevin Thai redid the whole sound system in his MX-5 because he knew I liked a hard bass. He was my first time. Being in an open-top car, I mean. All my other exes drove utes because of work. You ever been in a convertible? It's like sticking your whole body out a window.*

Sonny was dazed by the glamour of it all. She played dress-up with Michelle's spaghetti string tops, with her slippery-kiss lip gloss, with the idea of being a girl who went on drives late at night with the wind whispering all her worries away. What was it like to be desired?

'Don't you remember in primary? She was the biggest bully,' Najma answered, already beginning to crack a smile. She could never talk behind anyone's back without feeling silly and sacrilegious.

'No, I don't . . .'

Sonny remembered Michelle as the only girl who boys bothered being kind to. Boys who had conquered the handball courts always saved the Queen's square for the not-particularly-athletic Michelle and made her immune to all of the game's rules – no full, no foul, no double touch, no nothing could ever strip her of her royal title. In their eyes, she could do no wrong. In Sonny's eyes, she was a child prodigy, a girl who had taught herself to play hearts like the piano.

'Remember how my best friend in Year 4 was Meriam?' Najma waited for Sonny to nod before proceeding. Sonny thought about the name 'Meriam' for a few seconds before a face popped up in her head. Ah yes, Meriam with the long braid who liked to play puzzles in class at recess and lunch because the other kids made fun of her accent.

'I made BFF bracelets for us as a present because she was moving back to Lebanon. One time, Michelle sat behind us in the bus and she was like "You know what BFF means, right?" We were like, "Yeah . . . best friends forever." And she said, "No, it stands for Bitch Fuck Fuck."'

Michelle strolled past again and smiled at Sonny. Sonny waved. She wondered if Michelle thought she liked girls. *Did* she like girls?

Sonny appreciated the way Michelle's skirt hitched up as she mounted the stairs, rising to reveal that plateau of perfect skin. She remembered once seeing Michelle undress behind the demountables for volleyball practice; her first time seeing a thong in real life. It was the most delicate piece of cloth: sitting high on the waist, ivory lace against honeyed skin, bordered by buds of cotton. Could be torn or pushed aside with the nudge of a finger. If Sonny were to choose how to dress her privates, she would wear deadbolts, barbed wire, sandpaper, and an alarm system to ward off trespassers. No cotton. No lace. No white.

'Do you think she waxes or shaves?'

'The girl's all oestrogen, Sonny. I don't think she's even capable of growing body hair.'

'Not even . . . down there?'

'Maybe a few threads of silk. Or a patch of peach fuzz, at most.'

'Have you done any landscaping?'

'Never,' said Najma without blinking.

'Me neither. Do you ever prick yourself . . . when you . . . you know, reach into the rose bush?'

Najma immediately understood her friend's literary allusion but chose to avoid eye contact and pretend she hadn't heard. Just the other day, when her mother had been mixing garlic juice and Greek yoghurt into a paste for thicker, shinier hair, and warning her about various passions of the flesh, she had called masturbation a sin. All women are born with a predetermined amount of pleasure built into their bodies; therefore, she should take care to conserve her orgasms for someone she truly loves. Because type 2 diabetes was in their family history, kidneys were a similar concept.

Sensing that Najma had receded into another one of her thoughtful silences, Sonny tried to make talking seem irresistible. 'When *I* do it, it's like I'm directing a movie. I write the script, choose the lighting, the lens, get all the right angles. It's never actually me in my imagination. It's a really hot actress. Cameron Diaz, most of the time.'

'Really?'

'What, you think of yourself? That's pretty confident.'

'No, I –' Najma caught her tongue before she could continue. Whenever they talked about the logistics of sex, which was frequently, she would try to leave as much unsaid as possible, not because she distrusted Sonny but because she wanted to keep certain thoughts a secret from herself. Often times, after they'd had a discussion on the durability of hymens, or a discourse on what Islamic theology had to say about the moral implications of blowjobs, Najma would come to school the next day filled with an intense regret for oversharing and beg Sonny to forget everything she'd said.

'So it's just the guy? By himself?' *How sacrificial of her*, Sonny thought.

'No, I'm there but I can't see myself. It's a point of view thing for me,' Najma mumbled, imagining that tiny beads of sweat were beginning to form on her forehead.

'Oh. Naturalistic.'

There was another silence, but this time Sonny expected the explosion that was to come.

'It's just so much *work*!' Najma blurted. 'I'm so tired of having to use my imagination. My brain's already burnt out by the time I'm finished doing a million quadratic equations every night. It hasn't got any energy to direct an R-rated movie.'

'Well, there's some pretty raunchy stuff at Video Ezy,' said Sonny, trying to be helpful.

'Those aren't working out either. I keep having to beg my parents to rent *Titanic* every other week. They think I'm obsessed with steamboats or something.'

'*Titanic*? I mean, Leo *is* a demigod, but all you get from him is some passionate eye contact and a handprint on a steamy car window.'

'I know, I just can't help it. I don't know what's gotten into me,' Najma groaned, hunching over in shame. 'I've been staying up past midnight every day and locking myself in the living-room while everyone's asleep, just to watch two people make out on a block of ice before one of them dies of hypothermia.'

Sonny laughed and looked at her affectionately. 'Is that why you've been getting dark circles?'

'Yes! My . . . nightlife is really starting to take over. How have you been coping? Still reading second-hand smut?'

'I told you, it's not smut, it's *historical romance*. And it's not second-hand – they're pre-loved love stories.'

It was at the sweaty local op shop in the summer of '93 that Sonny first discovered *This Other Eden* in the fiction pile – colossal, dusty and red-edged. She devoured all five hundred pages of the gruesomely juicy romance between a helpless peasant girl and a moody aristocrat with more power than he knew what to do with. She was allowed to read *This Other Eden* and books like it in spite of the bosomy women on the front covers, because she'd convinced her mother that the mildewed pages and peeling corners meant they were key texts in the Western canon. And they were certainly classics to her, timeless in the short time she'd been alive. She loved them then and loved them still. But ultimately, Sonny knew that dreaming about Thomas Eden, Thirteenth Baron and Fifth Earl of Eden Castle, would take her nowhere.

'Words *are* known for being pretty suggestive,' said Sonny, with a pondering index finger pressed to her lip. 'But visual stimulus is so much more . . . stimulating. I haven't been able to focus in Ancient History since Miss Christopoulos showed us those pictures of the brothels in Pompeii.'

Najma grinned in agreement. 'The men in those wall paintings were so toned and athletic-looking. They must've been gladiators. You know, I wouldn't mind working in a brothel if it was still 79 AD.'

'All the prostitutes were slaves, Najma.'

'They were into BDSM back then?'

The rest of the day rolled by like a grey cloud, inching further and further across the horizon until it revealed that blazing sun: Mr Baker's Chemistry lesson. Sonny walked giddily to the science demountable and tried to look composed as she entered the room. She had rehearsed various greetings in her head, mumbling to herself 'Hey, sir', 'Afternoon, sir' and 'What's up, sir?' in order to decide which seemed most natural. In the end, she opted to be quiet, deciding that she wanted to maintain an air of mystery. This mental dilemma took place before every Chemistry lesson and almost always resulted in the same calculated silence (which sometimes included eye contact and a smile, if she was feeling spicy). *Mr Baker.* Sonny swooned at the sight of him: his adorable thinning hair and freckled face, his gentle blue eyes and thin-lipped smile. She had always admired his natural wit and sarcasm and cheered him on in silence as he debated the more vocal girls in her class. Today was a practical lesson on the Elephant's Toothpaste experiment, which allowed students to observe the decomposition of hydrogen peroxide.

'Didn't we do this topic last term?' Najma asked, turning to Sonny.

'I don't remember anything from last term. All I can remember is staring into his eyes,' she replied.

While Najma began, with a degree of suspicion, to colour in her 'Chemical Reactions' title page with a pink highlighter, Sonny eyed the emergency shower in the corner of the room pensively. What would happen if she 'accidentally' dropped the beaker when they were paired off to perform the experiment themselves? She imagined herself (in Cameron Diaz's body) running to the emergency shower, pulling the lever and pouting at Mr Baker as she writhed beneath the torrents of cool water. Her school shirt soaked and see-through, Mr Baker's eyes electric and indiscreet. She had joked about such a scenario with Najma before, but today she was consumed with a recklessness that frightened her.

Since Year 7, everyone had known of Sonny's burgeoning crush on Mr Baker. It had started off as a joke made in passing – why was she now contemplating it? Her mind raced, her logic fought with her instinct to make a move, and she could feel her ears begin to heat up. Her hand shot up in the air.

'Sir, can I go to the toilet?'

Sonny rushed out of the room and splashed her face with water over the sink. She smoothed her palms over her baby hairs, staring into the scratched, tagged and chipped surface of the mirror. Why was she complicating things? No-one knew of her intentions. At most, she might be reprimanded for overreacting, but she could easily explain that she'd been exercising *extreme* caution. No, that wouldn't do either. Everyone would see through her. What was wrong with her today? Why was she so intent on making a fool of herself? Did she want to be remembered, twenty years from now, as the girl who'd given her fifty-something-year-old Chemistry teacher a wet striptease – *against his will*?

Sonny began to walk back to class briskly, with a clearer head and a newfound sense of purpose. The beaker was safe; there was no way she would let herself commit the deed. But her concentration was broken by the sound of strange footsteps. Erratic whispers. High-pitched screaming. The ruckus of furniture being thrown around.

'Girls, get under the table!' the usually monotone Mrs Gillard could be heard yelling from the Geography classrooms upstairs, for the first time displaying a sign of kindred feeling for anything other than endangered corals.

Sonny didn't know where the perpetrators were but they sounded close, and she decided her own fate then and there: it was too late to run. She ducked behind the lockers and intended to wait out the massacre when she heard footsteps begin to approach. Sonny cautiously poked out her head and caught sight of the attackers. Tim Tam limped along defiantly, lugging his injured leg around as though he was minding it for someone else. She noted how livid he always looked but then he broke into laughter and his face became abruptly handsome. Alex and his shadow were one: intense and enigmatic. His long, unkempt hair along with his air of severity made him look like an Asian Che Guevara. Danny was the smallest of the boys and handsome in an elvish way. He walked in exaggerated sneakiness and his smile showed his crowded teeth. The boys clutched cartons of eggs against their chests and grinned in delight, greedily filling their pockets with the ammunition.

Then, a holy light beamed down from the mighty sky and shone on the final boy. Vince. His hair was gelled back so severely it looked like it had been styled by a Spartan. He wore his crinkled school shirt and microfibre pants, bright orange Nike TNs flashing like sunsets on his feet, the jade Buddha swinging from his neck with each springy step. A bottle of blue Powerade drooped in the pocket of his pants. His tan glowed against the pasty cream walls of the hallway, causing Sonny to wonder if the judge had allowed him to serve his juvie sentence on a cruise ship.

Vince reached for a door and swung it open. The four boys dipped into the classroom and unleashed the protein-rich projectiles onto a crowd of unsuspecting victims. Against the shrill screams, Sonny slumped blissfully against the wall. Dazed by the colour of his skin, her knees only getting weaker with the thought of him, Sonny pulled herself up and, stumbling a little, came out from behind the lockers. From the sustained chorus of screams, she concluded that the boys were still being held up by more urgent matters. She slipped out of the corridor and safely exited the building, nearing the sides of the brick walls as she made her way back to her classroom. The thought of running didn't even enter her mind; she was too busy imagining what Vince might've smelt like when *plop!* – two eggs splattered against the back of her head, coating her hair in a sheen of mucus.

Taunting laughter burst from the mouths of the perpetrators but Sonny didn't dare to look back. She couldn't find the words to confront her attackers or even yelp in surprise. Her only instinct was to continue on her path, to walk at precisely the same speed as she had before and not betray even the slightest intimation that she had, in fact, been egged.

As soon as she had turned a corner out of egg range, she stood still behind the brick wall. The office lady's heavy heels cracked rapidly against the floor, her shrill voice screaming, 'Boys!' Vince, Alex, Tim Tam and Danny laughed, cursed, dropped their eggs and ran, leaving behind an uncooked omelette in the corridor. Only then was Sonny able to walk back to the bathroom and wash the slime from her hair. She then made a second attempt at returning to class. Her heart pounded furiously in her chest at the thought of having been singularly victimised by a group of boys. The other girls were nothing more than collateral damage, faceless civilians muddled in amongst one another. She had first been isolated, *then* terrorised.

Who could have hatched such a cunning plan? It was immediately clear to her that Tim Tam was not the brains of the group. Alex had never once shown any interest in her and it was common knowledge that Danny liked the sporty type, girls with carved out calves and high-functioning respiratory systems. That left only one viable possibility. Vince had aimed at her, and only her. He must have intended some sort of secret message; otherwise why would he go to the trouble?

Sonny entered the classroom stiffly, overcome by all the thoughts circling her mind. Had Vince remembered her? Had he come into her school, knowing the principal's ruthless policy against egg-throwing intruders, just to see her, to let her know he had returned?

'Did it rain on your way back?' Mr Baker asked, concealing his heavy-hearted concern for her with cold acuity. Oh, what a clever fox he was. The distress in his voice was tucked away so neatly, so seamlessly, that nobody could sense it but her. On the surface, it was just a teacher trying to understand why his student had returned from the toilets with sopping hair, but Sonny knew better. Were his feelings towards her finally beginning to flower? It was too late now. He had served her well the past four years of high school, but now a new opportunity was arising and she could not turn her back on it. Farewell, Mr Baker, you sweet man, with your face that must have looked so handsome in the seventies, the twinkle in your eye when you explain the solubility of common salts, how you lick your thumb when you flick through sheets of paper, your way of peering up at me with your glasses sitting on the tip of your nose, how you struggle to hide your heart when you reach my name in the roll. Farewell.

'Some boys were egging the school,' Sonny replied matter-of-factly as she returned to her desk. All the girls stared at her, amused by the mention of 'boys' and relieved that they'd dodged that bullet of hair malfunction. If only they'd known she had come face to face, or back to face, with not just any commoner, but Vincent Tran, the crown prince of police custody, they would've begged to be in her shoes.

'My god, you girls stay here,' Mr Baker said, getting up from his seat. 'I'll have to report this to the principal.'

'No, don't,' Sonny almost shouted. 'Someone already reported it.' This did not feel like a lie; if they hadn't already, then they would shortly. 'They've probably already been caught.'

'Did you recognise any of them?' Mr Baker asked, his forehead creasing in distress. He was probably thinking of how to get a hold of the rascals who dared to taint her.

'I didn't see their faces.' But Vince's face appeared very, very clearly in her mind: the strong chin, the sharp jaw, the smiling eyes. *You're safe here*, she whispered as she – wearing a Victorian bodice with a square neckline and bishop sleeves – held him to her suddenly large breasts. By the time the bell rang for home, Sonny had convinced herself that if not a flame, there existed between them at least the dying warmth of the childhood they'd spent together. That was *something*.

'What happened, Sonny?' Najma asked as they walked together out of school.

'Nothing,' Sonny answered, trying to sound convincing but she couldn't keep the excitement out of her eyes.

'Tell me,' Najma whined. 'Did something happen with the' – she glanced around and lowered her voice – '*boys*?'

Sonny held her peace for exactly four seconds.

'It was Vince – he's the one that egged me!' she said, as though that was telling enough. She gripped onto Najma's wrist tightly and squealed.

'And?' Najma asked.

'And I think it's because he remembers me. You know in movies how boys always bully girls they secretly like? Maybe that's what's going through his head.' Sonny only began to realise how ridiculous this sounded once she said it aloud. Shamelessly self-indulgent. In future, she must keep these sorts of thoughts to herself.

'Sonny,' Najma said, trying to break this to her gently. 'I'm sure other girls got egged by him too.'

It was too late to backtrack now. The only hope she had left of preserving her dignity, her unblemished character, her family name, was to pour her heart out and parody its contents. 'No, Najma, I'm being targeted, like personally *attacked*.'

'Whatever you say,' Najma called as she crossed the street to walk home, leaving Sonny at the back gate of the Boys' School all alone.

She dreaded waiting for her little brother; the masses of teenage boys leaving for the train station just below petrified her. She felt as though they all stared at her. It never occurred to her that that could have been on account of her staring at *them*. Sonny tried to appear deep in thought but couldn't think of anything to think about. Then she remembered Vince's token of love. The yolk had been washed down the drain, but the feeling of being egged was still farm-fresh in her memory. How kind the world suddenly seemed. For once, heaven was thoughtful. Some god or dead ancestor had seen the life fading from her eyes and given her Vincent Tran as a light refreshment.

Sonny looked at the strip of houses back across the road by the Girls' School and noticed a small peach tree coming into bloom beside a boarded window. The sight puzzled her. The first peach petals usually appeared in the last weeks of winter. She thought of something her father once told her; how, theoretically, if you could control daylight hours and the temperature outside, you could trick a tree into thinking spring had come early. The idea of making something sprout on command had seemed so convenient. But standing there now, Sonny couldn't help but feel lonely for the only peach blossoms on the street, possibly in the suburb, possibly in the world.

Sonny kicked at the dirt. Where was Oscar? Had he accidentally followed the other boys to the train station? She peered through the chain wire fence and down at the platform on the other side, only to spot Vince stepping into the carriage. For a moment, she let herself forget everything she knew about little brothers, about the seasons, about how any fruit – even those with a stone inside – was at one time a flower, and watched him through the scratched glass of the train doors. She longed for him to just look at her. To find her in those long-misted memories, still standing there, waiting for him.

In an instant, Vince's head snapped in her direction and his eyes found hers. All his friends seemed to be staring as well. *Could it be? Could he remember me?* But Sonny shrank as she realised how he must have seen her: a short prepubescent-looking girl with dripping hair. Laughable. She looked away and bent down on one knee to tie her laces. Her eyes shot back and forth across the sky, away to something in the distance and down to her own scuffed-up shoes – but the only thing she saw was Vince's face.

'Why's your hair wet?' Oscar asked as he approached, but his sister didn't respond. She could be like this sometimes; so far inside her own head that she forgot other people had thoughts, too.

Sonny let her little brother tug her on the wrist as they began to walk home. Seeing Vince in the flesh and knowing that once upon a time she had been a part of his life gave her the courage to star in her own fantasies; no more Cameron Diaz, no more role-playing in other people's bodies. All at once, every fever she'd had since infancy seemed to rush back to her face. She imagined Vince's gladiatorial body, moving against crowds of schoolgirls,

66

pushing his way through the path, standing at the gate, waiting to whisk her away from oblivion.

This was the closest she had ever come to true romance. Gone were the days spent dreaming of one-sided love affairs with married-with-children-her-own-age Chemistry teachers and international movie stars. Here was a boy who knew her, or at least used to. Here was a boy who had once lived right next door, who had been a friend of the family. Sonny thought about his daily visits when they were children: both of them donned in some Salvation Army-donated hand-me-downs, the terror of kicking the ball anywhere near her mother's sacred lemon tree, the games they'd created out of a trampoline, a rotary clothesline and a patch of garden.

Sonny and Oscar reached home. They found their mother in the kitchen as usual: her hair clipped away from her face, her back turned to them, brooding over a pot on the stove. The smell of something warm and buttery wafted in the air. A honeycomb cake was baking in the oven.

'*Chào mẹ*,' they greeted. Sonny stood behind her mother and circled her arm around her wide waist. Oscar stood at her side and watched as his mother's freckled face smiled. She was in one of her good moods, for now.

'*Ừ, con về nhà rồi hả?*'

'*Dạ.* What have you been doing today, *mẹ*?' Sonny asked, looking over her mother's shoulder to watch the chicken stock bubble.

'What have I been doing?' her mother mused. 'I just stayed at home and *chơi* with the Kitchen God.'

Her mother smiled up at the small altar mounted on the wall. The red shrine was painted with golden Chinese script. No-one in the family could read the characters, only assumed them to hold

67

auspicious meanings. Sonny preferred to believe they spelled out pure nonsense, like 'heaven closing down sale' or 'rising phoenix farts smelly fortunes'.

Her mother wiped the sweat from her brow with the back of her hand and moved to rummage through the cupboard. The packet of powdered sugar sitting on the counter meant she was preparing to bake something else.

'*Mẹ*, why don't you go take a shower and rest? You've done too much work today.' Sonny frowned.

'It's okay, *con*, baking makes me happy,' she beamed as she cracked an egg against the counter and tipped it into a bowl. 'I can't study in your place – all I can do is feed you.'

Most of the cakes she made usually went to her friends because the children and their father didn't like sweets very much, but Sonny felt relieved by her mother's cheerful mood.

Sonny and Oscar changed into their home clothes and sat in the living-room. As she tried to help her little brother with his Maths homework, her mother shouted for her to help stir the batter and oil the cake tins. She squealed in delight as she watched her cakes rise in the oven. Sonny wanted to open the oven door and slam the cakes against the ground.

Oscar took his afternoon nap. Sonny lay lovestruck on the trampoline and contemplated all the possible interactions between herself and Vince if he moved back in with his family next door. She devised a plan to take the bins out whenever he did, check the mail whenever he got home from school and align her trampolining timetable with whenever he happened to be in his backyard. She imagined bringing her mother's cooking over to his house and being greeted at the door by a freshly showered Vince, who would pull her close to dry himself on her clothes, because his family had run out of towels. Or something.

Their father arrived home at five o'clock. Hearing his car screech, Sonny rushed to unlatch the gate and welcome her father home. She watched as he checked the mailbox and chatted with an elderly neighbour sitting in her rocking chair on the front porch with a cup of tea in hand. He spoke warmly of the weather and asked after her pet birds.

'*Anh!* What have you been doing out there?' her mother shouted from inside. 'Take these pots outside and wash them in the garden! You're out all day and you don't do anything when you get home! *Anh! Anh!*'

He excused himself hastily and rushed past Sonny. She stood there silently, with her blood slow to catch on fire, and only remembered to be embarrassed when she noticed the neighbour still staring at her. Slamming the gate shut, she ran to meet her father in the garden.

'Hey, Sonny!' he smiled as he hosed down the greasy pots. She reached for the dishwashing detergent and squirted it into his hands. 'Thank you.'

Sonny squatted beside her father and gave him a sympathetic scowl, a look that said *I'm sorry Mum is crazy*. The older she got, the younger her father appeared to her. With the passing of each day, he needed her protection more and more. But the fading afternoon pointed out a contradiction. The light that fell on her father's head made her see all his greying hairs. She saw, too, how the skin on his face was getting to look like worn leather and how time had sunken his eyes.

When they finished with the pots, he walked around the garden and told her all about the things he'd planted – how much sun they needed, how much water, when the fruit would come and how often. Her father had toiled all those Sunday mornings for this. The tangle of choko vines and bitter melon dangling from the arbour. Three dragon fruit trees standing tall and wild. The gracious lemon tree. The tough, prickly snarls of lemongrass. The plot of cooking herbs, only some of which she knew the names of, and the small section of flowers soaking in the remaining light of day.

But Sonny liked the banana tree in the corner most of all. Not for its plum-coloured blossoms, which her mother sometimes shredded to eat with *bún bò Huế*, or for the young, fumbling way its fruit grew in the shape of a hand with far too many fingers, but for its leaves, their cellophane shade and their frailty. It seemed to be her father's favourite plant too. Most days, home from work, he would stand beneath the banana tree and stare at the sky until her mother shouted for him to do something useful. Ever since Sonny was tall enough to reach them, she would split the leaves along their parallel veins to let more sunlight shine through to their garden, just a little at a time so no-one but her could tell. Now, as her father peered past the bunches of frayed banana leaves to watch the blue end of noon deepen, Sonny wondered if he simply blamed their condition on the weather, or if he knew it was his daughter's hands that had ripped a window from the foliage just for him.

Someone had broken into paradise. From the kitchen, her mother screamed another string of commands. Take the garbage out, wash the dirty towels, vacuum the house, leaf-blow the front yard. Sonny scowled again at her father in disbelief. He only shook his head with a smile, seeming amused by all his misfortune.

'I think I must've murdered a monk in my past life, and this is how I have to repay it.'

'It kills me when she yells at you like that, *ba*,' Sonny murmured, but her father was not looking at her.

She didn't think he'd heard her but then, 'Well, think of it this

70

way, baby. Every time she yells at me and I don't react, I'm accumulating wealth for my next life.'

Sonny contemplated this for a moment. 'I think you've spent that wealth in having a daughter like me.'

Her father laughed. Sonny listened closely, with the gratitude you feel when you encounter things that are always just passing by, never able to stay a while. 'I'm pretty sure the score goes back to zero after this.'

He looked at her warmly. The look a parent gives their child after a lifetime of dreaming to meet them, and a lifetime still to go. In his eyes, Sonny saw a glimpse of who she ought to become. She wanted to capture this image of him and let him live in it forever: beaming, surrounded by everything he'd planted, the wind billowing around him, the sunset behind the banana leaves, no woman's screeching to be heard.

'Sonny, you know what the happiest moment of my whole life was?'

'My birth?' she teased.

'No,' he laughed. 'Well, apart from that.'

'The storm,' Sonny said, a little solemnly, as if one had just appeared on the horizon. She knew what was coming.

'I know I've already told you this story a thousand times.'

'One more won't hurt.'

Her father laughed. 'Well, I'm getting old – you might have to remind me how it begins.'

'It was raining . . .'

'First thing in the morning,' her father said. His voice always started off small, soft, like a vapour. Soon, when he got to the bit about the poncho, the voice would become so warped and woven with his other personas that you wouldn't hear it at all, wouldn't know who it really belonged to. He'd force you to go looking for him in the fog. 'Raindrops on my face. Lightning's already tearing up the sky by the time I open my eyes. I gather a bunch of coconut leaves and build a little hut on the beach to wait out the storm. I'm stuck on the shore, but I'm seeing *everything* – it's as if I lost my eyes at sea. All this time, I never knew the world could be so big. Or maybe I just never thought I'd see so much of it, so I imagined it wasn't there. But now it's right in front of me. And even though the storm is only getting closer, only building in violence, all I feel is . . . calm. It's like, as long as I keep my head still, the earth won't spill over – as long as I never look away. Chaos, it's a kind of perfection. Not like calculus and geometry, but the way a piece of music can sound so perfect it makes you wonder if you're the one who wrote it, if it came from somewhere inside you. That's what listening to the storm was like. It left you with nowhere to turn but inside.'

He stared at her. They weren't the eyes of a parent anymore, thought Sonny, but of someone trying to convince you that you didn't exist. She had rarely seen his eyes so bright. The sun of that day was never allowed to set in her father's mind. Always, it would be early morning, lightning striking the inside of his skull. The story never got any sleep. Each time her father told it, there would be details added, new ways of seeing. That must be why, whenever she tried to write it down, her father's words would wrestle with the lines and refuse to lay flat. If he was not free, then his story had to be.

But in her imagination, the story listened to *her*. The storm would not come until she summoned it. Water would not stir until she herself swirled the bowl. Sonny saw her father at seventeen, handsome and limber, and brought back to life the little fishing boat. *Please no, not again*, moaned the creaking wood, coming together. *Why won't you let us rest? Let us rest*, begged the holes in the cotton sailcloth as they stitched themselves closed. Sonny would only reply in incantations. With the nudge of a finger, she pushed the boat out to sea.

For ten days, the refugees drifted. Just as the sun began to rise, the boat was pierced by a rock. The sea trickled in. The refugees were forced to jump. The water reached their chest. It thrashed around like a reincarnated snake. In the distance, a small island. The first time anyone had seen land since leaving. Families stayed anchored to the wreckage together, deciding to wait for more light, for the tide to get lower before they'd wade towards the island. Those who came alone, the young and fearless, were the first to swim to shore. Sonny saw her father carrying a seventy-kilo bag of rice from the boat on his shoulders, trudging through the ocean of corals and broken glass, finally feeling the ground with bloodied feet. The saltwater seeping in, his wounds stinging to be soothed.

'I'm sitting there with my feet poking out,' he said, wriggling his toes with a grin. He looked so young to her – like he hadn't even been born. 'It's high tide, the water's roaring into my hut. The rain is heavy now, pouring in through the cracks between the coconut leaves. I knew the weather would be like this. It's monsoon season. I came prepared with a poncho. I'm staring at the horizon, you know, looking for other refugee boats that might have gotten stuck out there. But what I'm really thinking about is all that wind, and all those waves – what's keeping it all going? You know, ever since I was a little kid, I imagined myself building a plane with no engine because I thought that if I could just take off then I could keep on flying forever. When the plane would dip, it'd give me the energy I needed to come back up, and so it'd keep dipping, and coming up again, just like the ocean. I was trying to figure out a thing called perpetual motion, but I didn't know the word for it back then. I didn't know that my ideas were violating laws of physics, either. I thought I was the only person in the world that ever dreamed of inventing a machine like that.'

You thought you were the only person in the world, Sonny wanted to say. Whenever it rained and her father would stare out the window, she could almost hear him praying for the heavens to fall through the sky. Her idea of him was almost almighty. Sometimes she wished he was smaller so he'd be easier to love. It'd been strange to be raised by a man like him, a man always just about to vanish. Even as a child you sensed something tugging him away from you (in fact, *the whole world* tugging him away from you), feared that he would grow restless of you, of this little home and this bickering wife. When a man like this, who has seen and known so much, comes home from his numbing work, you worry that he will one day stop being yours, that he will find his way back to the ocean, that mythical place he never once stopped believing in. He will stand alone on the shore of his sweetest dream and forget this life in favour of infinity.

Sonny envied the man who did not tremble when the sky hurled lightning at him, who thought of storms as misunderstood symphonies. Maybe one day, she too would fall in love with the world in the same sincere, solipsistic way her father had. Maybe then she would be truly free, by leaving everything behind – even him.

Dinner time. *Canh khoai*, fried fish and rice.

'How was your day at work today, *ba*?' Oscar asked. Sonny deboned the fish and put her father's favourite section in his bowl.

'That's it, no more. Thanks. Well, you know how it is. Same old stuff every day,' her father said matter-of-factly. 'It's bringing the money home. How was school?'

'*Làm ơn*, don't speak English at the dinner table! It's giving me

74

a headache!' her mother shrieked, silencing everyone. She wiped down the countertop with a scowl.

'Do you remember the woman who owns the grocery shop down at Cabra?' she added, finally setting herself down at the table. Only then did they reach for their chopsticks.

'The woman who owns the grocery shop?' her father repeated, reaching to scoop soup into his bowl.

'Yes,' she answered agitatedly. 'The shop that always sells over-priced cucumbers!'

'Overpriced cucumbers,' he repeated, seeming to be brooding over the mysterious woman – but Sonny knew her father's mind was wading in deeper waters.

'*Trời ơi*, does nobody listen to me in this house?' she huffed. 'The grocery shop in the alleyway!'

'What happened to her, *mẹ*?' Sonny interjected quickly, trying to steer the conversation her mother's way.

Her mother sighed forcefully before continuing. 'Her shop's been closed for two weeks now and I just found out why.'

They nodded at her, wearing expressions of exaggerated interest.

'Her daughter, only two or three years older than our Sonny, *bị ghiền*. She sold the TV, the microwave, all the jewellery in the house to get drugs. And you know who got her addicted? Her boyfriend. Her mother had to close down the shop to take care of her. But she's not getting better. People walk by her house and hear her howling.' Then she turned to her children. 'You see how *hại* drugs are, *con*?'

'*Ghê quá*,' Sonny and Oscar answered, pretending to look troubled. They'd heard countless stories like this before.

'Can you imagine what would happen if I went out and worked like other women? How could I take care of this family?'

their mother mused. Sonny knew how fascinated she was by the gossip; how this woman's sorry life made her temporarily satisfied with her own.

Her mother looked down at the dinner table and examined the free newspaper that was their tablecloth. The real estate section always advertised grand houses in the northern suburbs. It was not the swimming pools, however, which held her attention – she never did learn how to swim – but the spotlessness of the marble floors.

'Sonny, buy me a house like this when you grow up.' Her mother looked up at her radiantly. One day, her daughter would have an office job and wear the kind of clothes that needed constant ironing. One day, her daughter would marry well and build her a granny flat in the backyard. One day, her daughter would come home and cook for her the same Vietnamese dinners their family had always eaten together. One day, her daughter . . .

Sonny smiled, knowing her mother's fondness of her dimples. '*Dạ*, I will.'

'It will be so sad when our children grow up and leave us, won't it, *anh*? The house will be empty, just you and me.'

'Don't say that, *mẹ*,' Oscar said almost aggressively. 'We'll always live together.'

That night Sonny lay in bed and thought of how she could possibly leave home. She wished she could imagine her future without planning for her mother's. Maybe looking back on the past would shed some light.

She tried to retrace her mother's life: to be born the youngest in a family of eleven brothers and sisters. Raised and neglected by a single mother. Bathed, fed and disciplined by her older sisters. Food was rationed by the government and dinner was a sight to make any starving kid cry, a few grains of rice buried amongst mashed yams and fish sauce.

But as she got older, her siblings went out to work and began to rebuild the life the regime had confiscated. Things became a little easier as she reached her teenage years. Her family was still poor, but she hardly suffered because she couldn't imagine the world any other way. She had known leftovers all her life, had grown up gnawing at coarse pineapple cores because the flesh had been exported to the Soviet Union, reciting revolutionary poetry every day in class while her eldest four siblings had been recipients of a proper, colonial education. She didn't do well in school like her sisters, or have a mind for counting cards like her brothers, but she had discovered a love for baking. And she would sneak out to spend what little money she did have on sweet things, like her favourite *bánh phục linh* and fortune readings. She would tiptoe out of the house during her mother's mid-afternoon naps to taste coconut milk and toasted flour melt together in her mouth. Once a week she would visit the betel-addicted psychics who squatted in crowded market alleys for her horoscope, as though the stars above kept getting reshuffled.

She had not met her husband yet, but the wise old woman beside the coffee vendor in District 1, with the drawn-on Monroe mole that always turned blue from face sweat, knew all about him and promised to tell her everything she needed to know for only 20,000 *đồng*. She would lean in close to listen as the woman traced the lines on her palm and foretold while chewing on lime, cinnamon bark and dried tobacco with a ruby-red mouth.

Her husband would be a decade older than her, a man who fled the country long before the Americans flew home. He would come back a stranger with a little money and an accent, looking for a bride. The lady said they would be as inseparable as an areca nut and betel leaf, the kind of love that gets stuck between the teeth.

Once, while dreaming of his jawline and flicking through a dusty French cookbook she'd found at the bottom of her mother's wardrobe, she had the idea of baking her own wedding cake. *8 œufs. Might have to borrow a few eggs from Cô Tư's chickens.* Imagine her mumbling to remember the Romance-language lessons her second eldest had given her over the dinner table. *600 grammes de beurre non salé ramolli. You never need to soften the butter if you haven't got a fridge!*

Look at her, young and beaming, fanning the oven and watching light latch onto coal, smiling wide as the recipe rises to life. *Décorer avec des fleurs de mauve. Decorate with mauve petals? But purple is such a sad colour . . . Might bông mai do the trick?* Fortune uncertain, destiny still drying on a scroll as she carries the cake out of the oven. Watch her practise piping beef fat into flowers, powdered sugar sticking to her sweat. You have never seen her like this. This version of her is a stranger to you. When your mother was this young and this beautiful, you had not yet even been imagined. She had dreams, too. Desires just like you.

Chapter 5

To Ripen Or to Rot

Monday morning. The sun hissed like coal, harnessing all its heat against the poor kids in badly ventilated classrooms. With the suspension lifted, Vince returned to school and officially signed the documents to enrol into Year 11. He chose Drama because this subject took place at the Girls' School, Legal Studies as he had the invaluable advantage of having had first-hand encounters with the criminal justice system, PE because he wanted to keep his body in tip-top shape, and Maths and English, because they were compulsory.

First period was Legal Studies. Vince strode into the classroom with Alex, Danny and Tim Tam in tow. He scrunched his nose at the stench of the mouldy carpet. It had been in the room since the school was built in 1947 and had been rotting for decades. The fan swung shakily from the ceiling and stirred the sticky air around the room.

'Oh fuck, feels like I just walked into a sock,' Vince exclaimed. He did not dwell on the smell for long as he instantly spotted the wheelie chair in the corner, reserved for disability kids. Vince dragged it to a nearby table and swapped it with a standard chair. He sat down with a triumphant smile on his face and twirled in his seat. Alex sat beside him, and Tim Tam and Danny at the tables behind them.

Naturally, the other boys gravitated towards Vince. As feared, lauded and respected as he was, there was something about him that made people feel at ease in his presence, with the exception of senior teachers who only showed up for superannuation and free cups of instant coffee.

Mr Papas was one such teacher. He entered the classroom in his usual manner: silent and scowling. He was a lifelong bachelor, but his manner somehow always suggested he was going through a divorce. The man was almost sixty but he'd been balding since high school, when other boys were just beginning to grow beards, and his head was now as bare as a brioche bun – without even the slightest scattering of sesame seeds.

'Hey sir,' Vince shouted from across the room. 'I like your haircut.'

Mr Papas deepened his grimace and sat down at his desk with his coffee mug.

'Pleased to have you back, Vince,' Mr Papas said, glancing at him warily.

'Pleased to be back, sir.' Vince grinned. 'For now.'

'I'm sure you'll be more than familiar with the class content,' Mr Papas said. 'We'll be learning about some features of the Australian legal system today.' He passed a stack of comprehension activities to the nearest student and soon the papers were circulating the classroom. 'Everybody's got a sheet? Go ahead and start then.'

Vince, Alex, Danny and Tim Tam tried to pilot their papers into the bin at the corner of the room as they discussed how they would spend their night: a friend's house party in Liverpool or clubbing at the Pavilion.

'Get fucked,' Vince said, swinging on his wheelie chair. 'I got to recover first!' Two years without a drop and he'd been forced to chug seven cans the night before.

'Vince, can you put that chair back where it's supposed to be?' Mr Papas asked, his words seeming to echo from the depths of an astoundingly tepid soul. It was clear to Vince that Papas was not a man of extravagant passions. He only wanted to get through the school year without giving any detentions. He held sacred his boneless chicken lunches in the air-conditioned solitude of the Social Sciences staffroom.

'What chair?'

'The one you're swinging on.'

'See, if you just didn't swing then he wouldn't know. But you swang,' Danny scolded. The classroom erupted in laughter. Vince did as he pleased.

'Alright, alright,' Tim Tam said, resuming their private conversation. 'What should we do tonight then?'

'Come on, we've been waiting to take you out for ages,' Danny pleaded.

'Nah, that's sack, man. I'm sleepin' in tonight.'

'Vince, why don't we hear from you?' Mr Papas interrupted.

'Huh?' Vince said roughly.

'The first question, please.'

'Oh ... um ... the adversarial system originated in ... Somebody guess the answer and I'll tell you if it's correct.'

The class laughed as Vince leafed through the pages of his empty workbook.

'You boys go out,' Vince said. 'I'm gonna get some sleep tonight.'

'What's wrong with you? You're actin' like a fucking lightweight,'

Tim Tam said gruffly, reaching over his desk to shove Vince's shoulder.

'He's got to recharge so we can take him out tomorrow night, right?' Alex chimed in. Vince grinned at him, then shut his eyes tightly.

'Fuck, bro, my head,' he said in a hoarse voice. Alex placed his hand on Vince's shoulder.

'You want me to go get some Panadol?' he said quietly, as though headaches caused ultra-sensitive hearing.

'Nah, I'll be alright,' Vince replied.

'It's close, I'll be two seconds.' Alex put his hand up. 'Sir, can I get a toilet pass?'

The chemist was a twenty-minute walk away and by the time Alex returned, the bell for recess had already gone. Alex held the bubbler for Vince as he lapped up the water and swallowed the pill. Then the boys went to the toilets for a smoke.

Second period was Maths. Mrs Dewanji walked into the room. The ringlets of her hair were just beginning to grey but the rest of her burst with colour. Her red bindi and her gleaming gold bangles caught Vince's eye. She was a small, swift woman. The boys usually took ten minutes to finish off their arm-wrestling matches and games of Mercy, but she was already writing questions on the board.

'So, who knows the answer?' Mrs Dewanji asked.

The class quietened down for a moment before a boy at the front called out, 'We haven't learnt this, Miss!'

'What do you mean you haven't learn this?' she asked sceptically. 'This is basics from Year 7!'

The boys never hesitated to start fights with teachers but something about Mrs Dewanji was unlike the others. They were amused by her lighthearted rage, found it almost endearing the way her curly baby hairs quivered like she'd been electrocuted whenever she shook her head in disbelief. Mrs Dewanji was too small to be feared, and too kind to be cruel to.

'I can't believe I have to explain probability to you all over again – you are in Year 11!' she said, taking off her coat in the already-simmering heat. 'Let's use Terry for example.' Terry, who had been drifting off to sleep, lifted his head at the mention of his name. 'Terry flips a coin – what are the probability of Terry getting tail?'

'Fifty per cent,' the class called out.

'And what are the probability of Terry getting head?'

'No fuckin' chance, Miss, have you *seen* him?' Vince said. 'With a face like that, I bet that coin he's flippin' is payment.'

The boys slapped their palms against the tables as they rode out their laughter. Terry turned to Vince with a drowsy smile.

'Vince,' exhaled Mrs Dewanji, her hands on her hips, her belly puffed out. 'Can you keep your language down please?'

'My language or my volume, Miss?' he said with a smile, stretching his arms around his table and rocking it back and forth. 'I'll give you one, but you can't have both.'

Vince, Alex, Tim Tam and Danny decided to skip third period. All that learning had worn them out. They sat at the bottom of an emergency fire-exit staircase and played *tiến lên*. With a twist. The loser of every round received a strike on their bare back with a metre ruler stolen from a Maths classroom. In the end, each of them left the fire escape with bruises. Alex's back was most purple of all.

'You're getting better,' Vince said sweetly. 'One day you'll be able to clean my shoes.'

Last period was PE. The boys were forced to run laps on the oval. The grass hadn't been mowed in months and tickled their knees. A perfect camouflage. They dropped to the ground and crawled towards the gate. Tim Tam stood on Vince's shoulders and struggled over the fence. Once on the other side, they found the nearest convenience store and strolled around. The boys hid Paddle Pops under their shirts to cool their stinging backs. As Vince scanned the aisles in search of his favourite drink, Mountain Blast Powerade, his eyes lit up at an unexpected discovery. Eggs were on sale, close to expiration date, less than half price.

Monday afternoon. As the boys waited for their train, Tim Tam made the most of his time by committing his daily assault on the vending machine. Vince, Alex and Danny joined in. The boys kicked it, punched, yelled, rocked it back and forth and sent it rattling against the concrete floor.

'Just give us some Jumpy's, you greedy bitch,' Tim Tam groaned, beating his fists against the glass door.

The station manager locked himself in his little box, shut the blinds and huddled over his cold coffee. The boys used up all their might and when the packet was finally released, they had to take a deep breath before reacting. They looked at each other and laughed in disbelief as the coils finally pushed forward. They pounded at the vending machine to encourage it. But the Jumpy's refused to be rushed. It was cautious with its descent. The gears even seemed to hum a slow, mechanical tune as they let go of the chips. Graciously, the eighteen-gram packet slid into the compartment. Vince reached for the bag. He tore it open and held it under all the boys' noses before they dug in together.

'Nothing like a hard-earned meal with the boys,' said Vince.

As he chewed on the kangaroo-shaped chips, he was reminded of another kind of starch – raw wheat flour dissolving on his tongue. The taste belonged to a Sunday morning when he was seven. He'd accidentally joined the communion line and a priest had placed inside his mouth a piece of bread, as thin as a dumpling skin. On the drive home, his father pulled into the cul de sac on Wendy and stopped behind an old peppercorn tree to beat him. For receiving the blood and body of Christ even though he hadn't been baptised, for sinning against a sacrament. Vince remembered pressing down on all his new bruises, thinking about sneaking back into church, eating all the consecrated bread he could stomach until he was finally good again, maybe having a sip of the altar wine, too. Would that be stealing? Had anything ever been stolen from heaven?

Vince grabbed another handful of chips and kept crunching, feeling no longer concerned with the past. He only cared for the boys standing and laughing beside him now, and wondered if their happiness could be made to last a little longer, like daylight savings. *How long had he been gone for, really?* He looked around the platform as another train stopped opposite them and a thirteen-year-old poked his head out the carriage doors to call out 'Anybody want?' – heroin, that is. Vince remembered seeing a kid that looked just like him – maybe an older brother or a cousin – shouting those exact words, from that exact spot, before he left for juvie.

On paper, the sentence read two years. But what were the years made up of? Two summers, two winters; two autumns, two springs. It's hard to tell how long you've spent inside when there are no trees to tell the time by. But being under an open palm sky, as he was now, with sun spilt all over his skin, everything seemed to have a swing to it. His heartbeat was a rhythm, and if he listened close enough, so were the seasons. Leaves somehow always changed their colour on cue. He and his friends, on the other hand, must be more like the fruit growing off a tree someone forgot ever having planted; hanging there in the light, never quite knowing whether to ripen or to rot.

Leaning against the vending machine, Vince, Alex, Tim Tam and Danny watched as the train clock reached 2.50 pm, signalling the arrival of the girls. The Girls' School were always let out ten minutes earlier than the Boys'. The streets sang the arrival of their short skirts. The train arrived and the boys stepped into the carriage.

'Why's that girl looking at us so weird?' Alex asked. His neck craned in the direction of the Boys' School's back gate. 'She's been staring since the Lidcombe train left like ten minutes ago.'

Alex was used to getting stares. Most girls would look from beneath their lashes and then away as soon as they were caught; they knew the secret to seduction was having a secret. But these eyes were different. They weren't trying to uphold any enigma. They reminded him of the evangelist that stood outside Yagoona station, barefoot but never without his briefcase of King James bibles, whose eyes were always trying to undress everybody's soul willy-nilly.

The other boys all turned to see the girl in question.

'Vince, you used to know her, didn't you?' Tim Tam asked, nodding towards the girl now pretending to tie her shoelaces.

Vince shielded his face from the sun and squinted. 'Yeah. That's Sonny Vuong.' He hadn't said this name in a very, very long time. The first thought that crossed his mind was *She's still short.*

'You guys see her around?' Vince asked. The subtext of this question being: *Does she mix with our crowd?*

'Nah,' Alex said, 'only ever see her walk from home to school and back.'

Vince forgot about her soon after the train pulled out of the station.

The boys walked around Freedom Plaza with their hair slicked back and their bookless backpacks slung over their shoulders, sipping on sugarcane juice and struggling to hold onto their freshly fried banana fritters.

Cabramatta wore the summer well. Vince moved past its crowds, first cautiously, then curiously. The older men who squatted on street corners and spat on the ground became monuments in his mind. He listened to the fiery haggling between housewives and grocers in amusement. He watched the skill with which women chose their groceries: measuring the curvature of bananas, slapping a watermelon to listen to its melodic density, snapping the tips off okras and cracking apart sweet potatoes.

'They're selling *rau muống* for only four dollars a kilo down the street – if you wanted to rob me, you should've just taken my purse and ran!'

Vince wondered if he had ever noticed these things before he went to juvie, if they'd ever belonged to him until they were taken away. On Hughes Street, he stuffed his hands in his pockets and quickened his pace, looked the other way as he passed the butcher and tried to be happier than he felt. Found himself instead bidding a bitter farewell to that stupid detention centre, not even like grown-up prison where you came out tougher than before.

Remembering the taste of the tasteless TV dinners in juvie, Vince spotted Dennis and instantly cracked a smile. He had known Dennis since primary school. School captain, chess champion, environment club leader and always kind to everyone. His buck-toothed smile and the badges on his collar shimmered in Vince's memory. Usually he didn't mesh too well with the high achievers, those kids whose parents would pack them toasted seaweed snacks for school, who wouldn't even speak to you because they thought being dumb was a disease. But Dennis was never like that.

'Hey, Dennis! How've you been, bro?' Vince called as he approached the boy. He slowed when he realised how shaken Dennis was – even his eyes trembled in their sockets. His skin seemed translucent, like rice paper. Dennis looked around for Vince's voice, then finally seemed to recognise his face.

'Vince? Vince? Help me, Vince,' Dennis whispered.

He looked around, seeming afraid to blink. Then he seized Vince by the collar and brought his face so close Vince could've counted his eyelashes. Vince could only grab hold of Dennis's fists and stand still, every muscle in his body tensed.

'They're out here to get me. Don't let them get me.'

'Back the fuck up, man,' Alex spat, shoving Dennis's shoulders. The boy stumbled backwards, looked around and ran headfirst into an alley. Vince readjusted his collar and pinched his shirt back in place. He looked to where Dennis had been standing just a moment ago, as if he'd left behind his ghost. Vince ran an unsteady hand over his hair and kept his eyes on the ground, trying to keep his balance.

'His brother put him on it. He took a bad trip and now he's all messed up in the head,' said Tim Tam. 'Thinks there are hamburgers trying to eat him.'

'Hasn't been the same since,' Danny muttered, scuffing his shoes against the ground.

'What're you talkin' about? A bad trip to where?' Vince asked impatiently.

'To where!' Tim Tam snickered.

'Somewhere nobody comes back from,' Alex said. *A place darker than death.*

'Acid. He's on acid, Vince.'

The slang was no stranger to him, but he couldn't imagine those words ever touching Dennis. It wasn't meant to happen to him. *Don't let them get me.* His voice dangled in a void, like the light travelling from long-doomed stars. How long had he been hurting?

The boys walked home. The others had their showers and left to take the train to the city. Vince did not let the water touch him today. He unpeeled his clothes and socks and fell onto the mattress. He tried to sleep but Dennis's eyes wouldn't leave him alone. They would not blink. The air stiffened. The moonlight did not move. Whatever held the sky together stood still. There was only Dennis, lost and alone, looking for the person he used to be. At 8 pm, Vince left the house and walked to Cabramatta again, trying to find him in the faces of everyone he saw but Dennis was nowhere. By now, the sky was struggling to keep its eyes open, and the poise of summer afternoon had hunched its shoulders to cradle the stars.

Vince's face, even in the dark, was clearly defined. As if in defiance of all those fights that had left him bruised and tender, puberty had sculpted his nose tall and wide, darkened his eyebrows and thickened his lips to resist injury. No matter what kind of light it caught, Vince's eyes were black and fathomless, like a puddle of water people come to drown in.

By now, most of the stores had closed and the streets were quiet. The only other people around were boys his own age, who looked as restless as he imagined himself. Vince remembered a kid getting in for armed robbery just a few days before his own release, who'd for weeks had his eyes set on a bakery on the corner, a widow who always closed shop by herself at night.

While Vince pretended to look idle, his feet had already started towards Hughes Street. What if someone had been watching her this entire time? Was he already too late? Vince dipped into an alley, rushed past the packing-up fruit shops, accidentally knocked over a couple of custard apples and raced them down the hill. Gasping for breath, he stood to face the butcher on the other side of the road and warned himself not to come too close.

There she was. Inside the store, all alone, standing by a sink and rinsing dried blood off her hands. He stared at her and wanted so badly to be able to hate her. But when he saw how skinny she was, he couldn't help but wonder if she'd had dinner. He watched from behind the display window as she sifted through kilos of chicken thighs, and wondered how someone could look so blameless, surrounded by all those faces of dead pigs.

Vince waited for her to pull down the roller shutters and followed her. In the car park, he stood by a lazy lamp-post, his figure flickering under an unreliable light. Vince watched as his mother's old car pulled out of the parking lot. Then he walked home, with the sky hanging so low that whatever it was holding seemed just above his head – the galaxies of worlds being flung in and out of orbit, clumsy, sunless planets sailing in the dark, perhaps bumping into a meteor once every four million years, all straggling in whatever starlight's left over. And then there was the full moon, looking like a lonely, unpeeled eye, entirely separate to the night sky. Its light was not felt anywhere but in and of itself. It was merely a shape to sharpen the unyielding dusk.

In bed, Vince again found himself staring up at the ceiling. Images of his mother's face and Dennis's shaky hands stuck to his mind like napalm to nerve endings. He watched the hours pass until it no longer hurt, fell asleep the way a frostbitten foot forgets how to express the cold. The mattress beneath his back fell away. Every tingle of warmth bunched up in the blankets was quick to dissolve. He thought even his troubles had abandoned him but the opposite was true. There is no pain as dangerous as the kind you cannot feel. *It's just pins and needles*, he told himself, *pins and needles, pins and needles, just pins and . . .*

Alex, Tim Tam and Danny returned at three in the morning with a Toyota Camry in tow. The next day, they took Vince clubbing for his first time. Vince had no difficulty finding girls who wanted to dance, only with remembering their names afterwards. Outside the club, he shoved a stranger and started a sidewalk brawl that charged down the street like an electrical current. The boys decided to call it a night first thing in the morning.

'Those girls were fucking weapons!' Tim Tam reminisced on the drive home.

Long after they left the club, flashing lights continued to haunt the inside of Vince's skull and he mistook a memory of a bassline for his heartbeat. He had a dizzy sleep and woke up several times, only to hold his heavy head above a toilet bowl.

The boys skipped school and lived in house parties for the next few days. Some days he couldn't even tell what the weather was like, was too busy retching in gutters to notice there was a sky above.

When the sun goes down, the insomniac dreams of having a nightmare, just to get some sleep in this too loud world.

Chapter 6

Murder in the Dark

Friday morning. Sonny and Najma sat together. Their bums burned from the sharp heat that the silver seats collected from the sun's rays. It was only eight o'clock and they already felt as sticky as an outdoor gumball machine on a summer's day.

'So yesterday my dad brought charcoal chicken home for dinner and obviously I over-ate. I started feeling sick so I went to the toilet and puked it all out,' Najma said proudly as she fanned herself with her physics textbook. The solar system on the front cover wobbled in her hand. Sonny wondered if the planets had body-image issues too. *Did Jupiter ever compare itself to Pluto?*

'Why do you look so happy?' she asked, with a squinting smile.

'Well, I realised that means I didn't *technically* eat it. My mouth got to enjoy it but my thighs don't have to put up with the penalty. It was so nice. I get it now – I get why people love doing it.'

Sonny couldn't help but look amused. 'Najma,' she said in the sternest voice she could manage.

'I'm kidding, I know bulimia is a serious thing, but honestly, it was such an enlightening experience. Prophetic, even.'

'It's like when you were kneeling in front of the toilet, you could feel God holding your hair back,' Sonny said, making a ponytail gesture with her hands.

'Exactly!' Najma laughed. 'No, *Astaghfirullah, Astaghfirullah.* I'm going to hell. I can already smell my flesh burning.'

'Tell me about it. It's so hot today, I feel like I'm melting.'

'Good practice for Judgement Day.'

'What?'

'In Scripture today, the lady was going on about Judgement Day – well it's not really a day, it's fifty thousand years. Everybody lined up, stripped naked and left to stand in the sun. Melting for fifty thousand years. But if you're a girl and you were modest and covered up in your lifetime, you'll get your very own cloud. To shield yourself from the sun.'

'Is she just making stuff up?' asked Sonny, wiping the sweat off her face with her collar. 'Because this kind of sounds like apocalyptic fiction.'

Najma considered this with a snort. 'Maybe the prophets were actually aspiring novelists.'

'*The Hitchhiker's Guide to the Afterlife.*'

When the bell rang for home time, Sonny walked to the school library. Having already dipped a toe in marine biology, fondled human anatomy and had a brush with art history, she was in search of something different. That day, the librarian had been organising his archives and left out a box of old newspapers on the counter. Sonny carried the box to a corner and flicked through a pile of old *Sydney Morning Herald*s without much catching her eye. A nursery home had hosted a bingo afternoon to raise money to purchase a piano for its residents. Lots of divorces in the last few decades – Blisse v Blisse, Stirling v Stirling, British actress Dawn Addams v Prince Vittorio Emanuele Massimo. And a wall had fallen, somewhere in Berlin.

But Sonny was held only by her own hand turning the pages. The crinkling and murmuring of history in a room filled with one person's solitude and aisles of shelved memories, all resting. After contemplating, for a moment, the smoke-silver dust the newspapers had left on her fingertips, she found a headline about boat people in the South China Sea.

Mon 14 Jan 1980. An international official who interviewed survivors at the police station of Pak Panang reported that an eight-year-old girl had been raped by an unknown number of pirates for 12 hours without respite.

She had heard her father speak of the journey before; about the hunger and the thirst, the eternity of waiting. At times he would breathe a mention of the pirates and their desire for young girls, but nothing had been so black and white, grey and decayed as this. Holding her breath, Sonny turned to stare out the library window. The sky was still there. So too was the sun. Tomorrow the courtyard below would be filled with rollicking laughter, the grass outside would shake off drops of gathered dew, and the trains would arrive more or less on time; always, there would be the promise of tomorrow, no matter how often tomorrow lied.

Sat 3 Oct 1981. Burnt-out remnants of refugee boats on the beach, tufts of women's hair, children's shoes, blood-stained clothing and torn brassieres were grim evidence of

94

the crimes. On the walls of a hut, the only building on the island, were scribbled brief messages: 'In memory of father and mother' and 'In memory of the misery which my three sisters had to endure for 21 days'.

Like a worshipper kneeling in the darkness of a wooden room, she felt faceless, fleshless. She could hardly feel her own presence. But her heart was still there, and when she looked inside it, she could only find an incensed need to know more, almost necrophilic. She knew the simple act of reading what her people had endured could become a sacrament, a superstition, something to initiate herself into their suffering. And so she read on, in search of the most gruesome details, until the seas stirred beneath her, until she could feel saltwater rising in her lungs, until she could see, in dancing detail, the boat snatched from dawn by thoughtless flames, and all prior suffering going up in smoke, until the cabin door closed on a loved one's cries and she turned around to see ten, fifteen, twenty grinning men, each waiting his turn.

After it had all been done, had they lain there, still losing blood but finally breathless? What had it felt like, to lean into the dark and know you must close your eyes a final time? If you were given one last chance to see if the sky was still there, would you look?

Sat 10 Jun 1989. Women and children sank first. The boy managed to swim away but some four hours later he was swept back by the current. He found a woman trying to stay afloat on two dead bodies.

Dreaming desecration was exhausting, but if she didn't do it then who would? Sonny felt strong enough, young enough, to carry these strangers' sufferings for them. It didn't matter that they were all dead. Some corpses can never decompose. Some moments hurt so much they can't ever be lost. We keep them in our pockets; the perfect antithesis to a charm.

At lunch the next day, Vince appeared at the Girls' School; the only boy in a hot spring of effervescing oestrogen. Sonny positioned herself on a bench behind the basketball ring, almost making eye contact with him as he commanded his half of the court. This was the first time Sonny had seen anyone use this court for its intended purpose, as it normally housed swarms of sleepy-eyed girls sitting and warming themselves in the sun. But now, with Vince's presence, they were watchful as ever, acutely aware of every gust of wind which disturbed the stillness of their hair, every ray of sunlight which might reveal a blackhead.

He had a torn-up lip and a badly bruised jaw. Sonny wondered how he'd gotten so hurt but his manner refused pity. She wanted any excuse to talk to him; to go up to him and ask for a spare coin, for a spare heart, for the directions to his eyes. If he were to look at her, and see her as she remembered herself, it wouldn't matter if everyone else forgot.

As she watched Vince leap and release the ball, his shot rapping loudly against the peeling wooden backboard, she let out a soft sigh and surrendered to her daydreams. Sonny saw herself again corseted in period clothing, gently treating Vince's wounds and watching him wince like a fallen tyrant at her touch. It was many fantasies, all whispering to each other.

Caroline, a girl who sat next to Sonny in Visual Arts, came up to her and squeezed her wrist tightly. Sonny squealed. They looked at each other, dazed by the magnanimity of the blessing: an attractive teenage male was on school grounds. No, not one of those indistinguishable apprentice electricians that were endowed with the mystique of a blue moon once they passed the gates. This here was a fine specimen regardless of its proximity to the school, a boy so handsome that your heart raced and threatened to break loose from its cage to leap into his strong arms.

'Why's he here?' Sonny shrieked under her breath.

'He's taking Drama. He's in my class, Sonny, look at him. Look at him,' Caroline said breathlessly. Sonny buried her face in Caroline's chest, stomped her feet and let out a scream, incapable of believing her luck.

'Did you talk to him? Was he nice? What was his voice like?'

'I didn't get to! Michelle was hoarding him the whole time.'

Caroline was still solemnly stating the number of times she'd seen Michelle lick her lips in class last period when Vince set off again from the centre circle. He bounced the ball three times and threw, holding his stance and his arms in the air as he watched it plummet through the hoop. The concentration, the wrinkle between his brows and the sweat pearling at his hairline. She loved (and loathed) his arrogance; how he stood before all those hormone-hungry eyes and made a show of himself. Sonny let out a high-pitched moan of pure, virginal ecstasy. Immediately, Vince looked around to find where the pained noise came from and his eyes landed on her.

Eye contact had lasted precisely three seconds before it was interrupted by Michelle, of all people. Emerging from the stairs, she crossed the courtyard, carrying a chilled can of Pepsi from the canteen. Michelle then reclined on the court and propped herself up on her elbows. Her hair just skimming the ground, her long, languid legs bathed in the sun's afterglow. She watched

Vince with a smile. He thanked her nonchalantly, cracked the can open and downed the sugary soda. Sonny's eyes zoomed in on Vince and mentally captured the glimmering trail of cola that dripped from his mouth.

She spent last period completely mortified. Why did she have to objectify him like that? Why couldn't she control herself? Why did she have to be a teenage girl?

But sulking would not accomplish anything. Sonny realised there were practical matters to attend to. By the end of the day, through skilful consultation with the Drama students, Sonny had determined Vince's class timetable. He would be at her school three days a week: first period on Tuesdays, third on Thursdays and last on Fridays.

Sonny arrived home, greeted her elders, put together an afternoon snack for Oscar and tucked him into bed, then meditated on the personal sanctuary of her trampoline. She reflected on her misconduct and promised she would no longer embarrass herself. She had to remain unseen, lurk behind a carefully careless gaze, and savour his splendour from afar. That seemed to be the only way she could keep herself safe. But had anyone ever fallen in love unharmed?

Back in primary school, she had been more courageous. Year 6 Sonny was a master of intrigue and romantic warfare. Having long understood that she had not been born in Aphrodite's image, she knew she had to join the boys, sit, eat, play with them, get inside their heads and think like them – essentially *become* them – if she was to mould herself to the essence of their appetite.

It took all year honing her handball skills, collecting the most coveted Pokémon cards and spreading all the filthiest puberty jokes she could think of. But it proved effective. The boys wholeheartedly accepted her as one of their own, and when they did, she expertly appealed to their self-love. With the end of the school year dawning, all five of the boys she liked, even Dennis the school captain(!), competed for her hand at the Year 6 Farewell Dance and she had the satisfaction of turning each of them down. It was the sweetest victory she'd ever known.

In the middle of Sonny contemplating if she had been exceptionally manipulative as a child, and if there was any possibility she was now a fully-fledged psychopath, her father came home. As usual, Sonny opened the gate for him and asked about his day. She followed his finger as he pointed out plants she thought of as being new additions to their garden, but which he told her he'd been growing for years.

'*Ba*, what happened to the flowers we used to have here?' said Sonny, pointing towards a small and empty plot of grass.

'They migrated over there, Sonny.'

'You moved them?'

'No, the seeds got carried away by the wind and they started growing there.'

'Really?' she asked thoughtfully. 'I never knew plants could migrate.'

'Think about coconuts,' her father said. 'Have you ever wondered why coconut trees lean over huge bodies of water?'

Sonny shook her head.

'It's because the coconut children on the trees need to drop into the water. That way the ocean can carry them to another island, where they can grow.'

'Where did you learn that, *ba*?' Sonny asked, struck once more by how much could fit in her father's head.

'Oh, nowhere. There were coconut trees everywhere in my village, so I just grew up looking at them, and thinking about them. I must have been nine or ten when I came up with this theory.'

The weekend passed by quickly. Sonny tried to enjoy however much of summer she had left: sipping sweet chrysanthemum tea, watching the sun beam down on her father's back as he mowed the lawn, the smell of grass and wooden shavings heavy in the air. After she finished her chores, she sat herself on the trampoline so that she was always within earshot of her mother. Happy slept in her lap, eyes gleaming and nose twitching in the morning sun, her upturned belly shaded by the Rosemary Rogers novel in Sonny's hands. Inside, reading was a guerrilla activity and relaxing was to be done in haste. Needless to say, she hadn't done 'it' in a while. Self-abuse was difficult to accomplish in a home that managed so well on its own.

The family's Sunday noon was spent at the shops in Cabramatta. Groups of men squatted on street corners, held cigarettes in the corners of their mouths, cupped their palms over the trembling light and tried to keep it alive in the almost-autumn wind. The butcher walked out of the store for her quarter-hourly cigarette break, exhaling smoke cinematically before sticking it in the crack in the wall to return to later.

Sonny's parents despised smokers. They likened the act of smoking in public to tossing rubbish onto the street, and eating it too – and furthermore, forcing strangers to gag on your leftovers. She feigned disgust to her mother as she passed the smokers, but there was something she liked about being touched – even by second-hand smoke, even for a moment – by someone else's life.

Sonny moved past the crowds and sifted through eyefuls of people. Free to roam, she found herself trapped inside other people. The grocer playing *bầu cua cá cọp* on the sidewalk, his silver fillings filled smile as the bowl was lifted off the dice. Where were his children? What had his face looked like before all those liver spots; as a boy, as a newborn? The old man with a wispy white beard and a *đàn tranh* lying across his lap, nails as long as plectrums, plucking his sixteen-stringed soul for loose change. There must have been a dynasty once, where men who looked like them were scholars and wearers of embroidered silk. Not like now. Not like this.

Her mother dragged her away from her thoughts and into the riot of fruit shops and fish markets. There, Sonny helped her dig through cardboard boxes of nectarines, swapping bruises for firm flesh whenever the shop owner turned away. Fish lay wide-eyed in crates of ice. Her mother smoothed her palms over glimmering scales and lifted the gills to determine their freshness. The barramundi was still breathing when she found it.

With the fish wrapped in a bundle of newspaper under her arm, she went into a lonely travel agency to send money back to her brothers and sisters in Vietnam. There were three workers cramped in the office, surrounded by posters of places they had never been to. Sonny and Oscar sat on the waiting chairs. Five clocks were hung from the wall, labelled Paris, Saigon, London, Sydney and New York. *Tick, tick, tick.* Could time be a place, too?

'Hello, what can I help?' the travel agent said as he answered the phone. His hair was limply combed over to the left side of his head, touching the edge of his ear. On his desk sat an unused mug with a fishing pun printed in Helvetica, the kind children buy their father at their school's market day, when they wish he was a little more like other fathers. Sonny had heard from her mother that he'd been one of only four survivors from his boat – his brother hadn't been one of them.

Sonny turned to the window to watch the passing people. Everyone her age seemed to have someone to hold hands with. She knew that boys could wait. Love or lust, it could all wait. She looked at the girls, with their bared thighs and budding everything – did they ever feel shame? She felt shame even for things she hadn't done. For things that had been done to her. Perhaps innocence was a lie a mother once told her daughter.

That night in the bathroom, Sonny spent four minutes picking at the stuff underneath her fingernails. Her showers were always as hot as the handle would allow; it seemed that nothing less than an ordeal would be able to get her clean. Holding her hands under the scalding water, she imagined it might get rid of her fingerprints, too. Hair was always growing in places it shouldn't. She held her mother's razor against the straggly bits on her knuckles. Why was the body of a growing girl so hard to take care of? It wasn't the scrubbing, shaving, washing, combing, drying, brushing, flossing that bothered her. It wasn't even the dead skin and sand – from where? – that always got jammed right against the nailbed. What tortured her was the filth she couldn't ever reach. The shadow of someone's mouth on her neck. A dirty word still clogged in her ear. An imaginary hand between her legs. An index tracing her jaw, her lips, her ribs; cataloguing its destruction.

It had happened three years ago. She was thirteen. He was a twenty-something-year-old relative. Young and magnetic. The first incident was a game of murder in the dark; he had caught her and groped her and she was too scared to even scream. She could not put her finger on what exactly was happening then. He told her it was normal. But it made her feel icky. In the midst of all that pricked and stung, there sprung a bud that begged. There was no language for this bewildering botany. But she knew that her secret garden was secret no longer.

How long had it carried on for? It was difficult to tell. The incidents couldn't be arranged on a timeline. They could only be stacked, one on top of the other. When they reached up to her throat, and Sonny finally found her voice again, she tried to tell her mother what had happened. Her words were treated as fiction at first. Then, after some weeks of silence, she was told that family must always be forgiven, no matter the mistake. Her mother had a knack for condemning to history what felt eternal. In the end, it was as though nothing ever happened. The relative was no longer invited for dinner but her mother often visited him, deemed it her responsibility to do his grocery shopping and deliver homecooked meals to his doorstep. Still did. By now, Sonny had learned to cry without making a sound. She'd smother her face with a pillow until she couldn't breathe – it helped her get to sleep, too. Although she was sensible enough to keep her suffering to herself, she couldn't help but fiddle with it sometimes. It was like the ache of a loose tooth, or the itch of an ingrown hair. A pain that needed to be touched.

She draped a towel over herself and stood before the mirror. In the warm fog of the bathroom, she indulged in the daily mystery of trying to figure out, once and for all, if she was beautiful. When she got bored of looking at her face, she climbed into bed and closed her eyes. She was tired. Maybe tomorrow wouldn't come after all.

Oscar's snores kept her from pressing on with such thoughts. She remembered instead the nights he would shudder in his bed after she'd forced him to listen to horror stories she'd made up, and how afterwards she would climb back down the bunk-bed ladder to give the world a happy ending. She summoned magic to mend all that had been broken, ushered in springtime to the haunted woods, had even given Bloody Mary a handsome prince and her very own ever after. She had always been such a storyteller, always wanted to trick people into believing her lies. She wondered if her mother knew this, and if that was why she hadn't believed her.

Her mother never knew any fairytales. The purpose of any anecdote, to her, was to teach children to behave. That was why she only ever told one story; because one lesson was enough. The main character was a man of virtue. A Buddhist monk. Shortly after his mother's death, when he was making offerings to her altar, his mind's eye showed him visions of her suffering in the lowest order of hell.

She was scorched by constant fire and lightning, ravaged by snakes and crushed against iron walls as punishment. Worst of all, she couldn't eat the food he'd offered her. Every dish combusted into flames the moment she held it to her mouth. Unable to watch her waste away in the underworld, the monk travelled through countless dimensions of misery to find his mother. It took him many years to reach the hem of hell. When mother and son finally met, they did not run into each other's arms. They did not look each other in the eye or exchange forehead kisses. He hacked off his own flesh to feed her. That was the end.

The story startled Sonny as a child but she only now realised what it revealed about its teller. Her mother believed that love, in its most noble and worthy form, was sacrifice.

To love her was to love purgatory.

Chapter 7

Swimming in the Soup

Recess time at the Boys' School. Vince, Alex, Tim Tam and Danny held their heads above the water bubblers and slurped gracelessly. For taking too long in the bathroom that morning, Tim Tam was condemned to the broken one. Streams surged unpredictably from the rusted metal.

'This water tastes fuckin' nasty, bro,' Tim Tam yelled.

'The principal's tryin' to poison us.'

'My fuckin' saliva tastes better than this shit.'

The boys laughed at the way Tim Tam lapped aggressively at the spurts of water, drenching his school shirt in the process. Tim Tam flicked the water into all their faces, a simple action that caused an all-out water fight in which a hose, a Year 7's apple juice and a teacher's thermos were used as ammunition. Once mobs of other boys volunteered to fight and maintain hostile conditions, Vince, Alex, Tim Tam and Danny decided to go to the toilets for a smoke.

There was only one kid there, seeking asylum. He was a

scrawny thing and noticeably new to the school, looking sadly hopeful in his starched and pressed uniform. He was washing his hands and struggling to get soap out of the dispenser.

'Never any in there, buddy,' Tim Tam said. 'If this school'll teach you anything, it's how to piss without using your hands.'

The boy looked at Tim Tam, registered his shoulder-length hair and the tattoo peeking through his sopping shirt, and bowed his head slightly. He slunk towards the door to make his escape.

'Oi, Year 7,' Alex called. 'You're on lookout duty, alright?'

The boy stared helplessly at Alex. Alex retrieved a packet of cigarettes from his backpack and handed them out. He tucked his own behind his ear and lit the others first.

Noticing the boy's cluelessness, Danny said, 'Stand there and tell us if teachers come,' and motioned towards the door.

The boy nodded and obeyed, reluctant to look anybody in the eye. He leant against the doorway and peered outside, relieved to be so close to the exit.

Vince took a drag of his cigarette and looked at the younger boy. 'Hey, you look familiar,' he said. 'Your cousin sells on the train, right?'

The boy shook his head.

'You sure?' Vince asked. 'Any brothers or sisters then? Oh . . . you're Sonny's little brother, aren't you?'

'Yeah.'

'You remember me?'

The boy nodded again and smiled timidly, like a dog with something in its mouth.

'How d'you know him, Vince?' Danny asked.

'We're family friends – our mums used to work the same nail salon,' Vince explained, then turned to the boy. 'How you finding high school? Who you hanging out with?'

'Don't you sit with the disability kids? The ones that drool and shit?' Danny asked. 'You don't look retarded. You mute?'

'No,' the boy answered. His voice was little more than a murmur but it still managed an echo.

'Lay off the kid. He looks like he's gonna shit himself,' said Alex.

'Wouldn't that be convenient?' Tim Tam grinned and gestured towards all the toilets.

The bell for the end of recess rang. Alex went into a cubicle and stood on top of a toilet seat to open the window. The boys fanned the smell away. The wreaths of smoke broke up quickly.

'I'll see you around. Anytime you need something, let me know. Oscar, yeah?' Vince smiled and placed his hand on the younger boy's shoulder as he passed him.

The next day, the boys slept in until Alex's phone rang and they all took off for work. Suddenly with an afternoon to kill, Vince decided to walk to a nearby friend's house. On the way, he saw an old lady crossing Gilbert Street. The woman walked in front of a moving car, forcing it to a halt. She strode along the road, her limbs flailing and her tongue swivelling around her mouth, running along the pale pink gums where teeth used to be. An impatient driver beeped as she passed. Still, she would not hurry herself. Drivers swerved around the lady and swore hotly. Vince ran to the middle of the road and tried to guide her across.

She shielded her brow to see him; her cloudy eyes adjusting to the light. *Bà ngoại* took her time to recognise Vince, then received him with a serenity that suggested she was not a public nuisance.

'Ay, kid! How've you been? Haven't seen you in so long, you sure grew up. So handsome.'

A man thrust his head out the car window to curse and throw his cigarette to the ground, but nothing he did could phase her.

'Sit down,' *bà ngoại* said to Vince warmly. Her smile was toothless, like a baby smiling for the first time. '*Đừng có ngại mà*. Make yourself comfortable.'

'*Bà ngoại*, we can't sit here,' Vince said, but she was resolute, her body already descending onto the gravelly road. 'Let's go. I'll walk you back home.'

'I don't want to go home. I want to lay here. It's a beautiful day.'

'Come on, *bà ngoại*. If you don't wanna go home, I'll *cổng* you wherever you want. Just get on.' She relented and circled her arms around his neck, allowing him to hoist her up.

'How have you been, *bà ngoại*?' Vince shrugged his shoulders as he tried to keep her limbs in place without causing her any pain. He was under the impression that all seniors suffered from arthritis. 'You don't look a day over thirty.'

'This rascal,' she shrieked, tugging at his ear. 'Teasing his elders.'

'Ow, ow!'

'I've been taking very good care of myself. I've even fallen in love, with a white man.' Startled, Vince tried to look back at her. 'His name's Johnnie Walker.'

Though their bodies were already close, their laughter bound them together with rope.

'Boy, I'm hungry. My daughter's cooking some *canh ngót* at home. You haven't had *canh ngót* in a while, have you?'

'No, I can't cook. If I tried to make *canh ngót*, the fish would come alive and start swimming in the soup.'

'Look at you. You're so skinny, my dead husband could knock you over. What did they feed you in there?'

'Corned beef, mostly.'

'*Trời đất ơi*, no wonder you look like this,' she yelled, as if he was coming apart at the seams. 'That stuff's no good for a growing boy! You eat dinner at our house tonight.'

'No, that's alright, *bà ngoại* – I've got food at home,' Vince said, thinking about the cupboard of instant noodles at Alex's house.

'I'm not giving you an invitation. I've already made up my mind.'

Bà ngoại was determined to stay out. She said she wanted everyone to see that, even at this age, she was still getting interest from younger men. Vince obliged and piggybacked her around a nearby park. She spoke about how he'd been as a child, how she'd never expected him to grow up so handsome, to have his mother's pretty, pouty lips, how he was always so sullen, how he and Sonny had been attached at the hip, how he was content to play even with her shadow. Vince laughed cheerfully as he listened to these stories of himself, of this stranger coming back to say hello.

Sonny stood on the front porch, holding onto the railing as she caught her breath. She had run all over the neighbourhood looking for her grandmother – past the primary school, past the Serbian tobacconist, past the double-garage haunted house that was always up for sale. Inside, she heard her mother screaming on the phone to her father and demanding he leave work early. Sonny jumped off the two creaky steps and was about to turn the corner to embark on a second search when she spotted *bà ngoại*'s silver hair in the distance, her thin arms slumped over the torso of a teenage boy.

'Look who I brought home for you,' her grandmother called, waving her hands in the air.

'Hey, I'm the one that did all the walking,' she heard the boy say with a laugh. That voice. Those words. The whole manner of speaking. As easy as the breeze. It could only be Vince.

If the testimony of her ears were not to be trusted, her eyes wouldn't lie. He was well and truly before her. Tall as a dandelion, with a smile so wide it seemed he was grinning from behind an orange rind. Unmissable. As Vince walked towards her with her grandmother wrapped around his neck – laughing, it seemed, at something in the air – Sonny wished she could be as untroubled. But she was still suffering the aftermath of her Friday foolishness.

Sonny ran to her grandmother and reached for her hand. '*Bà ngoại*, where did you go? You made me so worried.' She could feel Vince's eyes on her but couldn't bring herself to counter his gaze. Maybe slighting him now would make him forget her embarrassing, pornographic scream. Maybe if she treated him as though he was only a figment, he wouldn't be able to tell how often she thought of him.

Almost as an afterthought, Sonny said, 'Thanks for bringing my grandma back home.'

Her grandma? They'd both grown up calling her *bà ngoại*. Had she forgotten? Vince cleared his throat and walked up the porch. 'Don't worry about it.'

Upon entering the house, *bà ngoại* announced that she had a special guest over for dinner.

'*Chào dì*,' Vince greeted Sonny's mother as he knelt down to ease *bà ngoại* onto a dinner-table chair. Sonny's mother was standing behind the kitchen bench, chopping red chilli and celery stalks with a butcher's knife. When she looked up at him, she seemed just about startled enough to scream. But then she smiled, remembering who he was in spite of his reputation: the son of one of her closest friends.

'*Chào con.*'

Sonny's mother proceeded to ask him about all sorts of things: how was the food in juvie, how was he catching up with his schoolwork, had he got a girlfriend yet, what was he thinking of doing when he got out of school? Vince answered these questions politely and punctuated his sentences with a burst of loud laughter. But his mind was elsewhere as he walked around the living area which doubled as a dining-room, noting the three ceramic deities of Luck, Longevity and Wealth mounted above the doorway.

In the corner of the room stood the glass cabinet that he and Sonny had been forbidden from playing near as kids. It was once a mountain to him, mighty and immovable and difficult to avoid when he and Sonny chased each other around the house. But now it was just another cabinet. There was a strange collection of objects on display inside. The back was lined with collectible plushies, which were meant for children but which the children were never allowed to touch. There were beaded animal figurines on the top row, each representing a family member's zodiac. He and Sonny were both born in the Year of the Dog – he remembered her once telling him that the dog had been strung together with both of them in mind. It belonged to him, too.

But the things that were most numerous, the things that glimmered and seemed to sing, had only one name engraved. Sonny Vuong. The cabinet was filled with school certificates, award pins, goblets and a line-up of spelling-bee medals. Nothing so golden had ever been given to him at will. It reminded Vince that he was not in his world anymore. He wasn't standing on the edge of the platform, feeling the wind rushing to catch up with the express train. He was not the possessor of the toilet block, nor was this a place he could smoke at will. He could tell Sonny's mother was watching him look at the cabinet. He kept his hands in his pockets.

The family hadn't often had anyone over to dinner, much less a teenage felon. *Bà ngoại* called for Vince and patted the chair beside her, telling him to sit. She hadn't sat at the dinner table in years. Sonny's mother set a large metal pot in front of them, the soup still bubbling inside. Vince's stomach grumbled at the sight of it and he laughed at himself, but felt angry at his body for betraying him, especially in a house which looked like it had never known hunger.

Sonny sat opposite Vince and Oscar beside her. The younger boy looked at Vince with a reticent smile. Vince understood; it must have felt surreal to have some fresh-out-of-juvie guy sitting in his home and at his dinner table. Sonny, on the other hand, seemed to be looking everywhere but at him. It was as though he wasn't even there.

'How you going at school, Oscar?' Vince asked, to make Sonny more invisible to him.

The younger boy opened his mouth to answer – too late.

'He's doing very well at school, *con*,' Sonny's mother said. 'I'm lucky I don't need to spend money on English tutoring like other parents. His sister helps him with all his schoolwork.'

'Oh, hectic,' Vince replied blandly as he stared at the silver spoon in front of him. He saw his reflection in it, all his features bent out of shape, and wondered why mirrors always did their best to disfigure him.

Outside, a car screeched its arrival from the driveway but the smooth, unhurried voice of a radio presenter continued with the economic forecast. The engine was cut. The door was slammed shut. Sonny's father rushed into the house, his shoulders sagging in relief when he saw *bà ngoại* sat at the dinner table.

'*Chào chú*,' Vince called out as he got up from his chair to greet him at the front door.

'Vince! It's been so long – how've you been?'

'I've been alright, *chú*, how are you?' Vince replied, shaking his hand.

'Pretty good, man. You having dinner with us? Sit, sit.' Sonny's father led him to the table. 'So, what have you been up to?'

'Oh, just the same old sh–' Vince caught his tongue before he could complete the curse. 'Stuff, *chú*.'

'And how about school?' he asked, picking up a chunk of barramundi stomach with chopsticks and dropping it in Vince's bowl.

'School? Well, I've been going.' Vince laughed loudly. 'That's about it.'

'That's good to hear,' the older man said. He scanned Vince enthusiastically and grabbed his bicep. 'Wow, you look great, dude, look at your muscles! What have you been doing?'

'You think so? I've been picking up martial arts again.'

'Girls must be crazy about you, hey?' Sonny's father laughed, as though his daughter did not belong to that sex. 'I admire you, man.'

'Admire me?'

'Yeah, you've always got all the ladies swarmin' around you.'

'You can do it too, as long as you've got a car, *chú*. Just drive by girls and ask for their number – it's easy!' said Vince, his eyes creasing in a wide smile.

'Oh, I never had the guts to do that. Even when I was young, like you.'

'It was Vince that brought mother home for us, *anh*,' Sonny's mother interrupted as she set bowls of rice before everyone. 'Tell me the truth, *con*, was *bà ngoại* drunk when you found her? Was she causing trouble for anyone?'

'Drunk?' Vince lifted his eyebrows and looked at *bà ngoại* with a lopsided grin. 'That doesn't sound like *bà ngoại* at all. Actually, when I found her she was sitting at the park, getting some knitting done.'

Everyone laughed. Except Sonny. Vince swore he could see a smile just beginning to wriggle on her lips, but then she covered her mouth with her hand and let out a dry cough. Why was she acting so cold, like she didn't even know him? Perhaps he wouldn't have noticed this, or been so irritated by it, if *bà ngoại* had not made him remember so much. Hadn't they been little together? Why was she able to call this dinner table, this bowl of rice, this steaming fish soup, this stay-at-home mother, this respectfully employed father, this little brother (and even a fucking grandmother, just to spite him!) her own, while he was all alone?

'Why haven't you gone home yet, Vince?' Sonny's mother said. 'Your mother's been very worried about you.'

If she worried about him, why hadn't she ever visited? Vince snickered to himself. He couldn't expect them to understand. These people knew nothing about his life, could not even imagine it. His temper just beginning to pry itself out of his clenched fists, Vince knew he had to get out before he fogged up all the silver spoons with his infernal breath. Without another thought, he felt his body begin to rise from the table.

'*Tự nhiên con bị đau bụng quá, dì*,' Vince said, clutching his stomach. 'I think I have to go home.'

'*Sao vậy con? Bị đau bụng hả?* The bathroom is just there.'

'No, no, that's alright. I don't wanna dirty anything,' Vince said with a laugh, looking around the house strangely, as though he was already no longer in it. 'You guys enjoy, thank you for the food.'

But his bowl remained untouched.

Vince crossed his arms in front of him and bowed to *bà ngoại* before she could command him to stay. Then he strode to the front door, leaving the house in silence. Sonny's parents exchanged glances, then continued to eat.

'*Ba*,' Sonny said urgently, finally looking up from her bowl. 'What did his arms feel like?'

Chapter 8

On a Watermelon Seed

As if swept up in a storm, Vince's body carried him out of that spiteful house and back home. The boys decided to drive to Parramatta, have dinner there and spend the night at a karaoke room. Radio hits were their specialty. On this night, for the very first time, the boys belted out old Vietnamese ballads, the kind of music their parents used to listen to at night with all the windows open.

When the boys had downed a few more beers, and felt a little more courageous, they began to try their vocal cords at songs from before '75, before the Fall. Vince lingered around the platters of fruit and listened as Tim Tam took the microphone. He could tell the song was tragic and romantic, like all old Vietnamese songs, but most of the words escaped him.

By the river, the tree is still soaking in our silhouettes
Here, the ancient moon, the forgotten water
Their reflections are still here
But whose love am I bleeding for?

The song came from deep, deep down, from the belly. When Vince listened to Tim Tam sing, he didn't just hear his voice. He heard the way the howling formed in his gut, like a sob being plucked and tugged, forced against a wall, and it rumbled in the throat before it made its way out.

I spill my sadness into one of the closer clouds
The souls of seasons past follow me everywhere
Flowers once sprouted from beneath your footsteps
The sky sends raindrops looking for you.

How could somebody grieve, with an honesty that seemed to bleed, a love that was never his, a country that he'd never known, a memory he could never remember. Why had his history always felt so fucking mythical? Vince felt an absurd and meaningless pain. It was like digging a grave and having nothing to bury.

He couldn't even cry.

When night comes, even my dreams long for you
Our love was but a crescent moon, unfulfilled
In a thousand lifetimes, might destiny let us meet again?
I burn incense in the dark, I see your face in every sunrise.

Vince didn't know who'd written the song, but he felt glad for knowing that they had. He longed for everything he'd ever lost to have its own song. He wanted a book written on a watermelon seed he once spat out a car window. He wanted the earth to be perfectly described. Vince knew he wouldn't be the one to do it. But he thought to himself that he'd like to see it done. A phrase could keep a flower from fading. A breath could be enough fire to outlast the dark. Did the world ever end when everything's already been said? Or would it get stuck in the middle of a sentence?

'That was fuckin' beautiful, Tim Tam!' Vince shouted. 'Where the hell you learn to sing like that?'

'Same way you learn to cry, man,' Tim Tam answered with a laugh. 'Shit just came over me!'

With sore throats, the boys strolled the night's streets, grinning at each other as they approached an arcade. It looked just like the one they used to skip school and take a train to in Bonnyrigg. None of the boys could remember its name even though they'd spent much of their adolescence getting into fights there, whenever a kid from another school took too long on NBA Jam.

Vince remembered how fed up the owner had got with them, how he'd threatened to shut the arcade down and destroy all their favourite games, but he never did. Not until his wife died and he hired a gangster to set the place on fire so he could collect insurance money. It was a bakery now. They'd driven past it the other week but none of the others had recognised it, and Vince didn't have the heart to say anything. The bricks outside were still scorched black.

The boys walked into the darkness electrified by softly glowing games. Cigarette smoke filled their nostrils. Back then, if you fed an arcade machine fifty cents, it'd give you infinite fun. He wondered if it could be the same now.

Alex and Tim Tam challenged each other to an air-hockey match. Danny, in his roguish sweetheart way, leaned towards the claw machines, eager to win teddy bears for the three girls he was dating. As Vince cracked his knuckles and waited for his turn, and his imminent victory over whoever won between Tim Tam and Alex, he looked around at the other kids. There were girls sipping from paper cups, twelve-year-olds who had abandoned their machines mid-game to gather around the seventeen-year-olds' Mortal Kombat duel, older guys arguing that the youngsters were all cheats for practising on home consoles. Then, against the digitised groans of pain, the intergalactic explosions, the angry white noise of outer space, Vince noticed a boy, only eight or nine, sitting in the corner with a blue Lethal Enforcers gun tucked under his arm, braiding his little sister's hair. It must have unravelled while they were playing.

It seemed like a secret he shouldn't have seen. He tried to find something else to look at. 'Hectic!' he yelled as he spotted Street Fighter II.

He scavenged a coin from Alex and sat down to verse him. The buttons were sticky with spilt lemonade, just how he remembered. Instinctively, Vince flitted across all the other options to select Blanka. His favourite character flashed on the screen with his familiar green skin and blistering muscles. The savage from the jungle. Vince thrashed and shouted, jolted the eight-way joystick and pounded at the buttons as he summoned his signature move: electric thunder. He shouted his triumph as Alex's life bar dwindled and the screen flashed *KO*.

Afterwards, the boys ran amuck. They ventured into the Old West on horseback in Sunset Riders. They blew up colossal space rocks in Asteroid. They rescued the president in Bad Dudes Vs. Dragon Ninja. They raided the chemical weapons base hidden in the baby milk factory in Total Carnage. They destroyed the God of Destruction in Forgotten Worlds. They were concerned only about keeping this paradise afloat for as long as they could.

But after a while, Vince began to feel himself linger along with it. It was the kind of moment so luminous that he already sensed it coming undone. He knew his happiness was coin-operated. There was a dim, passionless suffering, the under-your-breath kind that mumbled its displeasure because it was bored with itself, like the regret of a brother for never having learnt how to braid his sister's hair, or for never having had a sister in the first place. Why didn't the glittering feeling last? Was it his fault? Was it because his hands were not made nimble enough to separate strands of light?

Vince wanted to feel something eternal, and he wanted it *now*. On the drive home, he swung the car through a crowded inter-section on Alma Street. Just a few illegal turns later, they arrived at their friend's parlour. Tim Tam got his sisters' names, Thanh and Thu, on both of his wrists, Alex got a dragon on his chest and Danny a phoenix on his back. Vince was last and his took the longest. He listened closely to the humming of the needle which punctured him again and again. The black calligraphy ran down the left side of his body.

野 生 の 力 を 思 い 知 っ た か

In the living-room, Sonny sat beside her father on the sofa. They ate sour cream and onion Pringles together. Sonny seethed in silence. The perfect opportunity had literally arrived at her doorstep and joined her family for dinner, and what had she done? Kept her lips glued and her eyes stapled to the table. What was wrong with her? Had reading all those romance novels taught her nothing? If she'd played her cards right, she'd probably be wearing one of his shirts by now.

Sonny offered the last chip to her father and almost got up to put the scraps in the bin, but she noticed him staring at the empty can. She needed to distract herself with someone else's thoughts.

'What are you thinking about?' Sonny asked.

'When I was a kid, I'd have a lot of fun with something like this,' he said, still gazing at the green tube. 'Back then, there'd be plenty of bullets lying around my village. We would take them, remove the gunpowder from the chamber and pour it in any empty container we could find. Then, we would light it up and it'd go flying! We were trying to imitate the illumination flares.' He held the can in his hand and looked out the window, as if to pray for a comet.

'Illumination flares?'

'Yeah, you've never heard of them?'

Sonny shook her head.

'They were these things that the military used, these heavy, heavy metal canisters. Whenever the Americans shot them in the air, all of the kids cheered. We watched them in the sky, burning so bright that we thought the stars were on fire! Well, what we didn't realise was that everything that goes up's gotta come back down, and it came down hard, right into my little brother's head. That's how he died.'

'You had a little brother?' she asked with a sudden sorrow. Her father had always referred to himself as the youngest in his family.

'Yes,' he answered, and Sonny wondered where her father's anguish had gone to hide. She couldn't hear it in his voice. 'He was only a year old. My parents told me they were in the fields when it happened and he was just sitting in the garden. Playing one second, next thing you know he's gone.'

'How old were you then?'

'Only a year older than him. I'm almost forty years older than him now.'

There was no hesitation in his expression, no visible pain, no faltering. It was a fact of life: sometimes babies die, sometimes people drop things from the sky without considering where they will land. It made Sonny remember how her father's very presence was a daily miracle, only to remind herself how often she forgot; like an absent-minded Aztec who forgets to sacrifice a child to help the sun rise, but who wakes up to dawn nonetheless.

Sonny went to bed that night wondering how much of a mystery was this man she'd known all her life. And to confuse herself further, Sonny thought of the incident in the afternoon; the untouched grains of rice in Vince's bowl, glistening. She dreamed of what could have been reality. What if she'd got up to scoop a bowl of soup for him? What if she had offered him some Coca-Cola? Would he have thanked her? Would he have smiled? What if she had walked him out so they could be alone together on the front porch?

Nothing. She felt nothing but her heart ached nonetheless. She fell asleep clutching at some blithering, self-invented pain.

When she woke up, Sonny opened the door to the backyard and found her mother squatted beside the lemon tree. She stepped into her rubber sandals and came a little closer to stand under the shade of the dragon fruit's sunbleached limbs. Her mother didn't see her. She was busy rubbing a paper towel against clumps of rock sugar and trying to scrape off the clamouring ants. A semi-precious slab of morning light transfigured the sweetness into crystals. It led Sonny underground, unexpectedly. She was in the mine of her mother's beauty, now seeing the wisps of hair that always knew to fall just beside her eye, the forty or so freckles that the sun itself had painstakingly painted onto her cheeks (the proof she pointed to when reminding her to wear at least SPF50+), the tiny ripple of a scar on her upper arm from some Third World vaccination.

Sonny didn't want to get lost in the dark, but she couldn't look away. She wanted to pretend she hadn't seen everything that glittered in her mother's face, but like a handful of blood diamonds smuggled across the border, there they were, haunting her.

Her mother looked up from the scrabble of ants. 'How was your sleep?' she called out, pushing her hair away from her face with the back of a hand.

Sonny rushed outside and crouched beside her. 'I had a good sleep, *mẹ*. Did you sleep okay?'

'You know I always sleep well,' her mother grinned.

Sonny looked at the ground. The grass glistened with dew and wet her feet. 'Did it rain last night?'

'Yes. *Mưa vậy cây mừng lắm*,' her mother replied. '*Mất vịt không?* I caught you already – why are you still clinging on?'

Sonny laughed and watched as she tried to reason with insects.

There was her mother with the sun behind her, with Vietnam behind her, with the war behind her, years and years of youth, untold and continental, all behind her. How much had her mother sacrificed? Sonny thought of her rushing from store to store, a weightlifter of a housewife with those groceries on her arms, the way she cut chrysanthemum greens a millimetre from her fingertips because she didn't want to bruise the flavour, how quickly she cooked congee whenever anyone caught a cold. Sonny couldn't understand why being a daughter had always felt like a debt. She could never tell whether she loved her mother for who she was, or for what she had done for her; it seemed love itself was a question she didn't know how to ask, and yet one her heart had already found a way of saying yes to. One thing was certain. You can tell how much you mean to someone by the amount of ginger they make you eat when you're sick.

Chapter 9

Life after Death Anniversary

Fourth of April. The boys woke up early in the morning to visit the grocery stores at Cabramatta. Alex went looking for his father's favourite fruits. Custard apples, watermelon and lychees. He studied cardboard boxes of fruit and reached up to inspect the cardava bananas draped on the metal piping above him with tying twine. The other boys left him and went off to buy other offerings.

Vince, Tim Tam and Danny waited inside the Chinese barbecue shop. The crispy-skinned roast ducks and pigs hung from hooks. The boys ordered a whole *vịt quay* and watched as the man behind the counter hacked it into pieces. The sweetness of soy sauce and star anise warmed the air. Then, the boys bought flowers and left together.

Back at home, Alex took out the portrait of his father and stood it on the table. Three teacups were washed. The dust that had accumulated over the previous year whispered down the drain. Three bowls of rice, with a pair of chopsticks laid on each, the takeaway box of roast duck, the flowers and the fruits were arranged on the table.

Vince watched Alex's face as he poured Jack Daniel's into the cups and set them before his father's portrait. He was curious as to how death had erased all of Alex's anger, made such a vile man perfect again in his eyes. Vince remembered how, when he was thirteen, Alex had changed all the lights in his house to ultraviolet because he heard it was harder to shoot up that way. Imagine having to distract your father from his own veins; imagine a life under all that purple light.

Alex remembered the first bite of frozen pizza he had managed to feed his father after two days of refusing even water. His father had hated being touched, so he would walk home from school thinking of ways to peel the clothes off his sodden skin, to somehow keep him from thrashing in the bathtub at least long enough to wash the rashes underneath his arms. Every night he would lug his father's body onto the bed and cover him in their thickest blankets, but he would still be blue. When he'd finally fall asleep, he would look childlike but not quite innocent. Always alarmed, always waiting to be rescued. Alex remembered wondering if he would ever wake up.

Then everything came apart, separated, ruptured; even that unholy light broke into red and blue on Alex's face. The ambulance came and took his father away once and for all.

He overdosed. The boys all watched as he was carried away by paramedics. A white sheet placed over his body. A body they had seen jolt, pound at doors, throw itself against walls, the twitch of that running nose, the stretch of the sad smile, the nervous, tinkering eyes. Now it was lifeless, robbed of all its mayhem. The finality of that stillness shook Vince. But he knew the man inside had been dead long before his lungs decided he wasn't worth the breath.

Vince remembered the way Alex's face closed, how his fists clenched and he cried, rereading letters from his family still in Vietnam who counted on him to send money back. Some had hurt Alex more than others. Like the one from November 1993, when his little sister had a fever for five straight nights with no medicine to ease her scorching, and still had to get up to sell lottery tickets on the street. Alex would think bitterly of her scrawny self asking people to believe in serendipity.

But the envelope that Vince remembered best of all had only Alex's address on it. It arrived just a few days after his father's passing. Enclosed, the seeds of a fish egg tree, Alex's favourite memory from being a child in Vietnam. The other boys only knew this because he kept having the same dream about climbing up the trunk, trying to pick its little red fruits – they'd always fall from the branch just before he could reach them. The boys had taken those seeds and planted them in the backyard together but the tree hadn't survived winter. Maybe that was why the dream kept coming back.

For weeks after the funeral, Vince would find Alex sitting on his father's bed and watching a movie. Sitting there as if he was stuck. Silent most of the time, but once he said, 'I still hear him breathing, bro. Right in my ear. He's saying it's okay, he's made it back to his mum's belly, and it's still warm inside.' The boys could only sit with him and pass a cigarette around, taking turns to smoke and to summon, through memory, a friend or not-so-distant relative they'd lost to the same fate, like a séance for every slum on earth.

Alex's father had been gone for three years now. Together, the boys lit incense and bowed their heads. Vince couldn't look away from the photo. He couldn't have imagined that that man's face could have once been so proud. Alex's father held his head high and purposeful, his nostrils flared. His gaze was looming, fatal, final. In the photograph, he could not have been much older than the boys were. Vince saw himself, all his brothers, now, at this age, framed in their death portrait. Wreaths of smoke rose, carrying their prayers. He wondered if anyone would know to offer him homegrown fruits and fried chicken ribs when it was his time, and to light a cigarette instead of incense.

Close friends arrived at their doorstep. They came to offer flowers to the altar table, light incense and say a prayer. After they set up the feast, the boys floated out to the front yard and placed an ash can on the grass. By now the afternoon light was waning. Alex tore open a packet of ghost money and the boys held the notes in their hands. *Ngân Hàng Địa Phủ.* One by one, they held their money against the cigarette lighter. They dropped the bank notes into the barrel and let them burn. Each inscribed with the value of '1,000,000,000' ghost dollars. The jade emperor, the gold ingot, the phoenixes and the dragons charred grey-white, like an exposed bone.

As Vince watched the paper disappear into wrinkles of light, he remembered how his mother would burn joss paper in the middle of the night. He saw her squatting by a little fire in the garden as if to warm herself, sometimes folding the paper into flowers, and furniture, and shirts, and shoes, and ingots, before throwing it into the flame. He remembered being only seven or eight years old and watching her from a window, feeling young and sullen, thinking she'd rather play with spirits than her own son.

It was the ghost month. In the seventh lunar month of each year, his mother told him, the gates of the countless heavens and hells were unlatched and spirits were free to roam the world of the living. For an entire month, she would eat vegetarian food and refrain from calling for him aloud, for fear that spirits would learn his name and trick him into following them. Vince hated his mother's cold tofu dinners, and the way she caramelised bean curd skins to imitate slices of meat – he had never been convinced. To him, it seemed that these realms had mingled all year round in Cabramatta; the dead had always been amongst them, passed out on street corners and stairwells. At the dinner table, Vince's mother would set extra seats that remained empty for the ancestors to join. He did not know this as a child. He had made the mistake of sitting on one chair and witnessing, for the first time, his mother raise her voice: *You're crushing your grandfather!*

They went back inside to eat roast duck with Alex's dead father staring down at them. Vince wondered what the conversion rate was like in hell, how much a gram of dope cost there. If Alex's father was capable of spending his son's sweat-reeked, back-bending, cheek-burning, palm-callousing dollars on drugs, there was no price he wouldn't pay. Hungry ghosts couldn't eat in the underworld; they were condemned with throats too skinny to swallow. Vince was willing to bet, though, that they shot up like every day was doomsday down there. Whatever made hell sufferable, he supposed.

Alex had gone to bed by 7.30. Vince, Tim Tam and Danny sat in the backyard and smoked in silence. The air was bitterly cold and Vince could hardly breathe without thinking of the spirits which might, at that moment, be surrounding him.

'You look fucked, Vince. Haven't been getting enough sleep?' Tim Tam asked.

'I've been getting enough, it's just not any good. I can sleep the whole day and still feel tired when I get up, bro.' Vince's breath sucked and his eyes clenched.

'Maybe you should go for a walk, tire yourself out. Then you'll get a good sleep for sure.'

Vince thought about this for a bit, agreed with the logic behind it and stood up. 'You boys coming?'

'Nah, we'll probably stay home with Alex,' Danny replied. 'You know how he gets when it's *đám giỗ*.'

At this time of year, the boys often awoke to the sound of the door unlatching. They would find Alex, his face greased with the cold sweat of nightmares, walking out into the dark in his bed clothes. He was such a convincing sleepwalker; he never did stumble, always seemed to know where he was going, like a well-travelled sinner waltzing his way to the seventh circle.

Vince nodded. 'I'll be back soon.'

He walked to Cabramatta and did not feel any sleepier. He remembered loving autumn as a child because there would be fallen things to trample on when the bitumen became a bore. But now the dead leaves that thrashed in the wind sounded like an enemy's footsteps. He couldn't walk ten metres without looking over his shoulder.

Ahead of him was the ATM. Vince watched closely as the wad of clean fifty-dollar notes slid out of the machine and into liver-spotted hands. His thoughts ticked. The man was in his early sixties, wore wire-rim glasses and was built like a twig. There would hardly be any struggle. All it would take was a heavy-handed shove. This was the jackpot for a boy like him. But Vince wasn't feeling particularly like himself. So he let the old man stagger past, stuffed his hands into his pockets and walked in the opposite direction.

Vince faced the statue of the lion which guarded Freedom Plaza. It was past eight o'clock now and the evening chill nipped at his neck. He pulled the hood of his sweatshirt over his head and looked into the stone face, seeking comfort in the rocky formation of its rage. Vince wondered why he was out here, in the relentless cold, when he had Alex, Tim Tam and Danny waiting for him at home. It occurred to him then that he did not want anything they could give him. Neither did he want to run away. His desire was simple and impossible. He wanted to drown and rise from death anew.

Vince left the animal in captivity and started up the streets. When he would think about Cabramatta from inside his cell, it was always lit by that ceremonial light of summertime. The sugarcane stalls would be bustling and children would line up for a sip of sweetness. It was the same sun as anywhere else, but Cabramatta transported him – not to another country, but a crippled, blind and delirious soldier's memory of it. So much of it, of him, remained untranslatable. But just being there, walking under the gaze of elders who had lived for so long that their suffering was sacred, was enough to restore him. Vince would walk these streets as a kid, a tiny boy drowning in a t-shirt, every step sending him sliding to and fro in shoes which were more like vessels – 'You'll grow into them soon,' his mother would promise.

Soon. It seemed to be his mother's favourite word. But in the dark, pacing up and down the same street, starry-eyed, Vince felt as if the sky was trying to tell him that his time had, somehow, already passed. He'd been thinking about life, his in particular, and trying to make sense of it. Now, he saw someone who tore apart all his tenses, foreshadowed the past, recalled the present, made him uncertain of where he stood in the puddle of his sixteen years, give or take however many he had left.

Leaning over a cardboard box of bruised apples, a woman inspected each one with care, looking for a lost lover amongst all the spoiled fruit. Vince stopped. He had seen her buying groceries a thousand times before, but now the sight punished him. Two years, she had not visited him or written to him, had left him to wait for her like a pet.

Vince was determined to walk away, to find some bottle shop and work his way through that reservoir. But even when he was drunk, he would close his eyes and see that crumpled skin, those swollen eyes, that cheaply permed hair. And he knew he wouldn't be able to turn his back once he noticed how thin she had become. He watched closely as she approached the register and, finally, faced him. She was too busy counting change to notice her son.

Vince found himself searching her face and clenched his fists tightly upon seeing the very thing he dreaded most. The colour purple, his father's favourite shade of woman, painted her left cheek and sprawled across her jaw. The memory swallowed him whole. Feeling small, buried in the body of a trembling woman, the bed that slouched beneath them both, the echo of fists striking against wood, the never-strong-enough door, the never-strong-enough son. Was the weeping from him or his mother?

As she stepped out of the fluorescent light of the store and into the black night with several bags of fruit in tow, Vince came from behind and took the groceries in his hands.

'*Mẹ,*' he said, a little too coldly. '*Để con giúp cho.*'

'Vince, *con về rồi hả?*' she asked. Her voice was difficult to listen to, so strangely familiar, a sound you remember hearing from the womb.

He nodded.

'Since when?'

'Since a few weeks ago.'

'Why didn't you come home to me?'

'I didn't need to – I've got my own place,' he bit back, silencing her. He let himself seem heartless. It was better than thinking you had the right to love a person you could not protect.

The sound of their footsteps. The feeling of his mother's eyes on his face. Had he turned out the way she had hoped? They reached the car.

'I'll come back with you. I want to take a few of my things,' Vince said, hopping into the passenger seat with the groceries between his legs. He didn't have much left in the house, just old clothes he missed wearing. They were more comfortable than the new ones his friends had bought for him.

The night sky sulked above him. Vince watched his mother watch the road. All that time he had spent thinking of her face in the detention centre, this is what she looked like.

'Why didn't you ever visit me?' he asked, no longer trying to hack the sentiment from his tone. He sounded exactly as he felt: confused and mad with hurt.

His mother looked at him, then back at the road. 'Don't think that I didn't want to. I spent so many nights awake worrying about you. But your father wouldn't let me go.'

Vince nodded and continued to watch her face. Seeing her now, with the bruise on her jaw, he finally thought about what lengths his father would go to stop someone from disobeying him. But he couldn't be blamed for thinking she had just forgotten him. She had always been so frugal with affection.

'He said if I visited you then you'd never learn your lesson. He's just thinking of you, Vince.'

'Thinking of me.' Vince smiled bitterly, absurdly, and shook his head.

He felt his mother wince at his insolence and saw her hands tighten on the wheel.

'He's working again. At a factory, putting together refrigerators. He's getting better.'

'What's this then?' Vince asked, reaching gently for her sore jaw. She flinched and he shrank back into his seat. He noticed the instinct he had to make himself smaller and hated her for it. Her weaknesses were his.

'That was from a while ago. He's getting better.'

The rest of the car ride was quiet.

The car came to a halt. Vince carried the groceries to the doorstep and waited for his mother to open the door. He thought about how he had waded through so much shit only to arrive back home, back to the beginning again.

'Sleep here tonight, *con* – it's too late for you to be walking around,' she said as she pushed the door open. Trouble stalked the streets, looking for her son. She flicked on the lights and looked at him.

Before he entered the house, he had not known what he wanted to see. But it certainly wasn't this. Darkness, even with the lights on. A crucifix on the wall, beside a hole the shape of his father's fist. A photo of a long-dead-before-he-was-born grandmother on a cupboard. Vince laid the groceries down on the kitchen floor. He stared at his grandmother's face and remembered the story of her death. Hers was not the only one; his mother had a whole altar of people he never knew, who were always offered the fruits he liked most.

'No, I'll be fine.'

'At least let me make some food for you,' she pleaded.

'I said I'm fine!' Vince let out a breath, exasperated. 'Don't worry about me, don't do anything, *mẹ nghỉ giùm con đi*. Forget about my stuff. I don't need it, I'm getting out of here.'

'No, wait – Vince!' his mother called. 'Wait, there's someone I want you to meet.'

Judging from her tone, it must have been something endearing. Something innocent, something she was hopeful would change his mind and make him stay. But what could it possibly be? A teddy bear he used to hug at night? Had she been so lonely that she'd bought a goldfish?

Vince followed along unhappily as his mother led him into his old bedroom. He looked in to see if she had cleaned it out and found that all of his things were still there, only cramped in a corner. His bed had been pushed to the side of the wall, and his wardrobe beside the window.

'Everything's right where you left it. I just needed to move some things around to make room for –'

Was that a cot? At first, he thought the moonlight must be playing tricks on him. But there it was. And when he looked into it, there she was. Wisps of hair matted against her cheeks. Wearing the same secretly itchy, passed-down pyjamas that had once belonged to him. Her brows already darker than the night. So much of her was his. She stared up at him, curious. Her eyes looked as liquid as soft-boiled eggs, as black and bejewelled as the belly of papaya, as mysterious as the swirled cups from which fortunes are read. Vince felt himself swimming among the tea leaves. What kind of future could those eyes tell?

'*Me*,' Vince stuttered. 'Who, who's –'

He could do nothing but stare as the child's trepidation melted away. She smiled and reached for him with her eyes. She had recognised him before he could remember himself.

'That's your little sister.'

'Mine?'

The innocence in her son's voice startled her. Vince's mother looked up at him. His face was so young in the moonlight, younger even than the baby in the crib. She was reminded of that faraway time when he too was a child. Not big and brooding like he was now – a baby, who had always been so shy even around his own mother, who could spend hours playing with her hair, who would wrap his legs around her in his sleep, his brows knitted together, his ankles locked in place, fighting against letting go.

'Can't you tell?' his mother asked, reaching into the crib and holding the baby against her chest to show him. 'She looks exactly like her *anh hai mắt vịt*.'

'What's her name?' Vince asked, beholding the oracle. Could it be? Could this be his flesh and blood, his very own little sister?

'Emma.'

Emma?

Emma.

Vince had never before thought a sound could be so healing, to know that this little light had a name, to know two syllables could hold all the secret knowledge of the stars. *Emma* must be a synonym for destiny.

'How old is she?'

'Eighteen months,' his mother replied. This number did not mean anything to him. Vince instead examined her tiny fingers, her tiny feet and her tiny ankles, as if to confirm that, yes, this was indeed a baby-sized baby.

'Say hello to *anh hai*, Emma,' his mother crooned, chucking the baby beneath her chin.

'Hello,' Emma whispered in a raspy voice.

'*Aye, mày nói chuyện với ai vậy?*' Vince grinned.

'Hello, *anh hai*,' she croaked.

Vince thought his heart would be a little harder to hide after this.

'She always has trouble getting to sleep, this one,' his mother said. 'Wide awake way past her bedtime.'

Vince noted that this family trait had passed on to her. He poked curiously at Emma's nose.

'You play too rough with her! Stop it, or she'll have a flat nose!' his mother scolded, waving his hand away.

'Hold on, isn't someone meant to be looking after her?' he asked suddenly.

'I take care of her during the day, when I'm at home sewing – your father takes care of her at night.'

'Where is he now then?'

'Sleeping in our room. He must be tired from work.'

'Fuckin' hell.'

'Sometimes, I come home and she's all alone in her crib, sucking on one of my thimbles. *Như tim mẹ dừng lại.*'

'You can't let a drunk take care of her, *mẹ*! What are you thinking?'

'What am I supposed to do?' his mother said. 'We're living off my pay cheque, *con*. Your father and I forgot how expensive babies were.'

She looked down at Emma and pressed her nose against the baby's face, breathing her in.

'She's your father's *cục vàng*. He *cưng* her like nothing else in this world. She's very good at calming him down for me,' his mother said, smiling. 'Sometimes he gets so mad I think he's going to break something again, but then Emma cries and he can't do anything but hold her.'

Vince wrestled with himself for wondering why, as a child, he hadn't been able to make everything okay in the same way, why he could never take the sting out of his father's touch.

'Can I hold her?' he asked instead.

His mother looked up at him. He could see the smile syruping behind the sad eyes. Vince remembered being a child and dreaming of being coddled on her lap, wishing for her to look at him, sitting at the dinner table and wanting to ask how her day was. But she would always be tired after work. He wanted her to catch her breath, so he held his own. How could he even begin to fathom her sorrow, when all he had was her silence?

His mother placed Emma in his arms. She was even lighter than he'd expected her to be. Vince felt frightened thinking about how everybody he knew must have once been children too. Alex, Tim Tam, Danny. Alex's father. Danny's father. Tim Tam's two sisters. Dennis. Had they all been this defenceless? And yet, as Emma looked up at him, he couldn't help but feel as though he was the one being held.

Her mystic eyes caught the glint of his jade Buddha necklace and she reached for it. Vince craned his neck towards her hand and watched her face as she smoothed her fingers over the waxen stone.

'Will you eat dinner with me now?' his mother asked. Vince nodded. 'Good. Go change your clothes – I'll call you when the food's ready.'

'I'll know when the food's ready,' he said. 'Either the microwave beeps or the fire alarm goes off.'

His mother almost laughed. She watched as he cradled his baby sister in his arms, standing in the old bedroom he had outgrown. Sands of time had slipped through her fingers and gotten in her eyes. She walked to the kitchen, wondering who had taught her son how to love.

Vince looked down at Emma, who was now drifting in a dream. Her blinks were laden with lashes. She fell asleep holding onto his necklace. He pressed his nose to her head, then laid her down in her cot and pulled the edge of her blanket closer to her chin.

'*Ngủ ngon nhá*, Emma,' he whispered to her.

137

Vince changed into an old t-shirt and pyjama pants and ate with his mother. As he had suspected, the food was less than gourmet; overcooked steak and sodium-heavy soup. But she had made it herself and that meant something. He tried his best not to make his strenuous chewing obvious and prayed his jaw would not give out before the last bite. Vince turned to his mother and managed a weak grin.

'Is it that hard to eat?' his mother asked with worried eyes. 'Mẹ xin lỗi nhá.'

'What are you saying sorry for? Your cooking's what prepared me for the food in juvie.'

This was enough. This elastic meat, this crooked dinner table, this skinny woman with her swelling veins and her crinkle-cut hair – which, twice a year, for reasons he could never understand, she would pay for someone to soak in alkaline chemicals – this was enough, would always be enough. They ate their food silently, but did not notice the silence.

When they finished, she stood up to wash the dishes. Vince walked behind her and wrapped his arms around her shoulders. He pressed his face to the back of her head. There was sweat and chicken blood and salon ammonium and the baby-powdered springtime of the soap she'd always used. Melting into her smell, he wondered how he had strayed for so long from the first place he'd ever called home. But this thought, too, was disingenuous. Who was his mother, really? Even when she was in his arms, she was such a distance to travel. Light years away.

'I always tell you not to do work around the house with cold water,' Vince mumbled indignantly. He hadn't said a word to her in two years, but it was tricky to express time in Vietnamese; every verb seemed everlasting. 'Look how wrinkled your hands are.'

'If I listened to you, our family would have no more electricity left,' his mother replied, with a little chuckle. 'Do you want to shower in the cold tonight?'

She dried her numb hands with a dishcloth and reached back to touch his cheek. All she could do was look at him through the reflection of the kitchen window and say nothing, barely managing even to smile. All the words she knew seemed suddenly too small, too few, too incomplete. She stood there, waiting for the blood to creep back to her cold fingers so that she might finally feel her son's face, and ached for her heart to be whole again. This time, she would love him with all of it.

'Your little sister usually sleeps with me, but she can sleep in the crib tonight, since you'll be in the room.'

Vince lay awake in his bed. He listened closely to the world which rattled outside the bedroom window; listened to the rasping engines of cars speeding past, unexcitable ambulances, barely louder than a ripple the slurred singing from the only house on the street with a karaoke machine, and a little further away, the lemon-and-salt sound of someone's laughter piercing through starlight, with a terror that had not been there before. At 10.50 pm, his ears pricked at the sound of clumsy footsteps outside. A man, drunk and moaning and probably drooling, came stumbling down the path. With a violent cough, he stopped at the house next door, leaned over the fence and spat his throat-stuff onto the flower-bed below. Vince thought about the salmon-pink petals of Mrs Hussaini's poor hollyhocks and wondered if, tomorrow morning, he might find a lump of phlegm scintillating in the sun.

Another sleepless hour. Vince couldn't keep his eyes closed for too long, caught himself checking to see if Emma was still there in her cot every couple of minutes. While he waited for the sky to cheer up, for the sun to get on its way and hit that spot in the sky when everything's aglow but nothing's got a shadow, he stared at her little fingers still squeezing his jade necklace.

What could he give Emma? He wasn't good enough at maths to teach her about tangents and Pythagoras' theorem. How would she cope in school if he couldn't help her the way other elder siblings were expected to? It was then that he remembered Sonny's sparkling certificates, and the secret to all her success. Ever since primary, she had owned girly, organised stationery from Morning Glory: those grape-scented rubbers, flexible rulers, ball-pointed pens with swinging gem pendants, and pointy, metal contraptions that produce a perfect circle every time. Emma wouldn't have to borrow from any classmates; whatever she wanted, she would have it all. To love her was to believe in the future. He was impatient for the sunrise. He wanted tomorrow to come today. Sometimes, having hope is as simple as letting yourself forget who you've been.

Vince stayed at home the next day with his baby sister. He filled a salad bowl with soapy water for her bath but got distracted blowing bubbles, to hear her giggle when they touched her and to see her surprise when they popped. The siblings watched each other through these iridescent windows, each believing the other to be capable of magic.

'Emma, you see that one?' Vince said, pointing to a bubble the size of shrivelled blueberry floating just above her nose. 'It's been alive for ten minutes now! That's *ages* in bubble time. Let's keep it alive for as long as we can.'

'How, *anh hai*?'

'Keep looking at it.'

Together, they tried to keep the bubble always in sight and took turns at softly blowing it to keep it from landing. When it finally vanished, and the bathwater began to cool, Vince let more warmth trickle into the salad bowl. He was attentive to

140

the corner of Emma's eyes, the back of her chubby knees, barely grazed her ears, as though they were both sea shells, each with a pearl forming inside. Even the in-betweens of her toes were to him shrines inscribed with spells that'd be washed away if you weren't careful.

Vince's mother told him about the spare key she placed in her brown leather shoe at the front door. He stole a Honda Civic so he could visit her and Emma in the evenings. Over the next week, he came home to have dinner with her, watch over his little sister and sleep. Sometimes his father lay passed out on the couch. He always reeked of beer but Vince's mother insisted he was just tired from work. Father and son did not speak. They exchanged empty glances and avoided each other, a difficult task in such a tiny house. As long as there stood a wall between them, they allowed each other to carry on as though they were part of the same family.

Alex, Tim Tam and Danny were happy for Vince and he wasn't angry at them for not telling him. He was glad to have found out the way he did. There were other revelations too. Vince heard Sonny's mother scream for entire afternoons and wondered how anybody could endure that kind of treatment. That family had seemed so perfect when he had (almost) had dinner with them. Other fathers would simply stop coming home. Other kids would wait for bedtime, pop a toothbrush in their backpack but forget about the toothpaste, climb out a window, and soon enough end up on the street. He couldn't figure out what was holding them together.

'What is *happening* over there?' Vince asked.

'It's always like that in that house. That's why her children are so *ngoãn*, unlike my son,' his mother said.

She let a smile escape. It had been years since he'd last seen one out in the wild.

Chapter 10

The Stash

Since Vince left their house that evening, Sonny had become a soul tied to its senses in semantic knots. Her capacity to reason pretzeled logic in painful ways. At times she even questioned if she could make the ontological claim that Vince had been over for dinner since he hadn't so much as tasted her mother's cooking. Some weeks passed with no further interaction between the two. He didn't seem to bother much with school anymore. Of the twelve periods of Drama he'd had, Sonny had seen him twice. On both occasions, she tried to orchestrate their passing each other in hallways or courtyards but nothing came of it, not even a feeling. Vince had a strange power to look people straight in the eye and make them feel invisible.

Which is why, when she overheard his mother on the phone talking about how he had been visiting his little sister, her heart went out of her mind. Sonny was now more eager than ever to shimmy out to the front of the house and check for mail. She propelled herself ever higher from the trampoline to spy over the fence. When she hung the laundry to dry, she stretched her time translucent under a cobweb of old bed linen. Anything to catch a glimpse. He'd only come home in the evenings, so the most she could see of him was an outline through the living-room window. Even so, Sonny was too impatient for sleep those nights. She wondered if there was any chance their proximity made her appear in his mind. Might his mother have mentioned her name over dinner? Was he lying in bed right now? Could he be thinking of her?

One windy afternoon, Sonny's mother decided her hair was getting too long and took her to a nearby salon built at the back of somebody's house. Large bottles of peroxide and rolls of catering foil lay stacked in a corner. Just inside, the hairdresser's month-old baby slept noiselessly on a hammock. Sonny's mother reminded her that her hair was holding onto all her bad luck and needed to be chopped off ahead of exam time. No matter how Sonny tried to dispute her hair's ability to absorb misfortune, she could not change her fate. In her mother's mind, superstition was a science. And so, when the hairdresser asked her how short she wanted to go, she let her mother hold a finger to the nape of her neck, not daring to say a word. Sonny was so busy staring into the mirror and keeping herself from sniffling that she was unaware of someone watching her outside.

A fight in one of the surrounding streets had scattered when the police were called, and boys were seeking asylum in people's backyards. Vince had just jumped a fence and landed on a patch of cooking herbs. Having sustained an injury from the prickly culantro leaves, he held onto his ankle with both hands and hobbled along, cursing in pain. While he struggled to keep his balance, Alex and Danny were already at the other end of the yard, helping Tim Tam over to the garden next door.

Hearing voices from inside the house, Vince squinted at the window and saw some girl reflected back at him through a full-length mirror. He found himself holding his breath as the scissors chewed through the bundle of her hair, so black it was a silhouette of itself. When the shadow fell away from her face, it revealed yet another mystery: a stranger who might have once been someone special to him.

All was still, until a crying child snuck into the silence. The hairdresser stepped out of the room to rock her baby back to sleep, and then there was only the girl left in the mirror. Vince couldn't move. He felt silly for standing there on one leg, for not being armed with a good enough reason should anyone catch him staring; yet innocent and free and unashamed of his curiosity. How could you explain to someone a shape in the clouds or a sentence in Pig Latin? They either understood, or they didn't. Either way, you didn't need them to.

There was a horizon somewhere, and Vince felt himself getting closer to it; remembering who he was before he'd been forced to become somebody else. It was like returning to the garden you'd grown up in and finding a message you'd left yourself in the dirt. He saw his life flash before her eyes.

'Vince!' Danny called. 'What are you lookin' at?'

Huh? Oh, nothing,' Vince answered, shaking his head a little. He skirted past the star-petalled flowers sprouting from the hairdresser's garlic chives and to the other end of the yard. Jumping on the ceramic rim of a potted cumquat tree, he kicked a fruit-heavy branch as he bounded over the fence. Golden orange ovals dropped to the ground in a puddle. He heard the cumquats dribble against the concrete before falling silent, but left them there for someone else to harvest as he ran to catch up with the others.

All the thoughts inside his head were suddenly crisp and sun-drenched. Light, and filled with it. Hadn't his family once grown cumquats in their garden? If not, why did he know that their juice could be used to make a tangy *nước chấm*, and that the scientific name of the tree was *fortunella*? Hadn't someone told him the cumquat was the only citrus with a peel sweeter than its own flesh? Someone must have been Sonny. Vince thought it had been years since she'd last crossed the bridge between his ears, and yet, having seen her only a second ago, he realised she looked almost exactly like he'd always remembered.

Vince bit into the fruit of his memory, skin and all, and let the light explode on his tongue. He closed his eyes and saw Sonny standing on the grass with dew and dirt dampened feet, a crown of butterfly clips in her bowl-cut hair. She stared at him with a stern look, as if to ask what had taken him so long, how could he have left her waiting in forever like a flower fossilised while he went to grow up on his own, and who told him he could imprison her within his mind's amber?

Sonny. She was the one who used to tape together cubby houses from cardboard boxes they'd found on the curb, showed him how quiet the world could get with a flashlight and a handful of things to whisper. The one who knew just how long to microwave left-overs, who would mix burnt rice with butter and somehow make it taste just like cinema-fresh popcorn. The one who once cried when she saw him snapping branches off a eucalypt, not because she thought him wicked but because she swore she could hear the tree moan in pain – it was only the wind. Sonny, the first girl he'd ever wanted to hold hands with. It was not a romantic gesture; more, 'Here I am. Take me on whatever adventure you're on.'

Vince remembered how he used to despise the murder of crows perched atop power lines. The elders had called them bad omens. *Con quạ.* The name was burdened by a glyph, the sound itself signifying peril. But Sonny had always hidden scraps of her lunch to feed them. The elders would tell her to get away from the crows and call them cursed. But she never listened.

'Even the cursed have to eat,' she'd mutter to him as she laid a few sandwich crusts on the grass.

He would watch the crows swoop down from their tightropes to drop gifts at this little girl's feet: scuffed earrings, paper clips, sea glass. He began to trust them because they had the sense to love her.

Vince remembered how *bà ngoại* used to joke that the day Sonny learned to crawl was the day she began plotting to run away. She'd always linger near doors and windows left ajar, and even roped him in to her escapades. Perhaps, she proposed, the two of them would tiptoe to the front of their houses before the beginning of a new day and take the bus somewhere, to see what was out there. Or, they would go out to the garden, dig a hole and live with the worms underground – they were very friendly, she assured him.

At school, the other children committed themselves to collecting cicada shells and chasing each other into corners. Against the rumbling of laughter and alphabet recitals, Sonny sometimes just sat by the abacus, with the weight of her tiny existence propped on one elbow. When she let out a sigh, Vince swore he could feel his world tremble.

They held parts of each other that no-one else had ever known. Before his trouble began, the sun shone forever in her eyes and he had been content to play even with her shadow.

'Girls are like flowers. There's no need for you to bloom right now,' *bà ngoại* said in her mellow, drunken slur. 'Take your time, *con gái.*'

'But, *ngoại*, who would do that to their own daughter?' Sonny sobbed, folding herself around *bà ngoại*'s body, still warm with sleep. 'I was just getting ready for spring when she took a pair of scissors and cut off all my petals. Don't you feel sorry for me?'

Grandmother and granddaughter lay in bed with *Journey to the West* trumpeting from the television screen. Sonny anticipated the next line before it came; when you have seen something this many times, it is not so much watching as it is waiting. She snuggled her head closer into the curve of her grandmother's neck. The hem of *bà ngoại*'s shirt floated upwards, revealing a pleated streak below her belly button, from a surgery to fix the leak in her uterus from too many pregnancies. It reminded Sonny that, though her ancient smile hid the scar well, *bà ngoại* had not always been a joyful drunk. The truth was somewhere in those stitches.

'*Bà ngoại.*'

'Hmm?'

'Does it still hurt?' Sonny asked, pointing to the scar, wondering how a woman's womb could have given and yet been ransacked of so much life.

'No,' she replied with a chuckle. 'How could it still hurt after all these years? I can't even remember what it felt like. The only thing you don't forget in this life is the faces of your children. I still see your mother's brothers and sisters sometimes, when I'm trying to fall asleep. They stand right there, at the end of my bed, and try to crawl back in between my legs.'

Bà ngoại laughed heartily at the look of horror on Sonny's face.

'Why didn't you tell us you've been having nightmares?!'

'It's not a nightmare, *con*. It's my favourite dream. All my children, even the ones I never got to bury, finally come back to

147

me.' *Bà ngoại* watched with a fading smile as tears again dewed the ends of her granddaughter's lashes. '*Trời ơi*, what are you crying about now?'

'I didn't know you were so sad,' Sonny whispered. '*Con xin lỗi, ngoại.* I'm sorry for complaining about a stupid haircut.'

'Silly girl, who told you I was sad?'

'Aren't you?' she asked, fumbling. '*Mẹ* says that's why you started drinking ... because you remember too much. You remember everything you've lost.'

Bà ngoại smiled and reached over to hit her on the head. '*Con quỷ này*, being weak and old isn't enough – you want your poor grandmother to get dementia too?'

'I didn't say that!'

An echoing yell drew Sonny and *bà ngoại*'s attention back to the drama. The trickster Monkey King had been thrown out of heaven and crushed into a crack in the earth so that only his face was visible. A montage showed the years pass in a matter of seconds; a forest sprouting from the rocks while the Monkey King remained trapped with a wild mushroom growing comically above his head, a flower blooming from behind his ear, spiderwebs criss-crossing over his face. As he stuck his tongue out to collect pearls of morning dew, a bird passing overhead left a dropping in his mouth. The Monkey King glared up at the sky. Slowly, he withdrew his tongue, swallowed, and with a resentful, quivering lip, stared at a world a hand stretch away, and yet one he couldn't reach. A tear fell from one eye. He licked that too. Sonny remembered a line he had said in the first episode: *I said I wouldn't die, but I didn't say I wouldn't feel any pain!*

'The older I get,' said *bà ngoại*, shaking her head, 'the more difficult I find this to believe.'

'The Monkey King legend?'

'No, that's real. I'm talking about the acting.'

Sonny turned to her grandmother with a gaping mouth. 'But you love Dicky Cheung!'

'And I will love him until the day I die – don't go telling your grandfather I said that,' bà ngoại warned with humour squirming in her brows. 'But there's something wrong with this scene. He has the face of a man who has suffered. His tears are too genuine.'

'Too genuine to be believable?' Sonny asked, always eager to point out a paradox.

'Yes. A mythical being crying just like a human – that is impossible. The Monkey King may struggle the same way you and I do, but he cannot suffer like us,' bà ngoại said beneath half-closed eyelids.

Sonny grinned. Whenever her grandmother was in the mood to argue, she would seem suddenly twelve years sober. 'Why not, ngoại?'

'Because after drinking heavenly wine and eating the peaches of immortality, he could no longer understand time. He couldn't picture the future; he couldn't hold onto any memories. All humans are tortured by time. That is why a woman can go on waiting for her children to grow even as she takes her last breath, and why the past lives and dies inside her, like a baby born still. But immortals do not even feel time – they laugh at the idea. They belong to the present, just like mosquitoes. To them, there is only one eternal moment, nothing else.'

Sonny rubbed her still stuffy nose against her shirt and tried to breathe in through her mouth. 'But isn't it lonely there, in eternity?'

'My clever granddaughter,' bà ngoại muttered, using her sleeve to wipe a strand of snot from Sonny's cheek. 'Have you ever seen a lonely mosquito?'

*

Autumn arrived one morning in March; unannounced and uninvited. Once-green leaves fell to the floor without a stir. The warmer months, the yawning sunrises and young rosebuds and promising of things, can make people feel larger than they are. But in autumn, we are all small again; we are only atoms, always just arrived in a strange and ageless universe, never-ending, never-beginning.

Sonny decided she had to live with her haircut, but wasn't in favour of learning to like it. She tried to avoid herself in bathroom mirrors, but her reflection found other places to hide, like the window she used to stare out of in Ancient History, and the sadistically shiny conical flask in the Science lab. Sometimes she swore she could see a spectre of a sneer on her face, as if her own ego was belittling her. *Your neck looks a little bare without all the hair. Did you feel that slight breeze coming through the corridor? Chilly, isn't it?*

Sonny felt sillier than ever for supposing that anything could have happened between her and Vince. Who was she fooling? What kind of boy would notice her when there were girls like Michelle strutting around? All this time she'd been giving away her love coin by coin, in a currency he didn't even accept.

So Sonny went on living the way she always had; safe and alone, sat on her trampoline dizzied by verbose passages of erotica, and trying to remember how to smile when her parents asked, 'How about school?' Which is why when Oscar came home one day and told her of a communal reserve of pornography, the prospect of an expedition was so enticing.

'There's this thing I hear the boys in my class talking about all the time,' Oscar said, glaring at the full glass of milk. 'They call it The Stash.'

'The Stash?'

'Yeah. A few boys in 7G jigged and went all the way to Lake Gillawarna to see it.'

'What's in it?'

'I don't know, some . . . dirty stuff,' Oscar said. He had wanted to see his sister squirm but she just stared intently at nothing in particular.

'Dirty stuff?'

'Yeah.'

'Hold on, what kind of dirty stuff are we talking here?' Sonny asked as she carried on drying the dishes. Oscar could see the sudden knots of tension forming in her back. 'Like lingerie catalogues or actual videos?'

'I don't know,' he laughed. 'What, do you want to go check it out too?'

He'd meant it as a joke but she appeared to be frozen stiff, only with a glass ramekin quivering in her hand.

'Sonny? Are you serious?'

She broke out of her mental frost and scoffed. But she still wouldn't turn to look at him. 'Is that how you think of me?'

'Why are you acting so serious?'

'Because this is a serious issue! Pornography is a crime, stupid – you can get arrested for it.'

'What?'

'Yeah, that's why I'm gonna need you to tell me exactly where it is.'

Sonny began plotting out the bus route from Cabramatta to Georges Hall. The bodice-rippers were beginning to exhaust her. She grew weary of having to walk in the tattered shoes of an orphan in the English countryside who'd been sold by her relative to a brothel, just to read a few salacious scenes. Sonny wanted so badly to see something real. What claim did boys have on The

Stash anyway? It sounded like something with universal value, to be shared amongst the global community, like a heritage site. Pornography was necessary to any human's quality of life, a birthright even. She would not be discriminated against.

Sonny reminded her mother she'd get home at 5 pm because she would be at the library studying. At school, she told Najma about The Stash and by the end of the day the two were on the bus to Georges Hall.

'Thanks for coming with me, Najma.'

'It's okay. I really wasn't looking forward to going home today anyway.'

'Is something wrong?' Sonny asked.

Najma turned away from the window as the bus swung past the charcoal chicken place on the corner of Magnolia Avenue, which had recently been featured in a double-page spread of the local newspaper for its poor hygiene practices. As it turned out, it wasn't any divinely inspired eating disorder that Najma had experienced but just your regular, family-size salmonella.

'Oh, it's nothing,' she said with a sigh. 'My mum's just been nagging me more than ever since she found out my soul is damned for hell.'

'She caught you watching *Titanic*?'

'No. I forgot to pray the other day.'

'Oh.'

According to local legend, the location of The Stash could never be pinpointed. Each time it was discovered, it was hidden in a new place so that no group or individual held absolute sovereignty. The girls didn't know where to begin. So, they followed the paved path which led to a perfectly round clearing in the woods. The recently mown grass suggested it was a place reserved for Sunday-morning picnics, as opposed to camcorder evidence of doggy style or, as the Romans called it, sexual intercourse in the manner of wild beasts. No sign of the treasure trove resided here. Sonny and Najma left behind the flat lawn and asphalt in favour of true adventure: soft soil trails. As they walked deeper and deeper into the suburban wilderness, they lifted every small boulder, peered between blades of grass and even tried sifting through the mulch from a playground they passed. The Stash was nowhere to be found.

As the sun swung across the afternoon sky, Najma and her shadow achieved the same length, becoming Siamese twins joined together at the sole. It was then, as she glanced over her shoulder at her second self, that the second pillar of Islam came crashing down on her. She hadn't prayed the other day. But it wasn't because she forgot.

'I know my mum's always done what she thought was best for us,' Najma muttered, slowing her pace. 'But the way she treats my brothers is just different from the way she treats me.'

Sonny matched her footsteps with Najma's. 'How different?'

'They get to walk around the house shirtless and she never says anything. Yesterday she comes into my room and tells me off for wearing pyjamas.'

'Not the Garfield ones?'

'Yes, the Garfield ones. My long sleeve, cartoon-print, knit pyjamas are too provocative to wear at home, Sonny.'

It was rare that Sonny saw her friend look so defeated. She couldn't think of any words strong enough to undo the disgust, and the desire, that men saw in women, that a mother could see in her daughter. Maybe they didn't exist.

'My life would be so much simpler if I was skinny. Not Victoria's Secret skinny. Just skinny enough to be less seen, you know? I feel exposed all the time. Like everyone can see through my clothes.'

153

In the midst of her misery, Najma noticed a rainbow lorikeet sitting on the branch of a paperbark tree and pointed it out to Sonny. Her frown was still firm, but her eyes were imbued with sudden softness.

The lorikeet spread its wings and revealed a blaze of orange on its breast. Najma expected it to take off and fly far into the distance. Instead, it swooped down, landed gracefully on the edge of an overflowing bin, and began foraging. She would have expected such behaviour from a magpie, a pigeon, or even a galah, but not a lorikeet. She hadn't known self-respecting birds could have such objectionable habits. It made her feel oddly at ease with herself.

'I think I know how you feel,' said Sonny, as they stopped beside the bin to watch. 'It's like your most private parts . . . don't even belong to you. But I don't think it's got anything to do with how much you weigh, Najma.'

As Sonny rested a consoling hand on her friend's shoulder, the lorikeet's royal blue head was busily digging through fruit roll-up wrappers and ambient temperature ice cream. It made Najma think of last Ramadan, when she'd gotten her period and had to lock herself in the bathroom just to eat. Then the bird popped up and looked at her directly, with a perfectly crimson beak stuffed with cigarette ash. *How could you tell a male from a female?* Perhaps by asking if it had ever been told to wear its colours more modestly.

'I think you're right,' said Najma.

Together the friends trudged through knee-high foliage, the leaves crackling beneath their feet. The trees shuddered at the brush of the wind's fingertips. Sonny and Najma struggled up a steep hill that overlooked a creek, clutching their itchy noses and scowling at the surrounding air. The breeze must have aroused some deposits of sleeping pollen. As they reached the top of the hill, they noticed a pair of ibises standing at the edge of the water beside a big shrub, sticking their bills curiously into an overgrowth of weeds. By the time Sonny saw the rusted lid of a tin box beneath the stirred green, she was too exhausted to even scream. She raced down the hill and felt as though the wind had granted her wings. Meanwhile, Najma was so mindful of the slope that she decelerated to give way to a militia of ants.

'I think this is it, Najma! Come on!' Sonny called out, watching as her friend's head bobbled in the distance. A few gulps of air later and Najma had made it. She threw herself onto the ground beside Sonny.

There it was. Sonny and Najma had imagined the ever-elusive, ever-explicit material must resemble an extended love scene out of a Hollywood blockbuster: a night under ivory sheets, shadows falling on flesh, pelvic movements that harmonised with the undulating sea. At last, they had discovered the infamous stash.

A chainsaw guitar solo seemed to tang strenuously in the background as they opened the tin box together. The first thing they saw was the underwhelming underwear section of a Target catalogue. As they nudged the first layer out of the way and dug deeper, they were struck with another anticlimax. There were no cassettes or memory cards. It was all paper. Worse yet, The Stash wasn't even targeted at them. It consisted of men's magazines, periodical literature which seemed to cover such eclectic interests as 'Hot Legs Spread For You, Pg. 12', 'How to Turn on a Dental Assistant: Drill Or Be Drilled' and 'Best Nips Ever?', along with the occasional gardening column. Sonny and Najma both flinched by instinct, but forced their eyes open again and tried to salvage whatever clues the artefacts could give them about the kind of girl the opposite sex was attracted to. The answer was definitive: not them. Disappointed but nevertheless intrigued, they chose a collector's edition which promised 'more than 80 erotic pictori-als' of women who were distinguishable only by cup-size: Sharon (48D), Donna (38D), Julianna (42D) and Nikki (40D).

Sonny (10 degrees concave) and Najma (training bra) huddled closer to the water to examine it. It was brighter there; the pale sun hit the surface of the water, sending its light to refract. Sitting on the bank, breaths hitched, each knowing this would change the way they thought of sex forever, they turned the pages together. That was when it happened. Tucked between the woman in a wet top on page 22 and the woman with no top at all on page 23, a thin stack of instant film. They flicked through the Fujifilm photos quickly – a bedroom in shadow, a creased pillow, a fuzzy eyelash or pubic hair on a duvet, a vaguely unwashed foot, the corner of a blurred window. Then, in appalling focus, a penis appeared, point-blank. Unclothed. Unerect. Worst of all, uncircumcised. Neither Sonny nor Najma had ever seen the male sex organ before, so they were unsure if nature had intended for it to be unsymmetrical, but they were certain this one was exceptionally crooked. How could a piece of meat arouse such anxiety? It looked as though you would need a saddle and years of equestrian lessons to tame it.

Sonny and Najma panicked. They lost grasp of the magazine and let 48D, 38D, 42D and 40D all tumble into the water. The girls looked at each other frantically. Najma silently pleaded for Sonny to fetch the magazine as she gathered the bedroom pictures floating on the surface. Sonny screamed softly as she eased down the slippery slope of the riverbank and plunged her arm into the water. Luckily the magazine hadn't drifted to the bottom; it had been caught by a mangrove.

'Come on, you can do it,' said Najma, holding onto Sonny's shoes to keep her from falling in.

After successfully fishing the magazine out, Sonny tried to

dry it against the grass. They slipped the photographs back in the crease and continued to peel through the sopping pages. As they did, a sudden tingle on the edge of Najma's spine alerted her to a presence other than herself, Sonny and their accompanying shadows. Sensing something amiss, she checked her peripherals.

'Oh my god. Why is *he* here?!'

'Who?'

'Vince!'

At first, Sonny only rolled her eyes, unconvinced. But as she looked over her shoulder, the world skidded to a halt. The birds stopped chirping. The wind stopped blowing. The water stopped rippling. All the atoms were suddenly out of breath, motionless. There was only Vince, in all his glory, conquering the land of mere mortals. Sonny felt her thighs quiver as she watched his athletic aptitude in action, his long legs moving with untouchable ease as he mounted the mountain. She couldn't tell which way was up.

Najma stared at the ground for a few seconds and then turned to Sonny with a look of resolve. She got up from her knees and swiped the bindis off her pants.

'Najma, what are you doing?'

'What do you think? I'm getting out of here!'

'What? We just got here!' Sonny said, gesturing passionately towards the rest of the magazines, still unexplored.

'Are you crazy? What if he sees us?'

'He won't! This bush is covering us. We can just hide here until he leaves.'

'Sonny, I'm tired and I'm going home. I've seen enough scrotum for today.' Najma sighed and began heading for some dense woodland to conceal her departure. She crab-walked stealthily into the tall grass and almost vanished from sight. Her face popped up suddenly. 'Are you coming or not?' she mouthed.

Then, pointing with displeasure to the soon-to-set sun, 'I gotta get home and pray.'

Sonny contemplated her friend's spiritual commitments as she glanced down at the magazine they'd only just rescued. Perhaps some adventures were meant to be had on one's own. Particularly ones involving 'Juicy Amateur: Georgia's Red-Hot Peach'. Indeed, one must have ample time and solitude to properly appreciate such elegant prose.

'You go first,' she said with a dignified nod. 'I'll just hide The Stash somewhere and head home after.'

Najma waved reluctantly and then wove her way out of the woods with a dexterity that Sonny hadn't known her capable of. Sonny held the drenched pages of the magazine together in silence. By now, Vince had come down the hill and was walking by her hiding place. There was only a gangly bush and a few footsteps of foliage between them. Just then, an ibis that had been splashing about in the water lunged onto land and headed for Sonny. Horrified, she sucked in a sharp breath and struggled to keep still as it ran its slippery bill along the heel of her shoes, dripping swampy water all over her socks.

Just as Vince passed and Sonny let out a sigh, the damned bird stuck its bill up her skirt.

'Ah!' she yelped.

Vince had spotted her. He left the footpath and walked towards the shrub.

'Hey!' he shouted brightly. Was she seeing things, or did he look happy to see her?

'Hi!' Sonny replied with a pained smile.

How unlucky could she get! For weeks she had wanted him to see her, had even managed to trick her subconscious into dreaming of him just so they could spend some time alone, and when he finally did, she looked like a medieval friar. Sonny wanted to rip her monastic hairstyle from her head and clarify that she hadn't, in fact, taken a vow of celibacy. As if that would change anything.

'What're you doing over there?' he asked. His hands were stuffed in his pockets and his smile revealed a sliver of those star-studded teeth.

'Huh?' Sonny answered nervously, looking at the magazine in her hand and trying to think of where to hide it. 'Err . . .'

Enlivened by her alarm, Vince sped up and now was only a few steps away.

She dunked her hand back into the water. The cold sent a jolt through her arm.

'Oh, just, um, washing my hands.'

'What you got there?'

'What? Nothing.'

By now, Vince had walked around the shrub and crouched down beside Sonny. He nodded towards her hand in the water and smiled viciously. His eyes were two pools of oil waiting for the lick of flame.

'Give it to me,' Vince said, turning his palm up. Just as Sonny was about to let go of the magazine in the water, he lurched at it, tearing it from her loosened grasp. Vince pulled the soaked porno out of the water and seemed to disbelieve his own eyes. He took a moment to peel through the sodden pages before he looked up at Sonny, whose face was now as red as a boiled beetroot that had just been caught with a dirty magazine. 'What the fuck?'

He hunched over and broke into laughter, his forearm supporting his weight on the ground. If it was any other girl he would've still found the situation eccentric, but he could, perhaps, wrap his head around it. This was a different matter entirely: Sonny Vuong, his childhood friend, the girl who, as far as he knew, had never been in any kind of trouble, who always looked so high and mighty and otherworldly, hiding behind a bush, alone, to read GIRLS NEXT DOOR! EVEN NUDER THAN LAST ISSUE.

'No, listen, you don't know the whole story!' she groaned.

'Okay, tell me the whole story then,' offered Vince, giving her a moment to prepare her case while he flicked over to page 32. Sonny tried to make out his expression as he contemplated the photospread of Georgia, lounging open-legged on the edge of a bed. *Did he like his peaches red? What colour was hers?*

She only remembered to reply when he looked up at her. 'My brother told me about The Stash and I went to investigate so I could, um, report it to the police?'

Vince laughed even harder.

'You're that desperate, huh?'

The tone of his voice was no longer teasing, but there was a smile on his lips, vague and semilunar. A crescent of teeth uncovered, the reflectance of a tongue let slip. *Desperate for what?* Sonny wondered. Could he be referring to the activities depicted in the magazines? Was this really happening? Was she going to have her first time out in the open like this?

'How's that sit with you? Your parents having you on lockdown every day and all.'

Oh. Sonny let out a breath of relief and disappointment. 'You get used to it,' she replied.

'You know what I think? I think you just wanna get out. You're on the verge of . . . something. I can see it.'

He's mocking me again, she thought. It was difficult to tell.

'I'm not gonna pursue a porno career,' Sonny said defensively.

'What?' Vince said, laughing. 'No, that's not what I meant.'

'What did you mean then?'

'Nothing.' He smiled, amused by something he saw in her face.

'How'd you get here?'

'By bus,' Sonny answered miserably.

'You gotta catch the bus home?' – she nodded – 'What a fuckin' mission. Do you need a ride back? I'm going to my mum's now anyway.'

Sonny wanted to decline his offer, to walk off coolly with her hips swinging and the two or three strands of hair she had left fluttering in the wind. But a car ride would get her home infinitely faster than a bus, and answer questions which kept her up at night. What did his car smell like? What did he look like when he was driving? Did he accelerate when he got to speed bumps? Did he have any respect for amber lights or were they just a reluctant shade of green to him?

In the car, Sonny faced the side window and avoided his gaze. She wouldn't say it aloud but this was her first time in a moving vehicle without her parents, her first time outside of home with a boy. On the sudden, she remembered the fine-grained photo of the world's wonkiest wiener and couldn't get it out of her head. Her eyes darted to Vince's lap. *Surely his was more proportional. But had he been circumcised?* She cleared her throat nervously, feeling a need to say something lest her thoughts got too loud and he overheard them.

'So, what's happening around here? This area,' she asked, gesturing towards her face. The sun glared at Vince through the windshield. Such uncompromising light would have humbled almost anyone else, but it only redefined his beauty in harsher terms, allowing Sonny to study not only the deliberate armature of his face, the sharpness of the hollows and the fullness of the peaks, but the stark grazes and bruises. In a strange way, those marks made the rest of his face look even more flawless, and the flawlessness only exacerbated the state of his injuries.

'I got into a fight,' Vince said in a merciless tone, giving the sun the side-eye. Not getting any response from Sonny, he turned to her and found her grinning. 'What?'

'Oh, nothing. Nothing at all.'

Vince didn't know how to react. He would have been prepared for a soft swooning noise, or a concerned voice probing for more detail in his mysterious answer. Not silence.

'I like my bruises,' he said. 'I reckon they give me character.'

Sonny was pleased to know he'd been sitting there, trying to muster up a response.

'Isn't that what your personality's there for?'

Vince laughed sarcastically. 'I like your hair, by the way. Looks . . . light.'

Like a halo.

'Thanks,' she said unsurely. She couldn't tell if that had been the first genuine compliment she'd ever received from a boy, or if he was just being snotty. 'What were you doing at the park by yourself anyway?'

'Not much. Just wanted to go somewhere to clear my head. Be around some nature. Have a smoke.'

'Start a bushfire.'

Vince looked at her and laughed. It sounded like the real thing this time.

As much as she longed for the road home to go on forever, she could tell they were getting close. The thought of her mother standing by the window, or her father checking the mail, and seeing her get out of Vince's car, began to breathe doom down her neck.

'Can you let me off at the corner of our street? Actually no, maybe a bit further away. Here, maybe?'

'Right now?'

'Yeah.'

'I can't, there's a guy behind us.'

'Oh, okay. Keep going, keep going.'

'Want me to pull over here?'

'No, keep going.'

'How about here?'

'No, too close.'

'Sonny, we passed your house already.'

'Shit!' she exclaimed. 'Can you pull over here? I can walk the rest of the way. Thank you.'

He was just about to drive off when she grabbed onto the door. 'Hey, this stays between us, right?'

'The Stash is for everybody, Sonny. Don't be greedy.'

A quick, nervous burst of laughter from Sonny, and then, 'You know what I mean.'

Vince looked at her sceptically, eager to torment her for a little longer. 'Yeah, okay. Your secret's safe with me.'

As soon as she closed the front door, her mother's voice drew her into the kitchen. With her back turned as she dug an unfertilised egg out of a plucked chicken, she told Sonny to take the bowl of sliced green mango and *muối ớt* to her grandmother and wake Oscar up from his nap. It was when she entered the bedroom that Sonny discovered something had gone missing.

'*Bà ngoại*, what happened?' she asked, pointing to the empty space above Oscar as he lay asleep. 'Where did my bed go?'

Her grandmother only grinned as she dipped the sourness into toasted chilli salt. There weren't many places in their house that could fit her half of the bunk bed. Sonny went searching in the garage, out the backyard, next to the mailbox, under the trampoline, but it just wouldn't show up. Finally, she tried opening the door to the tiny laundry room at the back of the house and heard a *thud*. There, where the washing machine used to be, taking up so much of the room she couldn't figure out how it'd got through the doorway, was her bed.

She didn't need to wonder why her parents had done this. She ran to thank them both for giving her a place of her own to study for her upcoming exams and then jumped on top of Oscar's mattress, her hands quivering with care as she peeled the Backstreet Boys posters from the wall and carried them away. Because the laundry room opened to the backyard, and was tucked far away from the bedrooms, she knew she could stay up reading without her mother being able to tell that her light was on. But her books were left alone tonight. Now was not the time to imagine sunsets, but to look out her own window.

The first night in her new room, Sonny lay in bed and thought about how her name had tickled the tip of Vince's tongue, and the way two syllables could be a song when he spoke it. She thought about him and how, when he looked at her, she felt herself come alive again. Meeting Vince was like meeting someone who knew you before your own death, when you used to exist.

You're on the verge of . . . something. I can see it.

What had he seen? Could the verge in question be the zipper of his pants? Sonny giggled. No, what did he really see? Could he tell everything she wanted to run away from?

That night Vince thought of her, too. He ate his mother's congee and caught himself smiling. He sat on the toilet and wondered how somebody could be so unrehearsed, so goofy, so fucking *dễ thương*. As Vince watched his little sister sleep in the half-dark, he hoped she would grow up a bit like Sonny had, like nobody else he had known. Like the unnamed flower that grows amongst apocalyptic weeds, lending its bloom to anyone who still bleeds red for beauty.

Chapter 11

Betwixt Two Front Teeth

Friday afternoon. The bell had gone and the children were unleashed once more. Boys raised hell at the train station, challenging each other to race across the tracks and up the shaky embankments. At first, the girls only spared them an unimpressed glance as they checked their legs for ingrown hairs. But as the platform announcement voiced the arrival of the next train, their cool evaporated. The boys only continued their thoughtless games, howling with laughter against the girls' screams. They made a muse of terror and dared it closer.

The train rattled in the distance and then came into sight, moving towards them ruthlessly. The boys only laughed harder as they scrambled up the platform. They collapsed onto the hard ground and said nothing. Some pressed their cheeks against the cool asphalt, others faced the sky with shut eyes. The air was so clear it hurt to be alive.

'Shit,' a boy muttered after a moment. 'That was my train.'

*

In Drama that day, the girls witnessed versions of Vince they'd never before seen. Each warm-up activity revealed another boy; the girls felt as though they were speed-dating his split personalities.

Bus stop: one student sits on a chair on stage. Another enters. The aim of the activity is to do whatever you can think of to get the seated person to give up the chair. No bribery allowed.

The girls feigned sickness, a broken leg, a break-up. When it came Vince's turn, every one of his classmates expected him to turn the scene into a hostage situation, craft a weapon from thin air and threaten abuse.

He entered through the curtain with a sombre look.

'Hey' – he glanced at the girl on the seat quickly, then shoved his fists in his pockets and stared at the ground – 'you come here often?'

She looked up, mystified at his mild voice. 'Um, yeah I do – every day, actually.'

'So, you saw the cat that got run over here last week?'

'Yeah,' she answered, hesitating at first. 'Yeah, I did. Flat as a pancake.' She paused for laughter from the audience. 'Poor kitty.'

'Yeah . . .' Vince said. His eyes were electric and he looked at the ground as though the dead were rising all around. 'His name was . . . Mr Whiskers.'

'He was your cat?' she asked, astounded.

'He was my best friend.' He gave a rueful smile and let his voice crack, only slightly. 'I still remember the first time I saw him. He was a newborn. His mum had him in a cardboard box on the side of the road. Probably left as soon as she could get back on her four feet. It was raining down like hell that day. I was walking home when I heard the softest little *meow*. Took a look in the box – all his brothers and sisters were blue, lifeless.' Vince bent over and peered into an invisible box, into an invisible pair of eyes. He squatted down, scooped the air gently and held his cupped hand against his abdomen. 'I put him under my jacket and took him home with me. Stayed up all night trying to keep him warm. He's always been scared of the cold – but I can't get to him no more.'

'I'm so sorry for your loss,' the girl offered, with knitted brows and a hand clutched to her chest.

Vince stared into the distance, holding something precious and in pain against his shirt. He listened for a heartbeat.

'Loss? I haven't lost him.' He looked around anxiously. Vince stared at the audience, his mouth slightly agape, his eyes trembling like cups of water. A wave of calm washed over him as he let his shoulders drop. He closed his eyes as though to return to a pleasant dream, then looked back down at his cradling arm. 'Here he is. He's right here,' he said to the girl, with a shadow of a smile. 'See?'

The girl sank to her knees beside him, held herself up with her palms on the ground. She examined the empty space of his palm. 'I see. I see him.' She looked into Vince's eyes and gave a concerned smile.

'Good, you can have him then!' he shouted as he scrambled to his feet and jumped on the chair. He crossed his arms in victory.

The library was warm and quiet. From her spot by the window, Sonny took no notice of the clouds that hung low in the sky. She was dream-distant. Somewhere monsoonal, where the air was so heavy with fish sauce and sweat you could keep it in a bottle. When she finally looked outside, she decided she didn't want to be struck by lightning on her walk home, quickly returned the books and left. On the way to the back gate, she saw a boy sitting alone on the basketball court. It could only be one person. This was the first time he had attended his Drama lesson in a while. He had a book in his lap and was mumbling to himself. Could it be? Was Vincent Tran reading? *For pleasure?*

Sonny felt a jolt pass through her entire body. He sat beneath the sky and his heavily gelled hair glistened in the light. His face leaning down to look at the page, she could only see his dark eyebrows and the tip of his tall nose. He looked so statuesque she expected birds to land on his shoulder.

Sonny slowed her pace in the hope that he would notice her. She bent her knees slightly to get a better look at his face. Her heart wobbled at the sight of the unambiguous cuts on his cheekbone and his bruised bottom lip. Fresh injuries.

As if some fairy godmother had heeded her call, Vince's head lifted. It was only when he looked at her that Sonny remembered their last meeting, the dirty-magazine day. She brought her hand up to cover the sudden embarrassment on her face.

'Hey!' Vince called loudly, waving at her. 'Sonny!'

Even as she pretended to keep walking, she could feel her legs scrambling towards him.

'What are you doing out here?'

'Just practising my lines,' Vince replied, beaming.

'For what?'

'Shakespeare. *The Tempest.*'

'Oh, who are you playing?'

'Caliban.'

'The deformed guy? Wow, great casting,' Sonny said. She was shortly rewarded with the uplifting roar of his laughter.

'Oh, I wish you could be in it too but Shakespeare didn't set out any role for . . .' – Vince flicked to the characters page of the play – 'lonely teenage girl with chronic porn addiction.'

Sonny pressed her lips tightly together, accepting defeat.

'You know the play?' Vince asked.

She nodded. 'I know bits of it.'

'Did you study it for English?'

'No, I tried to read it. Your character's got some of the best lines.'

'The best lines? Man, I can barely pronounce this shit – I don't know what the fuck he's on about.'

Sonny smiled, readjusting the weight of her backpack on her shoulder straps, readjusting her weight on the balls of her feet.

'What's your assignment?'

'A monologue. Basically just choose some of his lines, put them together, perform it, this and that. It's due in four weeks, on Friday.'

'You've got heaps of time,' Sonny said. She sat down, crossed her legs and smiled at him. 'I'll be your audience.'

Vince tried to read aloud to her, but after a while struggling, he tossed the book behind his shoulder and lay down on the chalky court. 'I give up. How did people talk like that back then?' he groaned. Vince clenched his eyes and held the back of his neck with his hands. Sonny tried not to pant as his triceps made a provocative appearance.

Then, as if remembering she was still there, he looked up at her and smiled. 'I shouldn't have skipped out on so much school when I was younger.'

Sonny picked up *The Tempest* and squatted down beside him. Sitting the book on his chest, she looked at him expectantly. 'You can do it. Just treat it like you're learning a new language.'

'No-one talks like that no more, Sonny.'

'You don't need to talk to anyone. Sometimes, you just need another language to think in.'

Sonny and Vince sat like this, reading together. She watched him and nodded as she listened, noted the way his eyebrows pulled together as he tried to pace his breath. When he had trouble, she eased him along and read the passage out to him, sounded out all the syllables individually until the words became whole again in his mouth. They highlighted their favourite lines together and compiled them into a monologue, which they wrote on pages Sonny had ripped from her Chemistry workbook.

Slowly, slowly, something shifted in Vince. He was as giant as ever, but she only now noticed how gentle he could be. It was like watching a tree yield to the wind. She hoped the sky would withhold its teary tantrum for just a little while longer.

Be not afeard. The isle is full of noises,
Sounds, and sweet airs that give delight and hurt not.
Sometimes a thousand twangling instruments
Will hum about mine ears

It was getting to dinnertime when the swollen clouds gathered around them like crooks. Sonny and Vince packed up their things and walked to the back gate together. She gave him a single sheet of paper to keep – the one where she'd copied his monologue – reasoning that her handwriting was neater than his. In truth, she wanted to keep all the evidence of his hand to herself. Sonny would inspect, later in bed that night, how he wrote in a careless scribble, how endearing his mistakes were, how his print was so languid it looked cursive, how he rarely cared to dot his i's. She would analyse what this revealed about his nature and came to the conclusion that the disarray of his script showed that he was impatient, brash, hot-tempered, but also honest, affectionate and open. *Of course.*

Perhaps, if Sonny was clever, she could extend their time together and Vince would offer to drive her home.

'Looks like it's gonna rain,' she said, looking up at the brewing sky. *Subtlety is key.*

'Do you usually walk home?' Vince asked.

'Yeah.'

'I'll drive you?'

Vince had parked a couple of streets from the school. Who knew a Honda Civic could feel so far from the rest of reality? The world was somewhere else. Maybe it had been misplaced, but Sonny couldn't find it in herself to go looking for it. She only held these little details to her heart and stuffed them forcefully into the memory compartment of her brain: his gently choking cologne that flooded the car, the matchbox, the comb, the empty pack of Marlboros, the split toothpicks in the glove compartment. Sonny rolled down the windows and watched the streets pass by. Her life felt finally, inexplicably complete. As though she was looking at herself from an imaginary viewpoint.

Vince looked curiously at her, wondering why she seemed so visibly happy just to be driven home. Could it be as simple as escaping the rain?

'Well, this is my stop,' Sonny said as Vince dropped her off at the end of the road. He then parked in front of his house.

They reached their doorsteps at the same time and stood there for a moment, watching as the first stroke of lightning splintered the sky. When the arrowing rain came, they exchanged a glance and a smile and went into their houses. Sonny greeted her mother quickly and fell into bed. Even if there were no more conversations and car rides to be shared between them, she would be okay. She thought of him now and made him last forever.

Vince began to attend all of his Drama lessons. Whether at home with his mother or with his friends, he would take extra long in the bathroom to rehearse his monologue in front of the mirror.

On Tuesday, Vince was there at recess. Again, he brought his basketball. Michelle sat on the sideline and watched him play while she ate in her very careful way, softly churning the lettuce leaf into a paste in her mouth so no vegetation would get stuck between her teeth.

Sonny and Najma sat on the sheltered silver seats. Sonny crumbled at the sight of Michelle's contemptuously long hair and even longer legs. She squinted at her pretty face and wondered if she had been born without pores. Michelle was the only person whose good looks could match, or rival, Vince's.

Najma looked quizzically at Michelle's salad. She could tell from the fresh, unexploited plastic of the container and the pale, unseasoned complexion of the chicken that it had been purchased from the canteen. Beside her, Sonny had just unwrapped her banana-leafed lunch to reveal a mound of purple sticky rice. She remembered asking Sonny in Year 7 why her rice was always different colours. It was because her mother cooked the grains with natural dyes – leaves from the magenta plant to make it purple, pandan for green, turmeric or mung bean for yellow, and to achieve an impressive blood orange, the pulp of a fruit she kept in the freezer called *gấc*, which a relative had smuggled through the airport on the way back from Vietnam under a toupée. For some reason, it was as she imagined the unusual fruit under an unconvincing hairpiece that Najma realised she had never seen Michelle bring food from home before. Not even a sandwich.

'That salad looks really plain,' Najma said, sucking hesitantly on an antacid tablet instead of a lolly. She felt guilty for pretending she hadn't heard when her mother called her back inside that morning to bring the left-over *biryani* to school. 'Would it kill the canteen lady to use a little cardamom on the chicken or something?'

But Sonny wasn't listening. She had just noticed Vince approaching. As she dug into her decadent lunch, it was as though her soul left her body, hovered over the courtyard and tracked the speed, angle and trajectory of his path. She prayed that he would turn the other way and not see her as she was – her baby hairs felt turbocharged, she could sense a grain of purple sticky rice caught betwixt her two front teeth, and she worried about burping up one of the butterflies in her stomach – but he had already spotted her. There was no hiding now.

'Hey,' Vince said, nodding at them. Najma waved anxiously. He sat beside Sonny, reached into his pocket and took out a folded piece of paper. It was his monologue. It warmed her to think that Vince had been carrying around something she'd written on, that proof of her existence was kept on his person. 'You busy?'

'No,' Sonny replied, trying to swallow her rice quickly.

'Sweet. I don't really get what's going on in this part.'

It took all of recess to make him understand, but Vince liked to have Sonny listen to him when he read correctly and to be teased by her when he didn't.

Whenever he looked away, she and Najma would exchange quick glances which articulated nothing but their confusion. They felt, for the first time, the other girls look to *them* with green-eyed longing.

When the bell rang, Vince folded his monologue carefully and slipped it back in his pocket.

'I'll see you guys soon,' he said warmly. Then he turned to Najma. 'I'm Vince, by the way.'

She nodded, and said, 'I know your name,' as though hearing of him beforehand made her seem well-connected. Immediate regret painted her expression.

'Okay,' he replied, laughing. 'But I don't know yours.'

'Oh, it's Najma,' she said, then clenched her eyes shut as she lamented her birth. The two girls watched in sacred silence as Vince left.

'I can still smell his cologne,' Najma said frantically. 'Quick! Don't let it go to waste.'

How selfless of him, to leave a trail of his smell for them to remember him by. The girls snorted the scent aggressively, like lines of coke in the air.

'He smells so *blue*,' Najma said with a muffled moan.

'He does. *Cool Water*?'

'By Davidoff? Could be, but I feel like that's too obvious. It's definitely a sophisticated, older man's scent – something aquatic.'

Sonny pursed her lips and hummed in agreement. 'I'd call it a sensual reinterpretation of ocean air. But it's not just saline, there's a mineral sparkliness to it.'

'Elaborate on the sparkles, please.'

'It's juicy, cool, with prominent bitter citrus notes. Bergamot, probably.'

'Yeah, there's definitely a lot of depth to this one,' said Najma wistfully. 'The masculinity of oakmoss, but there are some softer hints of aromatic herbs as well. Rosemary and sweet clover, crushed and scorched by the Mediterranean sun. A really crisp, dry summer smell.'

'Did you say summer spell?'

'No, but we should stick with that. Sounds . . . hot.'

'Okay, a summer spell . . . I think I'm getting closer,' Sonny whispered, squinting in concentration. 'Almost there . . .'

With her eyes closed, Sonny breathed in softly through parted lips because it felt like the most natural thing to do. She followed the vapour as it drifted over her tongue and slid past the back of her throat. This time, she was not only able to smell Vince's cologne, and to taste it, but to feel his spirit press against the moist, mucous membranes of her nasal passage. She imagined a thick, thunderous mist, the leftovers of a violent storm, and the sound of waves crashing against the shore. Vince emerged from the haze, with saltwater dripping down his abs like newly formed crystals. As he rose, he parted the ocean like Poseidon, revealing his bronzed thighs, and between them, his long, hard, sand-speckled –

'I've got it!' announced Najma, clicking her tongue with a grin.

'What is it?!'

Acqua di Gio.

'Yes, yes, yes,' Sonny mumbled to herself. The glinting seawater. The subtropical climate. The warm, embracing spices. Finally. All her senses made sense. 'Of course, he'd wear Armani!'

Chapter 12

The Flesh

Vince was finding it difficult to amuse Emma – there were only so many places to hide in that house. She was getting more independent and more restless with the passing of each day; he'd had a fit when he caught his little sister rummaging through a cupboard to play with sewing needles. The garden should have been her Eden, but it was all dirt and scraps. He would do something about that when spring came around. Until then, he could only look for ways to pass the time. Vince dug through his wardrobe and found a knotted plastic bag of his old toys – a yoyo, a few plush bears, a broken xylophone, and a pair of walkie-talkies. He examined these souvenirs from his infancy with wonder. So, it was true: he had had a beginning and it had been a good one. He had been once very young and very happy; here was the evidence.

The bell rang for the end of recess. It was time for Scripture at the Boys' School. Vince, Alex, Tim Tam and Danny snuck into the Art faculty's kiln room to smoke. Before Vince left for juvie, the boys used to amuse themselves by crashing different Scripture classrooms – it was like sneaking into a movie you knew nothing about, missing most of the first half and trying to figure out how it was going to end.

Buddhism didn't seem to have an ending – you'd just keep getting born again and again, indefinitely – which was probably why it made for such a boring Scripture lesson. The class would just be ordered to chant *amituofo* together until one of the boys (usually Tim Tam) started making a *buzz* noise, and the others claimed they'd seen something flying around the room, prompting testimonies from the rest of the class. In the end, it was always Danny that would save the day, and incidentally kill the joy, by getting up to let the imaginary bee out the window. Compared to incessant, karmic suffering, the Abrahamic religions seemed to have a much higher production value – big-budget explosions on the Day of Judgement, a special-effects-loaded Second Coming.

'Oi,' Alex announced, holding up a recently fired and unglazed vase, made using the same coil technique they'd been taught in Year 7. He knocked it against the corner of the shelf, once, twice, to hear the hollow, then let it go. The vessel fell to the floor with a *crash*. 'Remember when this cunt almost bashed a priest?'

Vince stared at the mess on the ground and remembered walking into Catholic Scripture that day. He'd been sitting by the window, carving his name in the desk with a pair of scissors, when the priest appeared. Clothed in black save for one square of glaring white, he wrote his name on the board in a flash of chalk: Father Harding.

'He deserved it, bro,' muttered Vince, squinting through the smoke, choking a little on the disturbed silica dust.

'How come I don't remember any of this?' asked Danny,

crouching down and smoothing his fingers over one of the ceramic shards.

'You were away,' said Tim Tam. 'You had to take your uncle to the chemist.'

'Oh. So what happened?'

'He was telling us this story about how a guy confessed to him about killing his own fuckin' mum,' Vince muttered. 'And he thought he was being haunted by her ghost. So the priest went to bless his house and told him he saw her spirit, wearing a white gown. He told him that his mum forgave him, and she said she'd watch over him from heaven if he promised to repent. How fucked up is that?'

Vince sat inside a shiver. Every priest he met reminded him of his father – pathological men who seemed obsessed with mortifying the flesh, but were really only obsessed with the flesh. With keeping it in chains, hanging it from trees, plunging it in water, seeing if it would sink, putting nails through it, hammering it to crosses. He thought of his father's many crucifixes – the Son of God dangling from keyrings, necklaces and rear-view mirrors. If a man could take upon himself the sins of the world, what would happen to the world?

'First time I seen you get so angry, Vince,' said Alex with a laugh. 'Priest didn't know what to fuckin' do with him. He just closed his eyes and started praying right there.'

Vince remembered the scorn that had come before the fury. For a moment, he only sat there shaking his head with a closed-mouthed smile, as though bits of Eden's apple were still stuck between his teeth, as if he knew something you didn't and was already paying the price for it. It wasn't until the priest started talking about sin and forgiveness that Vince finally picked up his chair and hurled it out the unopened window, shattering it

178

instantly. Then he grabbed his desk and threw it at the priest. Vince's eyes were cold. He had crystals stuck in his hair, a glacier of broken glass beneath his foot.

Father Harding dug at the collar strangling his neck, like the string around a Christmas ham.

He stared at Vince like a demon his imagination could banish just as easily as it had conjured it up. Closing his eyes, he mumbled his holiness, something about separating the spirit from the flesh.

At last, something in Vince felt real.

I am the flesh! Oi, open your eyes. Look at me. I'll kill you myself, you fuckin' murderer!

On Sunday night, Vince had a dream about hell. It was a dream and not a nightmare because he saw his father there. At around eleven, he was woken by screams. Thinking the house next door was burning down, he ran into his backyard, prepared to jump over the fence. But he couldn't make out any smoke. The roof was unignited and the windows were disappointingly flameless. There was only Sonny's mother, standing beside the dragon fruit tree and swinging a doormat with a wet patch from her fist, her voice loud enough to make death metal sound melodic.

'Look at that *con quỷ*! Every day she makes a mess for me to clean! Being a slave to the people in this house isn't enough, I have to serve dogs as well?'

With her tail between her legs, Happy scampered away to the opposite end of the garden. Hunched in the dark and half-awake, Vince came closer to the fence. He saw the dog circling a thicket of lemongrass with a slight limp, blinking her confusion.

'Tomorrow, you go to school and ask your friends who wants a dog – I've had enough of this demon!' Sonny's mother yelled as she hosed down the stain. 'I've been working all day and I still don't get any rest.'

Then he saw Sonny. She had been standing at the door and watching Happy struggle to find a spot to lie down amongst the itchy plants. When her mother turned off the hose and hung the sopping doormat from the clothesline, she was caught by the glare on Sonny's face.

'Look at yourself!' she shrieked. 'Your parents are still alive and you cry like that!'

Vince only noticed how pink and puffy Sonny's face was when he heard this. Before that, he could only see the anger etched between her eyebrows as she chewed the inside of her cheek. He hadn't ever heard Sonny talk back to her mother before. Not once.

'Why didn't you get this angry when that person hurt me?'

Sonny hadn't stuttered, although he could feel her wanting to flinch at her own words. How long had this question been inside her, Vince wondered. Her jaw was firm, her face almost proud. As he stared at her face, he realised the expression was not grief alone, but an obsession with it. There weren't many things that could happen to someone to make them look that way. And it was then that he understood.

'Why are you bringing that up again? *Thời gian trôi qua*, you still haven't let it go? You know I don't want to talk about that! Don't you ever think about how I might feel?'

'What have you got to be sensitive about?' Nothing about Sonny's manner suggested she had asked a question. 'It didn't happen to you! You never asked me about it, never asked if I was okay.'

'So, everything is my fault! I'm evil, I just like to hurt my children.' Hot tears spilled down her face. 'You'll only know how to love me when I die, don't say I didn't warn you. But by that time, it'll be too late to cry!'

Her mother stormed back into the house. She dried a clanging of dishes, turned off all the lights and slammed her bedroom door shut. Oscar, who had just got up for a bathroom trip, stood in the dark. He was too sleepy to decrypt the noises he heard; he stood for a while with the pee frozen inside of him.

That left only Vince. He watched as Sonny ran to the other end of the garden, through the lacerating lemongrass, and kneeled on the ground to pull Happy into her arms. The dog wouldn't stop shaking as she stared helplessly into her eyes. Sonny tucked her into her cardboard box house, pulled the blanket over her and scratched her to sleep. Then, she crawled onto the trampoline and brought her knees to her chest.

Around her, the night unspooled. Sonny wouldn't move. She didn't want to go back to bed ever again; only wanted to be as cold, hungry, awake and supermassively stuck in the dark as she was now, forever. Her pain was an expensive painting that all forms of light tarnished. It was precious to her. Her heartbeat was all she needed to hear. Maybe the secret to feeling alive was having an inner rage to check your pulse against.

Vince couldn't look away. Her vulnerability startled him. Her tears shimmered as though she'd squeezed an evening star into an eye drop, but she didn't make a single noise when she cried. Why her? The world truly had no mercy, truly did not discriminate; it wanted to shove its bad in all the places it could.

The void didn't seem to make her any wiser. Sonny gave up on gazing. Her eyes fell on someone's figure. She moved to the edge of the trampoline and held onto the fence. There he stood, as still as a totem, watching.

'You heard everything?'

Of course, he heard, she thought. It would've been impressive not to.

Vince nodded uncertainly. 'I won't tell no-one, Sonny.'

'You're keeping too many of my secrets.' She smiled and, as she did so, her eyes surrendered their first tears. 'Usually when she screams at me, I can handle it, you know? I don't talk back. I can put everything aside and say sorry. It doesn't matter who's right or wrong. But this is different.' She looked down at her feet and then back up to him. 'You know what she said when I finally said something? She told me, "It takes two hands to clap."'

He nodded gravely. 'Can I come over?'

Sonny glanced inside the house. All the lights were turned off. She nodded to him. The trampoline jolted under his sudden weight. He sat beside her and she watched his face in the moonlight; his first and second fingers already slightly yellow with tobacco stains, his eyes, a mirror to the night sky. He looked like he wanted to wrestle with the dark.

'Was it,' he began, unsure as to whether or not he should look at her, 'was it someone close to you? Family?'

Sonny felt herself nod. Vince nodded too, to assure her that he heard, and looked down at his crossed legs. Sonny saw his fists clench at his sides. She rested her chin on the tops of her knees and stared ahead. Another tear was about to spill down her cheek but Vince took a tissue from his pocket and wiped it away.

'Is that tissue dirty?' Sonny asked.

'No . . .'

'Then why was it in your pocket?'

He looked away innocently, in the manner of making up an excuse. 'I just got these pants from the wash, so the tissue's been cleaned too.' It wasn't a lie.

She almost smiled but forced her face to darken again. He thought about the crows she used to save her sandwich crusts for. Did she think herself cursed like them? It wouldn't matter to him even if she was. He wanted to paint himself the colour of vengeance and go looking for whoever had hurt her.

'If you ever need anything at all, I'm always here,' he said. 'If you need someone to talk to, or you want somebody chopped up.'

In spite of herself, Sonny cracked a smile. He lay down on his back and motioned for her to rest her head beside his. She let out a breath and lay down.

'Things weren't always this fucked up. You remember how when we were kids, we used to argue about colours all day?' Vince asked.

Sonny laughed instantly, though it frightened her to think that the memory might have disappeared had he not been there to remind her. Colours were like private property back then. There was nothing else for you to own: crayons were to be shared amongst the class, paper planes would get lost no matter how big you wrote your name on them and everything that grew in the vegetable garden had already been christened by someone who came earlier. So, the children laid claims on colours.

'Your favourite colour changed every fuckin' day!' She had wanted all the colours in the world for herself and even went so far as convincing him that they'd belonged to her. Purple was hers because it was the colour of the sticky rice her mother made most frequently, red because she loved cherries and strawberries, green because her father's favourite colour was green so she'd inherited it; the list went on and on.

'Yeah,' said Sonny. 'You remember that one day, we were sitting on the trampoline. You were all like, "You can't do this no more, Sonny. You got to pick your favourite colour now. No second chances, no changing your mind, okay?"'

Vince laughed and Sonny thought about how some noises must have wings.

'You were such a goddamn drama queen. Laid down, looked up at the sky and decided you were gonna stick with baby blue.' He turned to face her fully. 'That better be your favourite colour still. You pinky-promised on that shit.'

Sonny closed her eyes. 'It might be black now.'

'Nah . . . you've always been baby blue,' he murmured. He turned onto his back again and stifled a yawn. ''Cause you always blue, always been a cry baby.'

Happy climbed out of her cardboard home and dawdled over to the side of the trampoline. Sonny and Vince sat up. Sonny reached down to scoop Happy up and held her in her lap. She scratched gently at her belly as Vince wondered why the dog's manner was always so helpless and perplexed.

'Why's she so scared?' he asked.

The question drew a whimper from Sonny. Her tears stood in her eyes, threatened to leap.

'Hey, it's okay,' he said, scratching the dog beneath her chin. 'Happy had a rough life, yeah. Came from a broken family, got beat around' – he looked at her wet, twitching nose – 'probably snorted a little coke along the way.' Sonny laughed and pulled on her sleeves to catch her tears. 'But she's safe now, with us. That's all that matters.'

Happy began to lick Vince's hand, a habit she had developed to deal with her nerves when she met new people. Vince shuddered at her tiny tongue lapping tirelessly at his skin but didn't pull her away.

'I forgot how ticklish you were,' Sonny said, laughing at his pained expression.

They sat in silence for a while. Vince looked at her, wordless. He wondered if there was any way to dissolve pain without stirring it.

As if she sensed what he'd been thinking, she sighed and said, 'Man, there's only one thing I know of that'll cure this sadness.'

'What?'

'I don't know if you've heard of it. It's called a Happy Meal.'

Vince took the dog from Sonny's arms and shielded her in his lap.

Sonny laughed. 'You know the way to McDonald's, right?'

'Yes . . .' he said distrustfully.

'Can we go and get some? It'll make me feel a lot better.'

'Sonny,' Vince laughed in disbelief. 'I think your mum will kill you.'

'And put me out of my misery?' she laughed. 'You think too kindly of her.'

'Well, why should I put *my* ass on the line 'cause you want McDonald's? I seen the damage that lady can do with a fly swatter.'

'Vince!' she huffed, pulling her brows together fiercely and jutting her lip out.

'You're still using the same old tricks, huh?' he said with a laugh. He had already given in; he only wanted to see how much of herself she was willing to reveal to convince him.

When Vince jumped back over to his side of the fence to grab his keys and wait in the car, she sat on the trampoline and simply stared. The still-drenched doormat judged her with displeasure. The banana tree, which her father had just pruned last week, reminded her that she knew better. The bitter melon hanging from the vines seemed, well, bitter. Even the sky was ashamed.

Not wanting to cause an upstir amongst her ancestors, she tried praying instead to god for guidance, but couldn't tell who the voice in her head belonged to. She thought about letting Oscar know that she'd be going out for a little while. But she didn't want to disturb his sleep, only to confuse him further. And what if she never returned? Would he stay up waiting for her?

Sonny held her head in her hands. Then she rose from the neatly folded self she had been a moment ago and let out a *huff*, feeling as though the world sometimes stops to listen when you breathe deep enough. She shivered past the gate and walked towards Vince's car. He had been sitting in there with the lights on. She stooped to look at him through the window.

Vince reached over to unlock the door. 'You sure you wanna do this?'

She fastened in and gave Vince a quick nod, her face firm with purpose.

As they drove out of the neighbourhood, the street lights began to get brighter. Sonny reached for the window crank and thrust her hand outside to feel the air. She rested her elbow on the window and smiled. The wind ruffled the collar of her fleecy pyjamas.

'You okay?' he asked. 'Is it too cold?'

'No, it's invigorating. I feel young again.'

Sonny pressed her face against the frosty breeze and turned to face him with a great smile, her eyes swollen and her nose still red. She grinned as they neared the McDonald's and pulled in to the drive-through.

'What do you want?' Vince asked, stopping at the microphone.

'I'll have a soft serve and a Happy Meal, please. Chicken nuggets, fries and apple juice.'

He nodded. 'I'll get two soft serves, a Happy Meal and a double quarter pounder with cheese,' he said, with the cold confidence of a loan shark.

'What kind of Happy Meal would you like?' a voice from the speaker asked.

'Nuggets, fries and apple juice.'

Vince pulled up to the window to pay for the order.

Sonny had been taught never to owe anyone money; and perhaps less ethically, this debt would secure her next interaction with Vince. She *could* speak to him at school on Monday, but did she have the courage to approach him when he was playing basketball with Michelle so near? Should she give him a handwritten letter with money in the envelope and leave it in his mailbox? Should she wait until she saw him next in his backyard? There were so many possibilities, just waiting for a chance.

Vince took their order in a paper bag and placed it on Sonny's lap. He put the soft serves on the dashboard. As he prepared to circle into the car park, Sonny opened up her Happy Meal and stared at it. Her eyes began to water again.

'Sonny?' Vince asked, his voice switching from the furious arpeggio of a moment ago to the soft, reverberating wind of a bamboo flute. 'What's wrong?'

She didn't turn to face him. 'I wanted Eeyore, not *fucking* Piglet,' Sonny cried, holding the plastic bag that contained a pink plush toy.

'What? What's the difference?'

'Eeyore's *blue*. He's always been my favourite.'

'Okay, it's alright. We'll get Eeyore then,' Vince said. He reached over to pat her on the head. '*Shhh*, don't cry – I'll get Eeyore for you.' Astounded by how easily she'd given in to her emotions, he reversed back into the drive-thru without another word. The car behind resisted with quick, fierce honks. Vince held his horn for one sustained bellow and stuck his head out of the window to dispense The Glare. The car behind withdrew in a hurry.

'Hey, we wanted the blue one, man,' Vince said, scrunching Piglet in his hands. He tossed it onto the counter and stared at the startled teenage boy.

'I'm sorry, man, you don't get to choose which one you –'

Vince took off his seatbelt and turned to face the boy fully. His chest swelled and heaved, the muscles in his neck leapt about and his eyes were so black that the poor kid could only see his own trembling reflection.

'Can't you see I'm takin' my missus out here?' Vince thundered. 'She says she wants the fuckin' blue one!'

'Jeez, alright, bro,' the boy scrambled through the Happy Meal toy compartments to find Eeyore, dropping sachets of ketchup on the ground.

'And get us some extra napkins too,' Vince said. 'Fuck me dead!'

Vince took the toy and the napkins with what Sonny perceived to be the most wonderful display of entitlement she had ever witnessed. She had always been so meek in her dealings with people; one of her worst fears was her mother telling her to ask for fresh chilli in a restaurant. Vince put the things on her lap.

'Thank you.'

'No worries,' he said, as if it were nothing at all, as if he had always left home with his wallet, car keys and a readiness to assault fast-food employees should the need arise. It was just one of those things.

Sonny shimmied her fingers in Eeyore's sockets to make the finger puppet clap and wave. Vince watched as she stroked its black mane and the pink bow on the end of its tail with such tenderness that he half-expected the toy to come to life.

With her other hand, Sonny took the soft serve and held it to her mouth, careful to maximise the satisfaction in flattening the tip of the swirl. She was safe here, with Vince beside her. Prince William's future wife might be bestowed with the title Duchess of Cambridge but Sonny had just been named Vince's *missus*, a victory which couldn't be measured in wealth or nobility, only in the beats her heart skipped when she was with him.

'Eating dessert first?' Vince teased. 'You're breaking all the rules today, aren't you?'

'I don't want it to melt.'

He pulled into a parking space and jolted the gearshift back. Vince took his burger from the paper bag and bit into it, then looked at Sonny with a curious smile.

'What?' she asked.

'Nothing,' Vince chuckled to himself. And then, 'I just never thought I'd be eating McDonald's with you this late.'

Sonny and Vince both smiled in disbelief. They did not look at each other but felt each other's presence as warmly as a beam of light falling across the face of a blind man.

'Do you like your mum?' Vince asked, interrupting the moment.

Sonny gave a laugh. 'I'd go as far as saying I love her. But she's never made it easy for me. How about you?'

'Me?'

'Do you love your mum?'

He was silent. He looked at the sky through the rear-view mirror, seemed to see something she couldn't.

'Sorry. You don't have to answer that.'

'I love her. I always have,' he said. 'But even when I was a kid, sometimes I felt like she didn't want me to.'

Sonny thought about something her grandmother once said: that children have a way of making us forget how much the world has taken from us. Maybe the world had taken too much from Vince's mother, more than he could forgive.

They didn't say anything for a while. Sonny fished the pickles from her burger and ate them on their own. The sourness gave her courage.

'Your dad?'

Vince didn't stir at first. He smoothed a nonchalant finger over an eyebrow as though he hadn't heard the question. 'No. Maybe I used to. Fuck, I don't know.'

'It's okay not to know. That leaves room for thinking.'

He nodded. 'How about yours?'

'I love my dad.' The immediacy of her answer made her uncertain of it. Sonny scratched her knee as a second thought. 'But sometimes it feels like he's so many people. Some of them you know, and some of them you haven't even met. You don't know if you ever will.'

They sat still, each of them wondering how love could get to be so jagged.

Vince cleared his throat and laid the half-eaten burger down in his lap, wiping the sauce off his fingers. 'I mean, thinking about my dad scares me more than anything because . . . because . . . what if I end up like him?'

'Vince,' Sonny said, looking at him fully now. 'You aren't your dad.'

He sighed. He'd said something he hadn't meant to. 'I know I'm not my dad. But you never really know. You can make promises to yourself and everything, but nobody knows who they're gonna be in ten, twenty years.'

'Don't you trust yourself?'

Vince shook his head with a snicker. 'No.'

'Do you trust your mum and Emma?' she asked, holding her breath. 'Do you trust me?'

His eyes flickered for a second. Then came back to light. He looked at her.

190

'Yes.'

'Then look at yourself the way we see you. You're not your dad. You'll never be your dad. You can stop running from him now.'

He let out a breath. She wanted to hold him. To say, why are you so afraid of the future? It's been waiting for you long enough.

The car came to a stop and Sonny was before her house once again. The lights were still out, the bedroom windows dim with disinterest and the blinds totally oblivious; everything as though she had never left.

Sonny reached for the car door, then halted. Before he could ask her what was wrong, she pressed Eeyore's snout to his face and kissed him goodnight. 'Thank you for everything, Vince. You're really nice.'

He watched her cross the front yard and wave at him a last time before worming through the gate.

Vince turned off the engine. In the dark, he pressed his fingertips to the cheek that had received the kiss, then to the other one, only to find that both sides of his face were burning. The air outside frosted his windows but the cold could not touch him here. He thought about the place inside people, where goodnight kisses come from. When someone, someone you know, someone you trust, someone your mother knows and trusts, forces their way into that place, you might live the rest of your life locked inside. And yet Sonny had reached for him, in her own way.

Something in the shape of a fist began to thud in his chest. Softly, slowly, it begged for his trust. All along it had been beating just for him.

191

Chapter 13

(The Heart)

It was Monday, lunchtime, and Najma was recounting the epic 'spiritual awakening' she'd had over the weekend. In an effort to put off writing an essay on the economic importance of the Nile to Old Kingdom Egypt, she tried to distract herself with an afternoon nap but had trouble giving in to sleep. Najma sought relaxation in the company of her mother's books. Abu Ali al-Hussein Ibn Abdullah Ibn Sina stated in *The Canon of Medicine* that boiling rosewater could relieve rapid heartbeats and sore throats. Another scholar mentioned the use of lavender in invoking lucid dreams, and myrrh for embalming. In one hadith, the Prophet himself called henna 'the lord of sweet-smelling blossoms'. The Arabic words lulled her into the sleep of Hellenic ruins. An hour or two later, when she woke up surrounded by the ancients, Najma tried to return Ibn Sina to his alphabetical place but ended up knocking over *The Metaphysics of The Healing*. Just behind it was a leather-bound book, pressed flat against the shelf, with a dust cover of purple arabesques; purposely, she thought, concealed from her.

'What was it?' asked Sonny, unwrapping her sandwich discreetly to avoid disrupting the suspense with the crumple of plastic wrap.

Najma leaned in close to Sonny's ear. '*The Perfumed Garden of the Shaykh Nefzawi*. Complete and unexpurgated.'

'Unexpurgated?'

'It means' – a heavily pregnant pause – 'uncensored.'

'Oh my god,' said Sonny, her eyes bulging as she tore off the crusts and undressed her sandwich. That which had to first warrant censorship in order to later be uncensored was certainly worth whispering about.

'At first, I was like *Perfumed Garden*? Pfft, it's probably just another one of my mum's books on extracting essential oils. But it's actually this medieval manual about how to have *sex*.' The last word was only mouthed, but further implied through her arched brows.

'People were having sex in the medieval times? I thought they would've been too busy fighting off the bubonic plague.'

'In Europe, yeah, but apparently my people were living it up at the kingdom of Tunis,' Najma replied, laughing. 'Anyway, I was just flipping through randomly until I found this one page. It had a detailed list of different types of lady parts. *El hacene*, the beautiful, *el neuffakh*, the one that swells, *el maoui*, the juicy one, *abou khochime*, the one with a little nose. But apparently, the one that reigns supreme, the cream of the vagina crop, is *el ladid*, the delicious one.'

Najma reached into her backpack and pulled out a solid ball of squashed paper. Carefully, she unravelled the sheet. But no matter how passionately she flattened it against the silver seat, the page was still as wrinkled as papyrus. It contained a passage she'd copied from the book before returning it to its hiding place.

Sonny couldn't help but giggle. There was a certain slapstick charm about centuries-old literature scribbled by a teenage girl in peril of getting called downstairs for dinner.

'Come on,' nudged Najma. 'Let's read it together. *El ladid* has the reputation of . . .'

It has the reputation of procuring an unexampled pleasure, comparable only to the one felt by the beasts and birds of prey, and for which they fight sanguinary combats . . . the highest fortune of this world; it is a part of the delights of paradise awarded to us by God as a foretaste of what is waiting for us.

'No freaking way . . .' She stared into Najma's eyes, beheld her like an immaculately conceived child. '*You* have The Delicious One?'

'What?' said Najma, bursting into laughter. 'No!'

'Then what was your "spiritual awakening"?'

'This . . . all of this.' She held the crinkled paper like a leaf, and imagined the words as vessels, seeping into the skin of her hands, dyeing her soul with bright red henna. 'I always thought that anything to do with my body was unclean. Even just thinking about it. Maybe I wouldn't have felt so guilty all the time if I knew that we used to write poetry about it.' She scratched the back of her thumb absentmindedly. 'Why didn't my mum tell me?'

Sonny took a bite of her lunch and chewed slowly, needing time to think. 'Maybe her mum never told her, either.' Then she looked at Najma, her mouth full and lips powdered with sandwich crumbs. 'Do you think she might've kept that book there because she wanted you to find it?'

Najma smiled to herself and decided to believe that was true, however unlikely. She felt like a detective who had solved the case without evidence, and tried to make up clues as she retraced her footsteps. For instance, though her mother firmly held that underlining, highlighting and writing in old books were all acts of desecration, Najma remembered once finding a page with a corner folded. It was in a medical book about pulse diagnosis, and the page that had been marked contained an excerpt from an Egyptian scroll. *To the back of the head, to the hands, to the place of the stomach, to the arms or to the feet*, it said, *(the heart) speaks out of every limb.*

The bell for the end of the school day rang and Sonny met her little brother at the gate of the Boys' School. They walked home slowly because, secretly, they wanted never to arrive.

All day Oscar had been thinking of her. A terrible thing had happened to his sister. He knew which relative it had been; the one who always offered to help Sonny with her Chemistry homework, who liked to watch scary movies with her, whose eyes would sometimes linger when she untied her hair. But how could he not have known then, when it mattered? How had he missed all the clues? Could he have stopped it if he'd paid better attention? And how could he tell her now that he knew? That he knew, that he was sorry he did not know before, and that he loved her so much that being near her, and aware she was hurting beneath the skin, bruised his own soul? Oscar reached out to hold his sister's hand and pulled it into his pocket. No words, just his hand closed over hers as he stared ahead, deep in thought, renovating somewhere inside himself to make room for all of her troubles.

Up the two creaky steps and straight through the door, once more, brother and sister faced the family shrine. Oscar squeezed

Sonny's hand a last time before falling to his knees. She crouched beside him and stared ahead. There stood the statuette of the *Quán Thế Âm Bồ Tát*, with her willow branch in one hand, a vase of blessed water in the other. How could a mother goddess be a virgin? Oscar wanted to scoff, but his throat strangled the noise into a whimper.

'Oscar,' Sonny said softly, 'what's wrong?'

He glared at the images of the deified, but they were no longer images to him. It was as though the spirits were present and facing the trial of his judgement.

'I wanna break them, Sonny. I wanna smash them so bad they bleed.'

He clutched the cool porcelain statuette in his fingers. It was hollow inside. What a fraud. An age-old scam. He wanted to whack it against the wall, or the concrete outside, or set it on fire the way Vince had burned the flag and hoisted it in the air for the whole school to see.

'Gods don't bleed, Oscar. You'll only cut yourself picking up the pieces,' said Sonny. 'And get really sore butt cheeks, too, when mẹ finds out you broke her favourite *bồ tát*.'

Oscar smiled through his tears. He wanted to go on with the rest of the day but did not know how to stop crying. Sonny hugged him and stroked his head.

'You know, Oscar – we can't stop bad things from happening to us, always. But we can make sure they end with us.'

Sonny pulled back and looked at him.

'Now come on, get up. You've got to drink your milk – you think I'd forget?'

They laughed together. Sonny wiped the rivers away and kissed his cheeks again and again, the way she always had before he decided to grow up and be embarrassed of being loved and cared for.

Oscar winced and managed to dodge the eleventh kiss.

'Are you okay?' he asked suddenly.

Sonny nodded.

'I've got you, don't I?'

They walked into the kitchen. Their mother had a severe look on her face as she scrubbed the pork belly with salt. Sonny greeted her and stood at her side, watching her massage grains of salt into pink flesh. She washed her hands and cupped the back of Sonny's head with her palm, pulling her in. She sniffed the top of her head, kissed her and scratched her scalp.

'*Con biết mẹ thương con*. You have to know that I live only for you,' her mother said, and made it simple.

Sonny nodded and cried the most bitter tears she'd ever known into her mother's chest. She felt as though she was holding her mother's portrait, still and perfect. The actual person was another subject entirely. Could you go on loving someone without ever learning to forgive them?

A few days passed by and life at home, inexorably, returned to the way it had always been. When Sonny was not vacuuming, putting the clothes out to dry, folding the laundry or helping her mother cook, she would escape into the backyard: the one place that remained largely spared from her mother's immaculate touch. This was her father's place, which meant it also belonged to her. Sonny looked lovingly at the herbs, the mowed grass, the dragon fruit tree and the rotten wood armature it was draped on, the occasional visiting ladybug, the jars of salty lemon preserve, and thought about how complete this picture would be under the summer sky. She was on the trampoline when Vince appeared over the fence.

'Hi!'

'Hey!' Vince called back. 'You ever get tired of jumping?'

'I get more tired of doing nothing,' she replied. 'Oh! You wait here, I have something for you.'

'I've got something for you too.'

They both went into their houses and came back out with their hands behind their backs.

Sonny stood on her tippy toes and reached over to give him the six dollars in her hands. With the advantage of his height, Vince looked over the fence easily.

'This is for the Happy Meal.'

'I told you not to worry about it, it's only a few bucks!'

Sonny shook her head and held the money out.

'I'm not taking it,' he said firmly.

After a while exchanging glares and examining the prominent cheekbones of that unwavering face, Sonny withdrew her hand. The coins sang as they fled down her pockets.

'Thank you for the Happy Meal,' she said. 'It meant a lot to me.'

'It's alright, as long as it made you happy,' Vince replied, smiling at her.

She stared at his arms, gently swollen with muscles, and realised he was wearing a short sleeve in such windy weather. 'Aren't you cold?'

'. . . A little.'

'Then why don't you wear something warmer?'

'I don't know.'

'Does it make you feel weak – to have to rely on winter clothes?'

'Yeah! When it's cold outside, I don't want a jacket. I'm tryin' to evolve. Anyway, Baby Blue . . .'

Sonny didn't even try to contain her happiness. So it was not just a one-off thing; he had come up with an actual nickname for her and half of it was *baby*. Her delight did not go unnoticed.

'I was looking through all my old stuff and look what I found!'

He handed her a pair of walkie-talkies his father once bargained for at a charity garage sale. He used to steal them for the games he and Sonny played.

'Aw, I remember these!' Sonny exclaimed, reaching for them.

'I changed the batteries – they still work!' And then, as though caught off guard by his own excitement, 'You can have 'em.'

'You can have 'em,' Sonny mocked in a gruff voice. 'I don't fuck with that Toys R Us shit no more.'

Vince laughed.

'What am I gonna do with two walkie-talkies? Here, take one.'

'And do what with it?'

'We can talk on them like we used to,' she said, perhaps a little too wistfully. He smiled at her slip-up. Sonny looked down at the walkie-talkie in her hands. 'I mean, I was just thinking you might need some extra help with your monologue. That's all.'

Vince stared at her blankly. Was she saying she wanted to come over and help him learn his lines? Presumably just the two of them, budged up together on his living-room sofa, after they'd both had dinner with their family, which meant this proposition would occur *at night*? What could this mean?

A loud voice broke into his thoughts, ordering Sonny inside to bring a bowl of cut pineapples to *bà ngoại*. It was then that he remembered the implausibility of her mother letting her study with him, and realised what Sonny had meant – that they could practise his monologue via the walkie-talkie's signals, together but apart.

Her knuckles turning white as she gripped the device to her chest, Sonny mumbled, 'Um, I think I've gotta go now.' She left him with only a sweet, sorry smile as she ran away, her slippers slapping against the concrete.

'Sonny, wait!' he called.

Just as she was about to close the door – the door which, for whatever reason, he feared would never open again – she turned back to look at him. Her eyes inquiring over her shoulder, her hair still swaying with the sudden motion.

Vince cleared his throat. 'What time can we call?'

Sonny feigned a headache for the rest of the afternoon and shut her bedroom door at 9.20. Under the flickering bulb of the bedside lamp, she pulled the covers over her head and hunched over Vince's monologue in her lap. The patterns of light she saw from beneath her blanket made her imagine she was lying under a tree. She touched his handwriting, pressed the paper to her face, smelt the ink, coughed twice before she finally plucked the courage to press the button and speak into the walkie-talkie.

'Hello?' No reply. 'Hello?' she tried again. Her confidence was already beginning to dwindle. Sonny pressed the walkie-talkie to her mouth as she tried a third time and then held the speaker to her ear, trying to listen for a sign of life. She hardly even noticed that her heart was pounding.

'Hi, hello!' Vince replied. Startled, Sonny tore the walkie-talkie from her ear. 'How's things at home?'

'Good!' Sonny said, only afterwards realising she was just happy to be speaking to him and things weren't *that* good. 'Better,' she corrected herself. 'How's your family?'

'Mum's good, Mum's healthy, but Emma, man,' he sighed, 'nó phá quá! She's doin' my head in, bro! I gotta find a way to keep this kid busy. I'm thinking of fixing up the backyard for her but that'll have to wait until spring.'

'I can't wait for spring.' Vince hummed in agreement. 'Winter's not even here yet and we're already dreaming about its hot sister.'

His laughter crackled through the walkie-talkie. He sounded so close. As Vince began to read his monologue, Sonny listened through the speaker and wondered how his booming voice could be so tender, so tragic, *like a thousand twangling instruments*. He would be her isle. He would be where she visited when the world caved in on her; soaked in sun and spring waters; paradise in a person.

The more he read, the more he talked. When he was seven or eight, his father started coming home drunk. The first time he fought back was when he was eleven. He'd shoved his father against the medicine cabinet. His father fell against the metal with a crash and staggered forward, held his palm to the back of his head, checked for blood and stormed to the kitchen. With a butcher's knife in his hand, he chased Vince up and down the street.

The trouble at home followed him outside.

His first suspension had been in Year 5. The teacher wouldn't let him go to the toilet so he stood by the trash can at the front of the classroom, unzipped and unleashed. He was thirteen the first time he stole a car. He couldn't remember what make it was, or even the colour, but he knew it was Japanese because the steering wheel started wobbling in his hand as soon as he hit 90 km/h. He'd been driving it on the wrong side of the road when the police came. He must've known what he was doing. Maybe he'd wanted to give fate a choice. To crash or catch him.

'I got a good behaviour bond that time or some shit like that.'

Sonny wondered what it was like to be in that car, speeding through this life, glimpsing the other side and yet holding onto nothing. Not a thought about a loved one, not a single sweet or safe memory. He made narcissism seem like a school of thought, and she was a willing disciple.

'How have you always been so brave?' Sonny asked. 'The worst thing I ever did in primary was steal worm juice one time for my dad's garden.'

'Worm juice? You were in the environment club?'

'I was in the environment club.'

'Seriously? What did you even do there?'

'We just watered plants and stuff.'

'Oh.'

'I'm sorry, was that not earth-loving enough for you?' They giggled together, but even as they did, Sonny was crafting her next line; all the banter she and Najma shared over the course of their friendship was preparation for this crucial moment. 'Every full moon we do yoga in the vegetable garden and braid each other's pubes. Oh, and then we make love to the worms. Is that what you wanted to hear?'

Vince laughed with such force that, if she were to come up for a gulp of air and unglue the walkie-talkie from her cheek, she would still be able to hear the noise leaking through his bedroom window. Instead she clutched the speaker even closer and swore she could hear his body shudder. Sonny wished she would always remember what his happiness felt like.

'Vince?'

'Yeah?'

'Why do you think you got into so much trouble when you were little?'

'Huh . . . why *did* I get into so much trouble?' She could hear his grin as he tossed over in his bed. 'I don't know, Sonny. I've always had a temper. I never liked to take shit from no-one. You go out, you see someone look at you the wrong way and you just go, "Yeah, let's have a crack." You bash the guy, bottle him, chop him up, and even after it's all over, you still feel angry. So you go out and do it again. It's like, if I don't have a fight, I don't feel right! I think lots of kids grow up feeling like that. When you're young and you don't have much, *everything* seems worth fighting for. And when you don't get love from your family, it's hard at home. So you and your friends go looking for it outside. There's so much heart between you. There's love, and love becomes even bigger trouble.'

'What kind of trouble?'

'You remember how I went away for a bit?'

'You mean for two years?'

'Yeah,' Vince said with a laugh. 'There were these dickheads from Liverpool Boys that'd go looking for the Asian houses in the neighbourhood, throw rocks through the window, slash tyres. We'd always fight them, but one day they took it too fuckin' far. Danny had an autistic uncle living with his family. When he wasn't home, some guy broke his uncle's bedroom window and threw in a cigarette, set the bed on fire while he was asleep. I still remember when I got Alex's call. I was home with my mum. It was a school day but I was sleeping in. His voice was shaking.'

'What did he say?'

'He said something bad happened and the boys were bringing the van to pick me up. Just grab your machetes, knock the door down, run into the house, find the guy, chop him up, and yeah. When I walked out the house, I think my mum knew what I was up to. But there wasn't much she could say. And I never listened anyway.'

He remembered the stillness of her back that day as she sat at her sewing table, her foot coming down on the pedal, the light that leaked from the window and turned his mother into a memory before him.

'The guy only ended up losing a couple fingers. Lucky for me, otherwise I'd probably still be in juvie. One of his neighbours called the cops, so we all split up. Some of us jumped the fence and hid in people's backyards but I just walked back home. I knew they were coming.'

Vince remembered walking through the front door with his shirt soaked in blood as cold as the colour blue. His mother hadn't moved from her spot since he left. Her back was turned to him and she was unstitching the hem of some trousers. Everything in the house was so still; it threatened to come crashing down at any moment. Vince threw his shirt in the laundry basket and got into the shower. He stood beneath the pouring water and scratched at the shampoo on his scalp. He rubbed the soap against the shower cloth and against his skin, feeling as though he were washing someone else's body. Then, he changed into his home clothes, slathered shaving cream on and held the razor to his face. There were hardly any hairs but he liked staring at the mirror and feeling the blade against his skin; not being able to recognise his reflection made suicide seem like an act of murder.

'Vince?' he heard his mother call.

'Dạ?'

'Vince?'

He followed her voice. She held the seam ripper between her thin fingers, slid a stitch into the crux of its fork and sliced through.

'Con làm cái gì vậy?'

Vince stood behind his mother and put his arms around her neck. He bent down and pressed his nose to the top of her head, breathing in. This was goodbye.

'Không có gì, mẹ.'

With his hair wet and the towel still around his neck, Vince sat on the sofa and waited for the police to arrive.

He told her about the detention centre. The food, the fights. He'd lost an arm wrestle for the first time in there and was so distressed about it that he poured a kettle of hot water on the guy and bashed him. He made most of his friends in juvie that way. Some mornings when he woke up, he'd keep his eyes closed for a little while, imagine he was back in Cabramatta, walking in the alleys, passing the old women on the floor selling limes from their garden, the forest-green glisten of dill under a grocery store sprinkler, the shop owner's son sitting at the register and teaching himself to tell analogue time, the bakery smells of sweet yeast and day-old frying oil first thing in the morning. He missed the graffiti on the back of the bus stop on Broomfield Street, sundried and hieroglyphic. He missed the public swimming pool, the chlorine of painless summers, even the old Band-Aids still drifting at the bottom. He wanted everything to stay as he remembered; equally, to recognise him when he returned.

Sonny paid attention to every word and began to notice how each fell into the cadence of a joke. She wondered how he could talk about severing someone's fingers and the tastelessness of tropical juice in juvie with the eloquence of a child recounting what he'd done over the summer. Vince seemed constantly amused at still being able to be amused at all. He was an open book, written in capital letters.

'Have you got any secrets, Vince?' she asked.

'Secrets?'

'Yeah. You're just so *you* that it's almost like you have nothing to hide.'

Vince was silent for a moment. 'There's this one thing I never tell no-one.'

'What is it?'

'If I told you, it wouldn't be a secret anymore –'

'Please?'

'– and it's a really long story.'

'It's only midnight. We've got all the time in the world.'

'Alright,' he said, taking a breath. 'It happened in Year 7, I think.' Sonny heard him shift again in his bed; something in his voice – the stillness, the gravity – made her guess that he was no longer lying flat but sitting up against his pillow. 'Yeah, Mrs Bennett's class. That lady always hated me for some reason. Always asked me questions she knew I wouldn't know, made me stand up in class, tried to embarrass me. One of the first assignments we got was to write a poem. I remember thinking, if I write something good, I can show her I'm not as dumb as she thinks I am. I worked on it every day at home, even in the library at lunch. One day, when she was giving us our marks, she said, "Vince, you have to stay back when the bell rings." The whole class heard. When everybody else went home, she took me aside and told me, "I know this isn't your work, Vince. Who'd you copy this from?" I was just confused, you know? I kept telling her it *is* my work. But all she said was, "Don't lie to me – I know *you* couldn't have written this." That was the first time someone made me feel like I stole something. After a while, she just let me go 'cause she didn't have no fuckin' evidence. I walked home droppin' tears, bro. I tore that poem up soon as I got home. Put it in the bin outside so nobody would see.'

Sonny ran an electrified hand over her scalp and tugged her hair in frustration. She knew teachers like Mrs Bennett. 'You never told your mum what happened, did you?'

'Fuck no,' breathed Vince. 'I didn't want the school calling up, talking in English to scare her.'

'Do you remember what the poem was about?'

'Not really. I remember what I called it, though. *I Will by Vincent Tran.*'

'You put "by Vincent Tran" in the title?'

'Yeah.'

'That's the kind of confidence only kids in Year 7 have.'

As he laughed, Vince turned to see his sister standing in her cot. Emma grabbed onto the bars and stared at him, prompting him to notice that the spaces in between were narrow enough to trap her chubby wrists. Cradling the walkie-talkie on his shoulder, he got up and reached into the cot to rock her in his arms.

'I thought you were asleep. How long you been listening to *anh hai* talk for?' he mumbled to Emma. He hadn't been planning on telling the future about his past so soon.

'Sonny?'

'Yeah?' she said, fumbling for Vince's voice in the dark.

'Has your mum always been like this?'

'Crazy? Yeah, she's always been like this.'

'Even when you were a kid?' He paused for an answer but received nothing. 'You've got no good memories of her?'

'I do. But even thinking about good memories . . . hurts. Because she's not the same person anymore.'

The loose threads of her childhood tugged at her – so distant they seemed like memories from a past life someone in charge had neglected to snip. Her mother's soft singing trickled in. She did not want to hear it but her ears opened to the sound.

Sleeping child, don't you know a parent's love never lies?
Father's arms will carry you home, whenever you are misled
When the monsoon blows dust into your black eyes
Mother's lap will be a lotus flower, for you to rest your head

Her bedroom flooded with afternoon light. Nap time. Her mother lay on her side, curled into a crescent moon, singing her daughter to sleep. Sonny was small again. Small and filled with admiration for the woman who had given her the world, and all its light. Small and sleepy but watchful: nap time was the only time her mother sang; each heavy blink felt like an eclipse.

Sleeping child, only the wind knows your fortune
You will be carried away, too far, too soon
Tomorrow droops from a fruiting vine
Cut it open, you will find it hollow inside

'Are you remembering something now?' Vince asked quietly.

'Yeah,' Sonny replied, 'this song my mum used to sing to me when I was little, to get me to sleep.'

'You were safe then,' he said, almost in a whisper. 'That person's still there, you know? No-one held a gun to her head and made her sing to you.'

They laughed for a moment.

'That song was from somewhere inside of her that loves you. Maybe she's just locked in there, and she can't get out. You know what I mean?'

Curled up beneath the covers, with the walkie-talkie on the pillow, Sonny closed her eyes and felt like Vince's body was right beside hers.

'I think so.'

'She might not remember who she was, so you have to remember for her. You gotta rescue her by remembering.'

Emma's eyes finally closed. Vince held his sister's hand between his thumb and index finger, then traced the bridge of her nose, the dip above her lip, the soft eyelids. He felt most at peace when Emma was asleep, when she slipped into a dream and looked as though she could hide there, safely, forever. 'Try not to think too much. I know thinking is all you *do*, but remember, your parents are still your parents, they're doing what they can to protect you. You take a look outside – anywhere! – and you can see what from.'

'I'm looking outside and all I see is stars,' she said, sighing into the night.

It was five in the morning when Sonny broke.

'Vince?'

'Hmm?'

'Remember that day you came and egged our school?'

'Yeah, what about it?'

'You were aiming for me, weren't you?' Sonny was too sleepy to mask the question in a teasing tone.

Vince laughed. 'Aiming for you? I don't know, there were lots of people that got egged –'

'No,' she interrupted with a yawn. 'I'm pretty sure you were aiming for me.'

Two hours of sleep did not look good on Sonny. No matter how much she washed her face, the restlessness remained in her eyes, and under them. She prepared lunch for herself and Oscar, poured him a glass of milk, then brushed her teeth, combed her hair and slipped on her school uniform; all the while feeling like she was interning as a mortician. Down the two creaky steps, brother and sister began to walk to school.

'Hey, wait up!' she heard someone call. Sonny stopped in the middle of the footpath and looked over her shoulder.

Vince sprinted towards her with one shoe on his foot and one dangling from his hand. He had crumbs stuck to his collar, blue Powerade-stained lips, no socks, no backpack – but his hair was as immaculately groomed and frozen in time as any other day. Last night had been the longest conversation of her life. Sonny looked at him from what appeared to be an unimaginable distance. Even if all language is futile, we dream of someone who might understand what we're trying to say.

Sonny squinted a little to figure out if he was the same boy he'd been before she fell asleep. He smiled and assured her he was. The two of them walked Oscar to the gate of the Boys' School and then together to the Girls' School. Enough had been said between them. They walked in a well-deserved silence. She didn't mind the gloom of autumn's mornings so long as Vince was there to walk her through them. He walked with summer in his step and didn't mistake the sound of falling leaves for someone else's feet. They were together under the bruise-blue sky and forgot, or let themselves forget, for a moment, where the world was hurting.

Chapter 14

A Thousand Prehistoric Nights

'Wakey-wakey! It's your first day on the job!'

'What?' Vince groaned. The glare of morning light broke into the living-room from the cracked window. Sprawled on the mattress, he squinted up at Alex before burying his face into a pillow.

'We talked to the big man and got you in!' Danny exclaimed, kicking at Vince's backside. 'Come on, get up! Boss doesn't like when people are late.'

He dragged his weight against gravity, pulled on his pants and staggered to the bathroom to brush his teeth.

'Should I wear one of your dad's good shirts? A tie?'

'Why would you wear that?' Tim Tam laughed.

'I don't know, make a good impression,' Vince grunted, spitting the toothpaste into the sink.

'What you're wearing is fine,' Alex said.

They got into their car and drove off. Vince rested his head against the window and tried to steal a few more minutes of sleep. But the car came to a screeching halt before he could get very far. He rubbed his eyes and stepped out of the car. In front of him, a unit complex.

The boys bowed their heads to the older teenage boy guarding the steel door and walked inside. As they made their way up the stairs, they passed the laundry room which had been emptied of its washing machines and fortified with an iron gate. The floor was a disgrace; the grime between the tiles bled through the ceramic. Vince got a sense that this scene before him, this moment in time, was not only happening now: it had existed long before him and would exist thereafter. How could you help eternity out of an ice cube?

A precarious fan dangled from the low ceiling. Each rotation looked like its last, as though it threatened to slaughter the people below if they did not kill themselves efficiently enough. Vince watched a blue-lipped man look frantically for his veins. Three others were taking shallow breaths, letting their eyes roll back and their heads fall only to catch them with a jolt. Surrounded by aluminium foils, straws, syringes. Their own souls hung over their bodies and watched in disapproval.

Look at these guys, Vince thought to himself, what a waste of fucking life.

The boys walked up the stairs and knocked on a door. Vince did not know where to look. There was the scrape of chair-legs. The rattle of a chain. The click of a lock. The grunt of someone getting their fingers around the second chain. An under-the-breath 'fuckin' hell'. Then the door opened. Vince walked in and bowed by instinct to three twenty-something-year-olds before he was introduced to the boss, a feminine-looking man with a long torso and even longer ponytail. He had the kind of eyes that crinkled and the outline of a gun bulging from his pocket.

'Now here's a kid that looks like he can do some fuckin' damage,' he said with a laugh.

Vince only nodded as the orders were given to him. He looked around at the room. What he saw: stools and a round folding table with cups of *cà phê sữa đá* and a game of *tiến lên* put on hold, microwaves, television sets, boarded-up windows. What he didn't see: drawers that opened into a trove of necklaces with the delicate characteristics of love tokens, and silver bangles that could only fit the ankle of a newborn. The stark grey metal of shotguns spoiled the jeweller's glimmer. Strangely, buckets filled with water sat like guardians in front of the bathroom door. Vince thought they were merely catching rain from a ceiling which wasn't leaking. He'd later learn they were used to flush drugs down the toilets in case the water supply was cut off during a police raid.

Alex, Tim Tam and Danny were given glassine envelopes. The boys shoved them in their back pockets, then walked downstairs with Vince.

The other boys sensed something wrong with him but they didn't want to make him talk. His temper was a difficult thing to restrain and was better kept out of drug houses; for his safety, and theirs. Vince stood firmly apart from the others, against the dirty brick fence. A stray cat contemplated him as it licked its coat clean.

'Don't fuckin' look at me like that, man,' Vince mumbled. 'This your turf?' He held his palms against the back of his neck, scratched his jaw, kicked at the air, spoke to nobody.

Then the boys split up: Tim Tam and Danny sold at the train station, Alex's storefront was an exchange of eye contact on the street corner, and Vince was left to stand outside the apartment front.

It was a still morning. The trees seemed stuck. Things in the air would fly pointlessly high. Around midday, a fly died beside his left shoe. Vince noted how it was bigger than most, probably about the size of a pea. Its wings were starched stiff. He had the ironic thought of chalking its outline or using the used tissue in his pocket as a white sheet. When he returned to it a little later, he saw a bunch of maggots spilling from its belly. He must have stared at the scene for a bizarre half hour, until Alex came back to tell him a nearby bakery had a happy hour for *bánh mì thịt*.

They drove silently for a few moments before Vince flipped the sun visor up loudly and glared at the light from outside. Alex only watched from the corner of his eye.

'Nice of them to let us have a lunch break. They take care of our super too, bro?'

Alex made no reply.

'What the fuck are you thinking, man? Just tell me that, what's going through your head?'

Alex jutted his chin out in annoyance. 'What are you talkin' about?' he said coldly.

'You know what I'm talking about. You know what that shit can do to you!' Vince shouted, his fist pounding against the dashboard. 'You know, you fuckin' know better than anyone.'

'I'm not taking it,' Alex heard himself say. He knew Vince must be wondering how stubborn he could be, how intent on hurting himself. It wasn't like that at all.

'You want me to remind you? This is the shit that killed your dad!'

'What do you think's keeping the rest of my family alive?'

Vince breathed out deeply and swore he saw steam. 'Fuck, Alex, these people got families out there too, waiting for them to come home,' he said as mildly as he could.

'No use waiting.'

'That's not true. Just because it's over *for you* doesn't mean it's over.'

Alex glanced at Vince and then dropped his eyes.

'I know it's not over,' Alex said, in a new bitterness, a new sorrow. 'It'll never be over. There'll always be kids runnin' around lookin' for their junkie dads, guys sellin' their girlfriends for a gram.' This pain was so bright and so bewildering that Vince couldn't look away long enough to think of a reply.

'You know what happened here last week?' asked Alex as they passed another apartment. It looked like every other one in Cabramatta, complete with an empty concrete court around the back for children's games.

'What?'

'I said you know what happened here –'

'I heard you.'

'Fuckin' say so then.'

'I did. I said what?'

'What? Fuck off. Listen. Cops say it's a drug house. Storm in, take the door down, raid the fuckin' place. Little kid I know, ten years old, he's playin' in the backyard, doin' soccer tricks, mindin' his own fuckin' business. They chase 'n' corner him, point their guns. They think he's swallowed the bags of coke they're after. A fuckin' ten-year-old!

'I go to check up on him when I hear about it. Kid's standin' at the front, tryin' to put the door back up. Tells me the cops went after him 'cause they thought he kicked the ball over the fence on purpose. He really fuckin' thought that – *ten years old*, bro. He wouldn't look me in the eye, and I couldn't look at him either. I was staring at the ground, and the ground got wet. He was dropping tears, bro. Tears. Kept on falling from the kid's face like . . . like . . .'

Alex trailed off. Rain, Vince thought.

'Kid won't play outside no more. Won't even go past the mailbox. Scared for his mum and dad to leave for work. You know – I'd swallow all the coke in the fuckin' world. If that'd put a stop to all this bullshit.'

'But it won't. So, you deal the coke instead. Pass it around like fuckin' herpes.'

Alex snickered. 'Don't try to be a hero, bro. Look around,' he said, looking dismally at the streets they drove past. 'What's left to fucking save?' Vince was not trying to be anyone's saviour – he only wanted to be safe.

Alex laughed. It sounded like a lump of poison in his throat. Vince wanted to reach out and touch him, but he seemed so far away.

'This is bad, Alex,' Vince mumbled, as if talking in his sleep. 'We don't have to do this . . . *be* like this.'

'There's nothing you can do to these people that they aren't already doin' to themselves.'

Vince fell against his seat as though he'd been struck and stared out at the window, at the footpaths and fences and passing front yards. Maybe death would wake him up. He looked down at his open palms and thought about grabbing the wheel and crashing them into a life-size, garden statue of a saint whose name he couldn't recall. It looked like it could take a hit.

'Nothing's gonna happen,' Alex said, in a kind of calm that held no pulse.

'It's already happening.'

'You've seen what we can make doing this shit. So we got to do some dirty work today. So what? Think about tomorrow. Think about everything we ever wanted. There's nothing we can't have.'

What about the fish-egg tree? Vince chewed the inside of his lip until he could almost taste blood on his teeth. Blood. Drops

216

of blood falling from branches. Little red fruit you won't live long enough to eat.

'You're talking to yourself again, Alex.'

Silence.

'How many guys have died on the street you're selling on?' Vince said, watching him. 'Wake up to yourself, man. You're digging your grave inside a dream – want a swimming pool just so you can drown in it.'

'Nah, not a pool,' Alex retorted. 'A mansion. With a balcony to jump off of. Better view.'

Vince exhaled, leaning his head against the grey sky outside the window.

'I get it,' Alex mumbled. 'You don't want to talk about the future. Let's talk about right now then. Right now, your mum's probably working on another order. Ten cents a piece. Seven, eight o'clock, she'll be back to the butcher's again. How long's she been taking the night shifts for? Come on, don't you wanna see her rest?'

Vince made it clear he would not touch the drugs, or hand them over to anybody. But he didn't hesitate to put the violent junkies in their place. They made his job harder when they'd start crying, when their faces softened and they looked, for a moment, like a child that's just figured out how to beg. That was only until they tried to sell you their sex. Most of the time, though, he'd be leaning against brick walls or walking up and down the street, looking out for cops, watching people pass and knowing they knew exactly what he was doing. But nobody knew he'd learnt his monologue by heart, that he could hear the iambic pentameter in a drug-addicted pulse.

His mother did not ask him how he got the money. She already knew the answer. She would be going about her daily chores when she would think of the cursed dollars that had bought her son's moral dignity and, more conveniently, a new cot for his little sister, and say, 'Vince, I never wanted you to do this for me.'

He would look at her, and say very carefully, 'I know. I wanted to do this, for us.'

With Emma growing up right before her eyes, learning to walk and reaching for things, wanting to explore the world, Vince's mother became increasingly worried about leaving her at home alone. She quit her job at the butcher and took more sewing orders. While his mother sat on the sofa, stitching buttons onto a blouse, Emma sat at her feet to play with second-hand toys. Vince outlawed playing in the backyard. Nothing angered him more than the sight of his little sister having to rearrange piles of dirt for her own fun.

Up until this point, Vince had tried to keep out of his father's sight and trod as gently as he could when the older man was at home. He was hardly prepared to face his father's rage when it did come.

Before the day had even broken into light, Vince was woken up by the bedroom door crashing against the wall.

'Aye, *thằng quỷ*! Get up! Get up!' his father barked, standing over him. 'You think you wear the pants in this family now?!'

'Huh?!'

'I said, do you think you wear the pants in this family now?'

Vince's eyes adjusted to the dark and he saw his father's face for what seemed like the first time. His steel wool hair and his snarl of a smile. Monstrous in the dim moonlight. He wore a

218

sadly sensible coat over his wife-beater, looking like a travesty of a real working man. For a moment, Vince could do nothing but stare in disgust.

Then he kicked the sheets away from his body, got up and towered easily over his father. 'Who's gonna if I don't? I don't see any other man in this house!'

There was red rage in his father's eyes, and then the blackest darkness. 'That's funny,' he said, with a snort of almost-laughter. 'That's very funny. You crack me up, *thằng quỷ*. You really think you're somebody, don't you?'

Vince looked over at Emma's cot. Her eyes were still closed, but her brows were scrunched together with worry. Either she was having a bad dream, or just about to wake up to one.

'Do you know how you came into this world? You came into this world with your mother screaming, clawing for an escape,' his father spat. He reached up and grabbed Vince by the collar, pulling his ear closer to his words. 'That's your beginning.'

Vince shoved his father off and seized his neck with both hands, pinning him to the wall.

'What are you always saying that for, old man?!'

He wanted to savour this moment. He wanted to lift him higher and higher, to make the struggle between every gasp for air last longer than the one before; it calmed him. But he didn't want to wake Emma. Vince dragged his father out of the bedroom, bashed his body against the narrow corridor, opened the front door and threw him onto the prickly lawn. His father only stared wildly and tilted his chin up to tempt him. Vince fell onto his chest and pressed his fist to his father's cheek, pleased at the fit. He swung. Blood poured out of his nose instantly.

It occurred to Vince then that he'd never seen snow. He couldn't remember ever imagining it, not even in school when they would cut snowflakes from sheets of paper to study symmetry. Now, like a child, he wondered how perfect this moment would be if snow came floating from the sky. Would it be fluffy? Would it melt on his tongue? He wanted to mimic fallen angels, to play in an eternal white stained with his father's blood.

'Vince, let go!'

He didn't have to turn his head to know that it was his mother, standing in the doorway. He heard the panic in her voice, but even louder than that was the accusation. She must have thought he had been the one who started it. He did not have to look up to know what kind of story her eyes were telling her. Love is not blind; it has its own way of seeing.

Vince wanted so badly to storm to Alex's house, but with Emma in the equation running away would solve nothing. His father stopped writhing, only looked up at him with a shit-eating grin. Vince held his throat a little tighter, pushed it down a little harder. At last. The fear had finally been reflected into his father's eyes.

'Ông cảm ơn ông trời đi,' he taunted one last time before he let go, moved past his mother in the doorway and shut the door behind them. He locked it with a click. His mother looked at him, pleading.

'He can't be around Emma when he's off his fucking face like that,' Vince said, frustrated that he had to explain this to her.

'Vince, you know how your father is when he's drunk,' she pleaded. 'He's going to get himself killed out there!'

'Only if we're lucky.'

His mother moved to open the door. His father was already waiting at the step, catching his breath, with his forearm leaning against the doorframe and the sleazy smile of someone who has been forgiven too easily. Vince could not see his mother's face but he knew what it must have looked like: anxiously in love.

'*Mẹ sẽ nói chuyện với ba con.* I can calm him down,' his mother assured.

He had heard that line too many times before – it was an empty promise she made to herself. Vince could hardly watch as his mother draped that man's arm over her exposed shoulder and hobbled with him back into their bedroom. Vince could only stand in the corridor as his mother closed the door on him.

He went into his room, hoping to get some rest but Emma was wide awake. He so badly wanted to see her smile; every wobbly tooth could be a mooring post for him to tie the rest of his life to. Vince took her in his arms and tried to rock her back to sleep. He took off his jade necklace and placed it in her tiny hands before laying her down in her cot.

Vince heard murmuring in his parents' bedroom and covered his sister's ears; when his father's voice was this soft, it could only mean one thing. He couldn't close his eyes when he finally got into bed. He felt that he was being watched. Not by anything divine. He was certain the sky pitched above his head had no eyes – if it did, it must have blinked the last century of massacres away. No, something in his blood was murmuring to him. It throbbed with the stories his mother had told him about the deaths of the strangers whose pictures presided over their altar.

Black and white footage of a young opera singer performing for army troops rolls in his head, so grainy it is as though he is watching through a curtain of rain. She is his grandmother. She wears his proud chin and his dark eyebrows. She dances as though gravity is greedy for her mass. She is singing but he can't hear the words. A bomb is thrown from the audience. The explosion is silent. Not even the scraps of shrapnel slicing through her throat could manage a sound.

221

There were other bombs too. Other bodies. A second cousin, a young farm girl destined to take one tragic step in a cassava field. A great-uncle's torso found in the mangroves, ribbons of flesh. An aunt, believed to have reached Malaysia, found floating face down in a prawn fishery. A boy from a nearby village, whose mother agreed to give every strand of gold she owned to anyone who would get him across the border into Cambodia, shot in the back of the head in the middle of the jungle, but only after being forced to write a note: *Mother, thank you for praying. I have arrived safely. Please send the necklaces.*

These were the historical deaths; and then there were the deaths he'd grown up with, deaths on every street corner, in every stairwell, at every hour. When your sky is patched up with someone else's last moment, you can't think of how you can begin, where to begin, if there's any room left for beginnings anyway when so much has ended.

In that faraway bedroom, the blinds were shut and the night was sealed in tight, yet Vince's father still fumbled everywhere to switch off more lights. He could only make love to his wife like this: in a dark deepened by drunkenness. He no longer noticed how she trembled at his touch. He undressed her desperately, aimlessly, the way a drowning man struggles for something to hold onto. He held her hard and rough. It was the only way he knew how. She'd slip through his fingers otherwise.

Even in the stillness of this room, with no splinter of moonlight permitted, the puckered knife scars on her ribcage and the skin all around rippling reminded him of a stormy sea. Her cry for help which had once felt so far away was now echoing in his eardrums. His woman, his first love, his one and only.

222

She was no longer the girl that they'd had their way with. Her skin sagged in places which were once firm, taut, untouched by time and gravity. Whenever she reached for his face, he would pin her wrists to the mattress. He did not want to look into her eyes. Anything but her eyes. He thought about those other men and wondered if, as he stroked her, she still felt her skin scorching in the places their hands had been. *Did she still feel them?* He closed his eyes. It had happened so long ago, there was hardly any pain left in him. Only shock. Like a third-degree burn plunged into a bucket of cold water. A wound wondering why.

At the refugee camp, he had held her hand as the old herbalist lady stuck a mulberry stick inside her, and refused to leave her side even as she slept two days away in the bed of roses between her legs; but the unborn disobeyed them both. All the *rau răm* in the world could not keep this baby from claiming its birthright. When the Australians finally flew them in, she was rushed to St Vincent's Hospital. She gave birth an hour after midnight. They named him after the hospital and made a vow to forget.

From what seemed to be far overhead, he grunted away. She could feel the mist of his breath hovering over her cheeks but he touched her the way only memories could. Wherever he was now, he was in peril. The sound of waves threatened him from every compass point.

Imagine life is an empty bag of rice. Just a few streets away, the local school has been bombed to rubble. The neighbourhood children play with land mines and collect used ammunition for fun. They polish the shells, hold them in front of the sunlight and compare whose bullet shines the brightest. They are young, but they already know that fearing for your life often gets in the way of living it. 1981. In the dark, the tiny boat pulls away from the dock. Twelve days pass. Drops of sweat loll suggestively on backs of necks, on foreheads and collarbones, only to dissolve in the monsoonal air. You would trade the ocean for a gulp of water.

One clutched breath hangs over the boat; a curse or an incantation. Two children die on board and their parents hold them to their chests, weeping, before lowering their tiny bodies into the darkness. You pray for water to be more than water, for wood to be more than the weight it can hold. Suddenly, a break of light. A boat in the distance. The people hold on to this drifting chance for dear life. Their stomachs have been empty for days, their bones ache against each other, but the sight of the vessel gives them enough strength to murmur hope out of their parched throats. As it comes closer, they realise it is a fishing boat approaching; no lights, no flag. They see the cargo pants, the headbands, the jungle of black hair. They know what these things mean.

Frantically, fathers drizzle their daughters with fish sauce and smear their faces with oil from the engine. You look to your wife and do the same. But her beauty shines through like a death wish. The pirates board the little refugee boat. All this time, you do not know what to do. Your instincts fail you. It's the same with everyone else. The rough days at sea with scarcely anything to eat and sitting still in one corner have numbed your body. The pirates throw babies off the boat. Unhinge the jaw of an elderly man and rip the gold teeth from his mouth with a pair of rusted pliers. They see your wife, and there is nothing you can do. Rough hands riding that ripple of black hair, making it into a rope. Teeth and tongue marking soft, supple skin. An oyster knife between a little girl's legs. You think about how purity is a word as hollow as a plastic pearl smothered in enough light to fool the world. You

224

wonder if you will ever live to forget this moment of two lovers perishing, each too weak to end the world.

You come to another country, scared but hopeful, to make a life for your family. You sit in a factory where the boss treats you like a *thằng khung* because you don't understand what he's saying. On the train to and from work, you are cornered by men who teach you that English is a language of spit and spite. Women hold their children close to their chests, as if you are the very monster she has not told them about. *Go back to your country.* Go back? Can't you see that I've gone through hell to get here? I could do suspect sketches of the devil to prove it to you, but he keeps wearing different faces, sometimes even my own.

Who is your wife? The only woman who still obeys you. Who is your son? Why don't his eyes look like yours? Why does he keep growing, and growing, and growing? When will he stop? It becomes easier to beat your children than to raise them, to stare them down than to look them in the eye. You are ashamed of your house, of your name, of your shoes. There are days the sky looks so deep that you fear falling over the edge. Everywhere is an edge.

But he didn't want to think about this right now. He didn't want to think of all those ruined girls either, their long hair, as black as a thousand prehistoric nights before the first fire. He only knew this bedroom, this drooping mattress, this groaning bed frame, this woman's warmth, as ordinary as an oven.

'*Anh xin lỗi,*' he murmured again and again. 'Forgive me.'

She held onto the nape of his neck to keep herself from sinking. In this act of faith, of one body becoming a revelation to another, all he could find was reason for apology. But she was wiser. No matter how fragile they were, she knew that nobody could make love without the desire to preserve it. Though sex and love are not the same thing, they are intimate with each other. Tonight at least, she knew she would be sleeping in the same bed as happiness.

Tomorrow, they will each wake up with an unbearable bitterness in their mouths. Disgusted at themselves, they will wonder if they might ever be kissed again. They will dress themselves very carefully. When their nakedness is no longer, he will let the light into the room. He will touch his forehead to hers. Brush a finger across her cheek, hope that it has healed. She will not flinch. He will breathe a sigh of relief. She will smile that lazy smile that he despises. He will put on his shoes and ask what's for dinner. As though he expects himself home in the evening.

For now, the morning doesn't yet exist.

There is no night dark enough to defeat the day's definition.

But their shadows come close.

Chapter 15

The Love Life
of Fruit Flies

At the Boys' School, Oscar had been stuck at the end of the canteen line since the beginning of recess. He fumbled the cough lolly coins in his pocket, where no-one could take them. Only four minutes until the bell for second period. Older boys were jumping the queue like it was a game of leapfrog, propelling themselves forward by way of his stooped back and not even looking back to thank him for his service as a human springboard. Oscar stared at the canteen ladies. Why didn't they ever say anything?

A hand weighed down on his shoulder. He turned around, slowly, to see who it belonged to. He'd been standing in the middle of the swarming canteen area but felt as though someone had just now intruded on his hiding place.

'Hey, Oscar! I thought that was you. How've you been, brother?'

He'd never felt so glad to be found. 'Hey, Vince, I've been okay.'

Vince stood before him, with a gracious smile, looking impossibly older than Oscar would ever be. It was not just his height, or how he was so strong it seemed his Adam's apple could be dislodged as a missile at any given moment. It was his eyes. They seemed ancient. He'd lived so long he imitated no-one.

'Just okay?'

'Yeah.'

'Things haven't been good at home?' Vince asked in a whisper.

This was the first time anyone at school had asked him about home. Oscar gave a smile, lopsidedly indecisive. It made him happy to share a secret with Vince, even if that secret was his own misfortune. 'Have you got a mum?'

'What's yours been like?'

'Just yelling and screaming all day. She never gets tired of it.'

'You been bringing too many girls home and she can't sleep?'

They laughed; Oscar, cynically.

'How do you deal with that? When your mum goes crazy?'

'I just kind of . . . disappear.'

'Disappear? Where do you go?'

'I don't know. Inside. It's the only way out, away from all the yelling.'

Vince nodded and jutted his jaw out. He tried to imagine what the inside of a person could look like – found himself thinking of himself as a room with an undependable door, someone sinister always just behind it. After a while, he said, 'I used to do that too, when things got bad. Hide inside.' Then he looked up. 'But you can't live there, bro. What class you have next?'

'Sport,' Oscar replied, the word leaving a bitter taste in his mouth.

Vince laughed, and his dagger-like eyebrows softened their stance. 'You don't like sport?'

'No. We're doing the beep test.'

'I see. You got the beep test.' He looked down at the younger boy, at his resentful eyes which looked like they were figuring out the distance between this world and the next, and his scrawny legs which seemed unprepared for the journey. 'Well, I've got a free period so I'll just be chillin' on the Middle Oval. If you want, you can tell your teacher you got to go sick bay and come chill with me.'

Oscar nodded and let him see his real smile for the first time.

'Sweet,' Vince said, laughing and giving Oscar a pat on the back.

Oscar checked to see what was still up for grabs in the canteen and noticed the queue was suddenly in order. The boys in line were still as rowdy as a cavalry, but no-one was being shoved in front of.

'Vince,' he said, almost flinching from the sound of his own voice, 'how come you don't push in like everyone else?'

'Oh, I never do that. I'm very polite on those terms.'

'Why?' Oscar dared himself to say.

'Because,' Vince said, and then laughed, 'I don't fuckin' know . . . Because it's important to me.' He thought about the time he bashed a kid in juvie for hogging the PlayStation and not letting anyone else have their turn. 'Gangsters got to have good manners.'

The bell rang for the end of recess. The line began to scatter and Oscar moved to the side, out of sight from the canteen ladies who shooed the kids away like a swarm of flies.

'What you want, Oscar?' Vince offered.

'I was just gonna get some cough lollies but I think it's too late –'

'Cough lollies? You got to eat *real food*, bro, you're growing! You eat eucalyptus all day and you'll turn into a koala,' Vince said with a grin. 'Get to class. I'll see you in a bit then.'

Vince stuck his hands in his pockets and strolled over to the canteen lady. Oscar waited just long enough to watch him lean over the counter and survey the food left over, his back muscles tensing under his white shirt.

Fifteen minutes later, Oscar eased down a hill to find Vince leaning against the grass with a cigarette between his fingers, the sky carefully rearranging itself around him. He blew his cheeks out into the blue, as though admiring his creation. Oscar looked for an auspice in the smoke, then noticed a pile of wondrous canteen food beside him – meat pies, sausage rolls, garlic bread, chips, Coca-Cola, banana milk, and beneath it all, four bags of cough lollies. They'd even given him straws and serviettes.

'Hey, Oscar, come sit,' he said, patting the grass. 'The Coke's for me. Your sister told me you never drink enough milk. They only had banana left, that alright?'

'Yeah, that's fine,' answered Oscar. The first and last time he'd had banana-flavoured milk was in Year 3, when he threw up in his school cap and had to beg the office lady not to call his mum. 'Thanks, Vince. How'd you get all this? It's too much.' He sat down against the hill and tried to look comfortable.

'It's all good. Don't worry, I didn't rob the place.' Abruptly remembering the cigarette he held in his hand, he flicked the light off and put it in his pocket for later as he fanned the smoke away. 'So, what's been on your mind, man?'

Oscar twisted and tugged on a handful of grass. He tried to translate his thoughts, to determine what was better left unsaid. 'Can you teach me how to fight?'

Vince laughed. 'He wants me to teach him how to –' he said to himself breathlessly. 'No, bro, I can't teach you how to fight. No way.'

Oscar looked at him as though he were denying treatment to the terminally ill.

'That all you think I'm good for?'

'No! I didn't mean it like that.'

Vince grinned and gulped down some cola. 'Who you want to fight, anyway?'

Oscar knew he could give no names. 'If someone hurts a person you love, you've gotta get payback,' he said. 'Right?'

'Right,' Vince replied. 'But –'

'But what? That's the law.'

'There is no law. Not for us. There are only jails,' Vince said, with a smile that was gentle and sorry. 'And you don't want to get yourself in there.'

Oscar looked away.

'You think it's cool?' Vince asked.

Oscar stayed silent.

'I thought it was too. But there is no greatness in any of this – this livin' on edge bullshit. They don't tell you that. No-one tells you. You don't find out till they put you away and you realise that you really have *nothing*. You have nothing and you come home to nothing.'

He looked at Oscar.

'When I was your age and my dad would, you know, kick my fuckin' head in – I'd be angry too. Go out and bash everyone. Didn't even think about it, just did it 'cause it made me feel better.' He drew in a breath and let it go, savoured the smoke of a world on fire. 'I remember in juvie, my psych tried tellin' me I was violent 'cause of my relationship with my dad. Said I got myself in trouble 'cause I wanted his attention or some shit. But I knew I wasn't begging for no-one's love. See, all the other boys in juvie had a missus waiting for them back home, but not me. They'd say "Aw, Vince, you gotta get yourself a girl," for, uh, you know, relaxation purposes. But I always thought when I get to love someone one day, I'm gonna do it right. 'Cause I knew I had nothing, and I wanted to *do* something with that nothing. And if you can love someone out of nothing, then you don't have *nothing* anymore. Out of nowhere, you've got the only thing worth having.'

Sometimes you listen to a person talk and know they are telling all the truth they can bear. It made Oscar think that everyone could be saved with a little honesty, or at least be worth saving.

'Do you have a girlfriend, Vince?' he asked.

'Nah, not yet. Got someone I think about, though. That's enough to keep you sane.' He threw a meat pie into Oscar's lap. 'You want some tomato sauce?'

Oscar tore off the wrapper and bit into it, his teeth sinking down the layers of pastry to meet gelatinous beef. 'No, I'm good. I just feel stupid now. I really thought I could do damage to somebody with these boney bones.' He looked down at his arms, the blue veins travelling through thin wrists, the bulging elbows that looked like knobs of ginger.

'Nah, they look pretty sharp to me. Could stab someone with 'em,' Vince reassured. 'It's normal to wanna start fighting, especially at our school. I just don't want you to get caught up in it like I did. Drink your milk, bro.'

Oscar nodded and poked his straw into the carton, seeming to measure the percentage of sugar in every sip. He wanted to gag on the artificial banana flavour, but forced his tongue to stay put. 'I always thought you were the kind of person that had no regrets.'

Vince laughed. 'Regret's good for you. If you have no regrets, then how you ever gonna change? Helps you figure out who you are – or at least who you *aren't*, and who you won't let yourself become. You get me?'

Oscar nodded.

'Good chat, Oscar. I gotta jet to the Girls' School for last period. You come to me if you ever need anything, alright?'

Vince strolled over to the fence and stepped over it with vaudeville ease. As he walked along the footpath, Oscar imagined the exposed tree root snaking through the squares of concrete would try to trip him, and then the stormwater drain might open its mouth and let gravity do the rest. He had the sense that the older boy was in perpetual danger, but a danger which could never injure him. Wherever fate might fling him, it seemed Vince would land like a cat.

'You're gonna do great!' Sonny waved as the bell for last period rang. 'I wish I could watch.'

'Nah, it's better this way,' Vince said, almost fracturing her heart. 'If you were there, I'd just see your face and crack up.'

With the sight of his smile, with the thought that her face alone could be cause for his laughter, her heart rummaged through its handy surgical kit and patched itself back up. The frenzy of emotions that took hold of her whenever Vince was near was a nuisance. The more she looked at him, the more self-control she surrendered. She stooped down to reach for the bottle in her backpack and guzzled the water, hopeful he would leave.

Without her noticing, Vince had bent down before her. She looked up to find his nose almost touching hers. 'What? No good luck kiss?'

She choked on the water rushing down her throat and spat it out. It streamed down Vince's cheeks, gathered in his brows, made a well in the corners of his eyes. He scrunched his face up in shock but could not help grinning as the water dripped down his neck and drenched his collar.

'Ha ha ha! That was a good one! You got me!'

Sonny sped off to class before he could even dry his eyes.

Vince changed into his blacks and stood in the centre of the stage. The blinds were drawn, the door was shut. The other Drama students sat on the carpeted blocks and some fiddled with the projector to help Vince sort out the stage lighting settings.

'This one?'

'Nah.'

'This?'

'Keep going.'

Then, a smoky almost-blue light took hold of the room, not unlike the ultraviolet that Alex had grown up under. Dust particles rose and fell, swirling in the air like things to be wished on. He felt like a being that shouldn't exist; half man, half myth.

'This one,' he said.

He still looked like himself, black-haired with cheekbones as knifelike as ever, but the light was unkind. Shades of violet overshadowed his face, making his eyes look as dreary as sunflower seeds. Vince hunched over so deeply he seemed to have swallowed his spine.

> *The spirit torments me. Oh!*
>> *Hast thou not dropp'd from heaven?*
>>> *Be not afeard. The isle is full of noises,*
>>> *Sounds and sweet airs, that give delight and hurt not.*

Caliban knew what it was like to be belted by spells, to bare your teeth and curse at the air, knew the way insolence burns like sulphur in the stomach. But in some sense, Caliban was freer than most. The other characters could be left in the ever and ever of fiction, to roam and remain in the exact words they'd been given, but he had somehow escaped. Perhaps the only slaves were those held captive in another's imagination.

> *Teach me how*
> *To name the bigger light, and how the less,*
> *That burn by day and night*
>
> > *Do hiss me into madness*
> > *And I will kiss thy foot: I prithee, be my god.*

Vince knew something was happening to him. His blood pounded through him like the drums of triumph after sixteen years of being at war with yourself. He found he could take everything that was inside him and push it further, so that what felt like a precipice became a stage.

> *The clouds methought would open and show riches*
> *Ready to drop upon me, that when I waked,*
> *I cried to dream again.*

As he said Caliban's last line, he looked into the hazy light of the projector. Then it shut off. The room was black and tongue-tied. Vince laid his palm against his chest and took a bow. The bell rang soon after. He walked out of darkness into day, feeling as though he had just discovered how to force a sunrise, and stood at the back gate with an extra kilowatt added to his smile. School-girls squirmed through the gate, each tickled with the thought that he was waiting for them. The fantasy shattered the moment Sonny appeared.

'Afternoon, Baby Blue,' Vince called. He felt as though he were greeting her as a new person, and hoped she would notice.

This was the first time Vince had called her this in front of other people. Sonny had always loathed smitten teens, both in theory and in practice, but in this instance she didn't feel a need to cringe. Said in his abrasive voice, any term of endearment was stripped of its sweetness; 'Baby Blue' sounded like a nickname for an inmate who had done time for suffocating infants.

'Hi!' Sonny pressed her lips together, wondering if he'd forgotten how she'd hosed him down with a pungent mixture of tap water, saliva and dental plaque just a few hours prior. 'How'd your thing go?'

'Hectic!' he exclaimed. 'Yeah, it went really well.'

'All your hard work paid off then!'

'*Our* hard work. You helped a lot.'

'I did?'

'Yeah . . . spitting in my face was a good idea. Really freshened me up.'

As Sonny pretended to shoo a fly and avoid Vince's stabbing remark, she saw Michelle walking towards them. She noted how dazzling she looked with her picture-perfect hair and envied the ease of that long-legged stride – it was as though Michelle walked perpetually on ice skates. She must be the reason Vince was waiting at the gate. Who wouldn't wait for a girl like that?

'Well, I'm gonna get home now,' Sonny said, with a pinch of a smile as she began to move past him.

'Actually,' Vince said, 'I was gonna ask if you wanted to get some pizza with me. So we can celebrate.'

She looked at him curiously. Did he not notice the billowing hair, the honeyed legs, the thorough curling and mascara-coating of each lash? Sonny was relieved he had no eye for beauty, but still would not allow herself to say yes outright.

'Oh, I don't know if I'm allowed to.'

'Good job today, Vince, bye, Sonny,' Michelle said in her silvery voice as she passed, moving lithely in between the two.

'Bye!'

'Thanks!' Vince waved briskly before returning his focus to Sonny. 'Come on, Sonny, let's go. We worked for this, we deserve it!'

'Hmm,' Sonny hummed, tapping her finger against her lips.

'I didn't bring my car today so we can walk. It'll be fun.'

Dare she accept this quest? The consequences were slim to none. Her mother didn't go grocery shopping anywhere near the school and her father was at work.

'It's my shout,' Vince sang.

Sonny continued to walk uncertainly, with Vince following at her side. She liked to be begged. It reminded her of how he had been when they were children.

'I don't know, Vince.'

'Sonny,' he sighed, clasping his hands together and holding his index fingers against his lips. 'We're just going for a little snack. Come on, we're already on our way! We're so close already.'

His laughter convinced her to give in. After a few minutes of walking, Sonny strayed off the path and stood on the dirt. Peering through the chain-link fence that separated them from the train tracks, she let out a whimper.

'What is it, Sonny?' Vince asked, standing beside her. All he could see was an embankment of overgrown grass.

'All my flowers are dead,' she groaned, holding onto the fence with both hands.

'What flowers?'

'The ones that grow here. I think they're weeds, but they smell so nice. I walk past them every day – I don't know how I didn't notice they were all gone.'

She only forgot about her flowers when they passed a charming little church on the other side of the road. On this particular day, the temperament of the letter board outside was a little less hellfire and a little more salvation. The sign read: *Come to me, all you who are weary and burdened, and I will give you rest.*

'Sounds like something a prostitute would say,' Sonny said.

While Vince stopped at the edge of the street to wait for oncoming traffic to pass, Sonny continued straight without second-guessing herself. When she was with Oscar she always remembered to look both ways, but on her own, avoiding eye contact with drivers had always been a greater priority than her safety. She stormed ahead when a car was just turning into the corner.

'Sonny!'

Before the car could come to a complete halt, Vince had lunged between her and the bonnet. He muttered an apology to the driver and grabbed hold of her wrist to walk her the rest of the way.

'Don't you check for cars when you cross?' he asked, stopping her at the curb for a response.

'Woah,' Sonny said, looking down at his fingers still latched on. She shook her head as if to unthink something absurd. 'I just imagined you were a boy for a second there.'

He let go, looked at his hand for a moment and then at her.

'I *am* a boy.'

'You know what I mean,' she muttered as she began to walk again.

Vince crossed his arms around his chest, following quickly behind. 'I don't think I do.'

'I imagined you were a boy*friend*.' Sonny's face fell as soon as her voice left her mouth. She had no idea why she'd said what she said. But she knew the b-word would contaminate the air if she left it to linger. 'I think I've been so deprived that when I interact with *any* guy, I start to imagine things that aren't really there.'

Vince jutted his chin out and raised his brows. 'Any guy, huh?'

As Sonny and Vince turned into an alleyway on the opposite side of the train station, they passed a totalled Toyota Camry. They saw snowflake images of themselves in the dented metal and in the glass of the smashed windows which frosted the bitumen below. Dirty toys that had been dumped in potholes sometimes squeaked under their footsteps.

'What kind of things do you imagine?' he asked.

'Huh?'

'When you're around a guy.'

'Oh ... you know ... the usual stuff. Butterflies in your stomach, fast heartbeat.' *Bodily fluids.* 'My body's just so unused to human touch that I think it plays tricks on itself. Starts feeling things that aren't there, just for the sake of it.'

Vince closed his eyes in laughter, stumbling a little as he walked.

'Okay, so, say you really did start to feel *things*, with me. You wouldn't be able to tell if it was real or just your body reacting?'

'I don't know, I guess,' Sonny shrugged. She was surprised that he was even taking her seriously.

A train roared in the near distance. The sound of heavy metal scraping against itself and carrying its own weight filled the air. Sonny cupped her ears to block out the deafening sound. When it passed, she let out a sigh of relief. As her hands dropped from the air, Vince caught hold of one with his. His large hand easily surrounded hers, encasing her in his ample warmth. *Racing heartbeat? Check. Butterflies? Check. Moist underwear? Give it a second.*

Sonny had not known that such utilitarian instruments as hands harboured so many sensory nerves. Her palm begged for more of Vince's skin; her thumb wanted nothing more than to twiddle with his. Vince curled his fingers around the hollows between hers and held the woven arrangement to their faces. She could feel her heart ripen in his hand.

'How about this?' Vince asked, smiling only slightly. 'You feel anything?'

He stood so close. A muscle in his jaw appeared to have a pulse. She looked into his eyes, still and serious, and wondered what thoughts they were keeping from her. Sonny wanted to throw her arms around his neck and pull him close. Breathe him in and make her body know that touch is not always treacherous. She had dreamed of a moment like this a thousand times before, and imagined just being near him would send every fear crashing out the window of her soul, and she would land on him like a fruit fly itching to lay eggs under the skin of a sugar plum.

But there were too many worries embossed in her goosebumps. All she could do was wonder. Could he make her nakedness sacred to her? Otherwise, could he uninvent time and make her forget everything that had come before him? Would a kiss answer the question – or keep her from asking it?

'Yeah,' she said, tugging her hand out of his hold. 'Your palm is sweaty.'

Vince only laughed at her shaken response and shoved his hands in his pockets.

Sonny looked around at the alleyway and imagined a desolate world where the two of them were the sole survivors. An apocalypse would make life so much simpler. Copulation, of course, would be the only ethical thing to do. She unwillingly imagined the two of them securing the survival of their species in the backseat of the beyond-saving Camry while the zombies advanced. Vince watched her from the corner of his eye and laughed at the impasto of expressions on her face, which ranged from cheeky delight to extreme shame.

'What's wrong with you?'

'What's wrong with *me*?' She pretended to look offended, then found herself contemplating the question. 'I don't know, I've been asking myself the same thing for a while now.'

And they laughed again, both knowing they were not laughing only at themselves and at each other, but at everything that had ever happened to them.

The total came to twenty or so dollars. Sonny swooned at the speed at which Vince reached for his wallet. At their table, they swirled tap water in their wine glasses and grinned as their orders arrived. She had never before seen hot chips presented in such a respectable manner: piled neatly onto a deep white plate and sprinkled with herbs. Garlic bread was next, and then the pepperoni pizza was set before them: cooked to an ashen crisp around the edges and oozing delicious sauce.

Sonny and Vince each folded a slice in half and held it to their mouths, grinning. The orange oil dripped from the pizza and the pizza dripped from their hands. They puffed their cheeks out to blow steam because the very rational idea of waiting for it to cool hadn't occurred to either, and swapped the sizzling pain in their mouths for inside jokes.

After Sonny had devoured three slices, she was ready to pick up the conversation again. 'So, tell me,' she began, wiping her mouth with a napkin in mock gentility, 'how'd your monologue go?'

His mouth full, Vince chewed quickly to answer her but ended up almost dislocating his jaw in the process. Sonny glanced down at her wrist, which bore no watch, and laughed as he winced and rubbed his chin.

'It was good!' Vince said. This would have been a sufficient answer for anyone else, but with her he felt a need to say more. 'I felt so fuckin' free, Sonny.' His hands were reaching, grasping for the right words.

'At first, you're standing in the dark. Nobody knows who you are. In a second, when the light comes on, the audience will be sitting there, waiting for your first line, your first move, waiting to have you figured out. But before they do that, you could be *anyone*. They look at you like you're some big fuckin' mystery. That's the freedom.'

As he said this, he was wiping his fingers on the napkin but only catching more grease. Sonny reached for the resealable bag in her backpack, where she collected wet wipes from KFC, and handed him a sachet.

'Thanks,' Vince grinned. 'I've been thinking about what you said the other day, about having another language to think in. Both of us grew up speaking Viet. But the voice in my head isn't Vietnamese. I think it used to be. It's weird. I feel like, in Vietnamese, I'm still just a *thằng giang hồ* that can't talk to his mum.'

He laughed unkindly at himself, then sipped some water. Sonny knew he had meant to say, *when I speak* in Vietnamese. But she found something in his mistake.

'And who are you in English?'

He was surprised by the question. His first response was to shrug his shoulders and stare at a nearby napkin. 'I don't know. English is even weirder. I always felt like I was talking in some shady, bootleg version of it. Like them movies they sell on the street corner – an imitation of the real thing.'

242

Sonny pinched a fast-food towelette around her fingertips philosophically. 'Maybe it only felt like that because you thought you had to repeat after someone else just to speak.' Staring at the water stain on the table, she nudged the corner of the wet wipe under her thumbnail and scraped away some dirt under the half-moon as her thoughts drew her deeper. 'But then you started using your own words.' She looked up at Vince with a smile. 'English used to belong to people like Shakespeare. Now it belongs to people like us.'

They walked home together, reaching up to touch the drooping leaves of trees. Vince would sometimes stop to climb over the fence of a backyard and Sonny would just keep walking knowingly, waiting for him to catch up with a knobbly, green guava, a pair of sour passionfruit or a handful of persimmons, his pocket knife slashing into the season's last offerings.

'Want some? Don't be shy,' Vince said, dropping the skins on the grass and holding the overripe persimmon in his hand like a salted egg yolk.

When they reached their street, Vince stopped in the middle of the footpath.

'Sonny,' he said. She shuddered at how young his voice sounded. 'If we ever get the chance to get away from here, we have to take it. Okay?'

The sun beamed down and warmed their blood. Sonny turned to look at Vince.

'What do you mean *if*? Somehow, I feel like we've already found a way out,' she said with a gravity that pulled him close.

'Somehow,' he repeated, his tongue pushing away a mango strand leftover to test the word in his mouth for sweetness. 'Okay. I believe in somehow.'

Chapter 16

Something, Anything

When winter came, it held the sun hostage and woke Sonny at four in the morning to the rattling of dishes. The blinds would be closed but the darkness swelled outside, draping itself against her window like black magic. She would walk to the kitchen and be faced with her father's back; watch as he ate breakfast alone, as he cracked an egg into his coffee and stirred it with a spoon of condensed milk, as he squinted down at the neatly transcribed catastrophes under a single fluorescent bulb.

'Sonny,' he would say, after noticing her shadow. The sudden concern on his face never ceased to move her, and make her wonder what she had done to deserve it. 'Why aren't you asleep?'

Without a word, she would move to hug him and run back to bed. She would lie still beneath blankets to cultivate her selfish heat while her father dressed (always inadequately) for the cold. When she listened to the door unlock, and the slip of fake leather as he wore his rain-moulded shoes and drove off, she thought of him still, as if to keep him warm while he was out in the world.

Sonny lay in bed and prayed the way she did as a child, pleading to the spirits of ancestors to protect him from slippery roads, to divert reckless drivers and to ward off armed thieves. She remembered staying up at night, sleepy but burdened by her own divinity, thinking that the more she prayed, the more she could ask to keep.

If there was anything beautiful about winter, it was how the cold coloured your summertime possessions. Think luminous, of languor and sunshine the yellowest yellow. Remember how the air would seem so pleased to just be near you, fall asleep to the thought of afternoon naps by an open window. Huddling over a bowl of green mango soaked in sweet fish sauce, slugs of cold pandan jelly swimming in coconut milk, dicing and dyeing canned water chestnuts into gems for *chè*, cardinal and pomegranate-red, the burnt caramel of your father's back which must have once been golden, ice cubes chanting down a glass you'd bring out to him in the garden. Winter is a reminder that – yes – even you have things too precious to lose, and summer is only a matter of time.

On the dinner table one late-June night, Sonny's mother delivered a sermon on the effect love has on body weight.

'*Cô Hạnh* used to be so beautiful,' she lamented about her next-door neighbour. 'It must have been more than fifteen years ago when I first met her, and I still remember how she glowed. But now she's so thin, and so tired, like a flower that *bị héo*. It's because her husband *hành hạ* her all the time. See, *con*, this is why your partner is so important. Love feeds you. If you get enough, then it plumps you up. That's why I'm fat, because your father cares for me too well.'

She laughed but the rest of the family only continued eating suspiciously, wondering how much longer the sunny weather would last. 'But if you look at *cô Hạnh*, that's a woman that's barely

245

scraping by. She's lucky she's got that son of hers, though. Even if he does *khuấy*, at least she can depend on him. He's bringing in such good money that she's already quit her job at the butcher.'

'Vince has a job?' Sonny asked with an astonished look on her face. Had he gone to look for work after they'd had pizza together only a week ago?

'Yes,' her mother replied, her eyes sparkling, daring her to ask the next question.

'What does he do?'

'What have boys like him always done to make money?' she asked in response. 'With a personality like that, you think he's going to go out and wait tables?'

The rest of the night passed by with Sonny's mind having gone on a journey elsewhere; solely relying on instinct, she did her homework, folded the laundry, brushed her teeth. She was glad that Vince was taking on responsibilities, yet anxious about what this job entailed. Most of all, she felt silly for letting him wear his shoes inside her head, leaving marks all over her thoughts. On the walkie-talkie that night, Sonny decided to bring the matter up.

'Your mum told my mum that you got a job,' she said expectantly.

'Yeah, I did,' he replied, and she could tell by the tone that he was trying to lessen the damage. 'The pay is good.'

'Is it?'

'Yeah, this place *làm ăn được lắm*. Customers come and go all fuckin' day.' He laughed and the suspicion flashed in her mind like lightning, brighter and more bewildered than before taking the form of a bolt.

'What kind of trouble are you getting into now?'

'Well, I've never really been *out* of trouble,' he said, and she

246

The man stopped in his tracks and glanced over his shoulder. From under his jacket, he pulled out an ice pick. Vince was only a few metres away by now. He ran, cut the space in between, seized the man by the throat and shoved him against a car parked beside the sidewalk, then smashed his wrist against the window, once, twice, three times.

The ice pick fell to the ground. Vince slammed his knuckles into his face again and again, and the man only stood there, slumped against the car door. His hands began to tire, and he had expected the man to be over with by now, but at the moment he slowed his next hit, the man came at him like a lightning strike. Vince was kicked in the stomach and thrown against the footpath. His skull throbbed against the asphalt. Alex ran towards them, and by the time he got there, the man had straddled Vince's chest and pounded at his head with balled fists, jolting him against the pavement.

Vince closed his eyes for a moment and opened them, feeling as though he was waking up into a new day. The bright, white daylight glared at him and he clenched his eyes shut in retaliation. Next thing he knew, he was in the passenger seat and Alex was driving. Alex drove by the train station and honked until Danny and Tim Tam got into the car.

'What the fuck happened?'

'Does he need a doctor?'

'This *fucking* junkie caved his fucking head in, out of nowhere,' Alex said. His knuckles were white as he gripped onto the wheel. 'I took the dickhead up to boss's room. We'll drop Vince off at his mum's and then go back, fuck him up a bit.'

'Stop talking so fucking loud,' Vince groaned, leaning against the window and holding his hand against his ear. 'I'm trying to fuckin' sleep here.'

heard him grin, as if he was proud he could score this against her. 'How can I say this?' Vince mused lightheartedly. 'Oh, you know that house on Melville Avenue, where people do your taxes?'

'Yeah . . .'

'I'm working at a drug house on the other side of the road.'

She laughed so that he wouldn't hear her tremble.

'Sonny . . .'

'You're joking.'

'I'm not.'

'You have to be.'

'I'm being serious. I promise.'

But this wasn't the kind of promise she had ever wanted from him. All at once, everything eclipsed. She looked at all that surrounded her with a sudden helplessness, and the streets outside appeared in her mind. There was such dirt and darkness, such single-minded suffering out there. How could it have happened to him? To this boy who had read aloud to her; who had made her feel so safe; who returned that lost song from her childhood. And now this.

'I'm not selling it or nothing,' he said, quietly. 'All I do is stand outside and guard the place, like a bouncer.'

She supposed that was the single misfortune of all lullabies. You are safe in your sleep, and yet the world is always there, waiting for you to wake up. Feeling as though she had just now awoken, she could only see Vince, standing deathly still in front of a drug house, flames framing the edge of his eyes. Like the monk, no-one could tell he was sending himself to the underworld just to see his mother eat. Infernos were made for boys like him.

Vince could only sit, staring at the old walkie-talkie in his hand, and wonder at the thoughts she was keeping from him. He was entertained by the slight trembling of his fingers.

'Sonny? You still there?'

'Yeah.'

He could picture her troubled face.

'Why won't you say anything?'

Because the words simply wouldn't come. Her thoughts were not only unspeakable, but unreadable, even to herself. There was only the repetition of a single phrase. *No, not him, not him, not him, no, not him, not him.* She wondered how many mothers had said the same prayer disguised as disbelief.

'What do you want me to say?' she heard a voice answer, only afterwards realising that it had been her own.

'I don't know. *Something.* Anything.'

'Your family doesn't have health insurance.'

If he was smart enough, he'd sense every nerve in her body entangled in those few words.

'What?'

Evidently not.

'I heard your mum say so on the phone to mine the other day. You're not covered by any insurance, so don't do anything stupid.'

They laughed because that was the only way they knew back to each other.

'Don't worry, I know I got to look after myself. I've got my girl at home, waiting for me now.' He smirked at her silence, before adding, 'I'm talking about Emma.'

As time passed, the older men had grown more and more fond of Vince. They appreciated his commitment. He could sniff out a police dog, he was good at their card games, and, above all, he had proven himself to be one of the fiercest fighters they'd ever seen. One morning, in the middle of August, Vince sat on the

brick fence under the sky's blue scream with his hands in his pockets.

'What the fuck is wrong with this weather?' he muttered to himself. 'Even the sun is cold.'

Visibly afflicted people walked by all the time – brothers and sisters, mothers and fathers, sons and daughters – but it hurt too much to see the world this way, so he trained himself to see each person on their own, not expected home for dinner by anyone standing over a stove.

Vince stared at a pigeon contemplating its image over a dirty puddle. When the water began to wobble, he looked up. A man was approaching fast, with a face the colour of clay and skin dented with ribbon tools, sweating buckets, melting away on a six-degree day. Vince could see his pupils even at a distance. Purple autumn leaf for a lip, cracked, dried blood on the corners of his mouth. He wore a blue and purple Nike windbreaker and stormed past with his arms crossed, one hand slipped beneath his jacket.

Heroin, no doubt. Vince looked to see where he could be so eager to get to: ahead, carbon copies of the same dreary apartment complex, a few stray cats, countless potholes, two streets of bare footpath, and a teenage boy dealing dope at the corner.

'Alex!' Vince called. 'Alex!'

Alex didn't hear. He was finishing a deal; a woman had just handed him some rubber-banded cash. He lifted his shirt and put the money in his waist pack before handing her a baggie.

'Fuck!' Vince muttered. He jumped to his feet and sprang into action, sprinting towards the man with thunderous breath. Every part of him fleeing. Caught by the wind and moving in mid-air. His feet struck against the pavement and he felt all his strength surge to his fists.

His mother's car wasn't in the driveway; she had probably gone out to buy groceries and taken Emma with her. The boys helped Vince into his bedroom and stormed out of the house again. They drove back to the workplace, smouldering as though they were in a sauna, their breath suffocating. Their legs shook in their seats and they drummed their fingers against the car window to the rhythm of their wrath.

Vince lay in bed the rest of the day, caught in a daze, slept, tossed, dreamed. When he tried to get up for a glass of water, he couldn't plant both feet on the ground without feeling as though the earth shuddered beneath him, without his brain wobbling in his skull like failed Aeroplane Jelly. He saw stars and streaks of lights in his left eye. Even his thoughts fought against him.

Vince used to be hell-bent on winning fights but that thought didn't occur to him now. What denied him rest was what he saw before he blacked out. What if that junkie had been a little stronger? What if he hadn't got the ice pick out of his hands? Then the last glimpse he would have of this world before the never-ending nothingness was that face. Hollow. Painless. Almost like a newborn again.

He woke at eleven, and still could not move from his bed. With a parched throat and what seemed to be the combined weight of everything in the night sky on top of his head, he threw himself onto his side to see Emma sleeping safely in the cot. To think that she was asleep beside him, breathing so softly she wouldn't even rustle an onion skin. To think that only a year and a half ago, when he was much younger and always on the wrong side of walls, Emma had been a stranger to the world. Yet here she was now; a baby, complete with fingers and toes and a heartbeat swollen with hope.

He reached for the walkie-talkie above his pillow.

'Sonny?' he said in a gentle slur. 'Sonny? You still up?'

Sonny, who'd been reading, scrambled through the family of stuffed animals on her bed for the walkie-talkie.

'Hello? Yeah, I'm here.'

'You remember how I said before, that everything is worth fighting for to me?' Vince asked drowsily.

'Mhm,' she hummed.

'I don't know about that anymore.' To gather his thoughts hurt his head, and trying to speak snuck needles into his throat, but he needed to get these words out if he was to ever sleep again. 'I used to be so angry all the time because I felt like, every day, the world was ending for me and I couldn't do nothin' about it. I didn't know what would happen to me or anyone around me.' He was trying his best to keep from mumbling. 'But it's different now.

'The world is still ending again and again, for everybody, but for *me* . . .' A jagged pain pierced his skull. He stopped to suppress a groan, then let out a breath and continued on. 'All I know now is, if the world is ending, I hope it ends with you. You're the last thing I want to see.'

Sonny's breath hitched in her throat and by the time she could speak again – only to say his name – she was faced with silence. He had fallen asleep, leaving her to lie awake with his words circling her head again and again.

When the boys visited Vince the next day, he was in an even worse condition. They observed his symptoms – vomiting, persistent headache, loss of balance, disorientation, sleepiness – and diagnosed him with a concussion. They drove him to Alex's house because he didn't want his mother to see him like this. The boss took care of Vince's family while he was recovering; men came by the house once to drop an envelope of money into the mailbox.

Everything was loud and bright and Vince only wanted to get away. He lay on the mattress in Alex's living-room and groaned, knocked his fist against his skull and tried to evict his headache. He needed to make room for sweet dreams.

'Yeah?' Alex called from the kitchen.

'What?' Vince said hotly.

'I thought you were calling me.'

'If I wanted to call you, I'd say, "Hey, stupid, fat bitch,"' Vince replied with a wry smile.

Alex grinned and strode into the living-room, tackling an already bedridden Vince, too faint to even move. He wrestled with Vince's motionless body to mock him. 'You wanna start something? 'Cause I'll fuckin' finish it.'

Vince could only squeeze his eyes shut in annoyance.

Alex looked down at him. 'You got a headache?'

'I will if you keep talking.'

'You want me to call your missus? Get her to come visit you?'

'Fuck no!'

This was the first time Vince had shown so much expression since he'd been hurt. He winced from the sharpness of his own voice.

'Why not?' Alex asked, pleased by his sudden passion.

'Just don't,' he muttered. 'If you see her, tell her I got the flu. Or whatever's going around at the moment – I don't fuckin' know.'

'Chlamydia?'

'Fuck off.'

'What? STIs are always in season.'

The next few days passed, its contents played out in Vince's absence. He was stuck somewhere inside of himself. The only thing he remembered was Alex, or Tim Tam, or Danny feeding him a painkiller and holding a glass of water to his lips and saying, 'Wake up to yourself. You're living in a dream, bro.'

Without Vince in them, Sonny's days inched by and by. She missed him terribly, and felt foolish for it. Had he been hurt? Had forgotten enemies finally caught up with him? Had being around drugs got him into a bad habit? The time that passed only deepened her suspicion: that after all that had been said about him, after his arrests and his time away, you'd think she'd have found a safer place to keep her heart. Sonny told herself he was more trouble than he would ever be worth. Now all that was left was to make herself believe it.

Almost two weeks had gone since Vince's walkie-talkie confession, and the memory of it – his soft, faltering voice – would not leave her alone. She stood in front of the sink and washed her cereal bowl, wondering where he was and looking up at the sky as if he would be suspended from a parachute. When Sonny looked back down at her garden, Vince's face beamed at her, at once eclipsing the sun. He was talking to her father over the fence. When she noticed that he looked just fine, her own symptoms went away. She hadn't known that love came in a liquid form, that a boy could be both snakebite and antivenom.

While he and her father spoke, Sonny picked up pieces like 'top soil' and 'spring-flowering bulbs' and 'free horse manure outside the racecourse in Warwick Farm'. She watched from the kitchen, taking particular care with this particular porcelain bowl. She looked down quickly when her father came back into the house.

Scrubbing away at the enamel of the already-sparkling crockery, Sonny asked, 'What were you talking to him about, *ba*?'

'Oh, I was just giving him some gardening advice. He wants to fix up his backyard for his family in time for spring,' her father explained. 'He's a sweet kid.'

He's a sweet kid.

'Sweet?' she repeated, as though to doubt it.

'Yeah, very thoughtful. He saw me struggling to climb onto the roof –'

'Why did you have to climb on the roof?' she asked, alarmed.

'Your mum wanted me to put some rat poison up there.'

Sonny scowled in disappointment. Her mother was always ordering him to do the dangerous work around the house.

'It's okay, Sonny. Vince saw me and climbed up there himself to do the job for me.'

'Is he sick?' she asked, trying to strip her voice of any sympathy she would not give indiscriminately.

'Yeah, has been for some time now. He said it's his first time getting out of bed in days.' Then he paused to look at her. 'How did you know he was sick?'

Sonny panicked under those all-seeing eyes.

'Just a guess. I haven't seen him at Drama class in a while,' Sonny said, drying her hands on the kitchen towel roughly. She looked at her father as if to ask, *How much do you know?*

'Oh, I see.'

That night, at 11.20 pm, he finally called.

'Hey, Baby Blue.'

'Vince?' *So he was still alive,* she thought to herself. *Not good enough.* She cleared her throat and tried to be stoic. 'I heard you were sick.'

Vince smiled to himself. 'Yeah, I caught something pretty bad,' he said, straining his voice. He needed to maximise his suffering just to see how she would react; felt himself entitled to some affection, even if it was as simple as hearing the concern in her voice.

'You can't just go and disappear whenever you get sick,' Sonny said. Would he get the wrong impression and think she'd been worried about him this whole time? 'It's – it's bad manners.'

'I'm sorry, Baby Blue. I've just been out of it for a while.'

'Have you been to the doctor?'

'I can fight it off myself,' he said, as a peace offering.

'I can help you fight it,' she said, as an invitation to war.

'How?'

'Come over to my room.'

'Now?'

'Now!'

'What for?'

'I've got something that'll cure you.'

'It's alright, Sonny, I –'

'Are you sick or what?'

'I am!'

'Well, then let me see you,' she argued, before adding, 'or are you just a big fat liar?'

Without another word, Vince got out of bed and went to the backyard. Whilst he was hurtling himself over the fence, Sonny had turned off her bedroom lights and was sitting on her bed, fidgeting with the touch lamp to figure out the perfect dimness to set the mood. Her head snapped to the door as soon as she heard his knock.

'Come in,' she called.

Vince found Sonny sitting on the side of her bed, contemplating, it seemed, the colour of her shadow. He looked at the posters of boy bands and the glow-in-the-dark stars plastered onto her walls. Something about the sight of piled books brought a feeling of admiration for her. Even the bodice-rippers. Vince adored the quaint cottage ambience of the floral bedsheets and the brass lamp, which burned a light they used to play shadow puppets against. The Bedtime Bear and the buck-toothed Bugs Bunny on her bed seemed to welcome him in. The Eeyore finger puppet he'd got her was sitting upright by her pillow. He laughed inwardly at the way the diffused lighting softened the two of them into almost-silhouettes.

'What?' Vince said, grinning at her as he closed the door. 'You couldn't light some candles?'

He backed away as soon as he saw the green medicated oil and metal spoon in her hands.

'Oh, no,' he said, and laughed quickly. 'Nah, I'm good, thank you.'

'It'll help you!' Sonny said firmly, holding her tools of healing like a broken glass bottle. 'You probably got sick in the first place 'cause it's cold and you think you're too tough to wear a jacket. I just gotta take the wind out of you and you'll be fine.'

She stood up and patted her bed, motioning for him to lie down.

'Sonny,' he winced.

'You can handle it. It won't hurt any more than any of your fights.'

Vince huffed, got on the bed, and took off his shirt. Sonny's breath sucked as she drank in the sight of his bare back. Shadows fell on his skin and carved out the curvature of his spine, his rippling muscles, the basin between his shoulder blades. He lay down and waited. Sonny made a show of kneeling between his legs, sitting on the edge of the bed and twisting her back towards him, only to give up on all these positions with a huff. Finally, she straddled the back of his thighs; but not before remarking, 'I know it's hard but you're just gonna have to control yourself, Vince.'

They laughed together and Sonny dabbed the oil over his back, kneading it with the heel of her hand. The smell of menthol and herbal love filled the air. Vince flinched and grabbed hold of the bed sheets before the cold metal spoon could even touch his skin. He heard her smile from behind him, or, rather, on top of him.

'Sonny,' he pleaded, turning over his shoulder to look back at her. 'Be gentle, please.'

She laughed loudly as she started her work.

'Oh, what the *fuck*,' Vince groaned. He stared up at the black buttoned eyes of her toys, trying to find some consolation. '*Amituofo, amituofo, amituofo, amituofo.*'

Sonny scraped his back with the edge of the spoon in firm motions. She worked from his spine and scraped outwards as he squirmed beneath her. He was warmer than she could have imagined. The smell of menthol rose from his searing skin, mixed with his sweat and something unmistakably masculine. Sonny's breath hitched in her throat and she wondered if he felt the same nerves that she did. What would her parents suppose they were doing in her bedroom if they were to wake up in the middle of the night to his groaning?

'Will you please be fucking quiet?'

'Sorry.'

After no time at all, the streaks on his back turned deep red and purple.

'You *trúng gió* really bad,' Sonny said, twisting the cap back on the oil. 'But it's a good thing we got all the wind out of you.'

'Yeah, thanks.' He turned back to give her a grin and pulled his shirt over his head.

'Vince? What is that?'

'What?' he asked, swiping his hands over his shirt frantically to check for cockroaches.

'That!' Sonny cried, pulling up the hem of his shirt. 'When did you get that?'

'Oh, *that*!' he said in relief. He pulled the bottom of his shirt up higher so she could see the entirety of the anatomical artwork, which included his hard-earnt abdominal muscles. 'A while ago – I got it at Parra with the boys.'

'What does it say?' she asked, touching it as if to test whether or not tattoos smeared, finding any excuse to feel him.

'You ever played Street Fighter?' – Sonny nodded – 'You know Blanka? It's his victory quote. When he wins, he says, "Now you know the power of the wild!", or some shit like that.'

'Oh my god,' she cried, crumpling over herself and burying her face in the pillow. 'You know what? I'm just glad it wasn't an ancient Chinese proverb.'

When they finished laughing and Sonny finally lifted her head, she wiped away a tear stain on the pillow. 'So,' she said, drying her eyes, still giggling. 'I heard you're starting to work on the backyard.'

'Oh, your dad told you about that?'

She nodded. 'Are you gonna plant flowers like how your mum used to?'

'Yeah! I've been thinkin' where to get them.'

'Hmm . . . when we were little, we'd just creep into people's front yards and steal their flowers.'

'Hey, that's not a bad idea! Alright, let's go flower picking sometime then!'

'I think you're getting a bit ahead of yourself. You can't go anywhere like this,' she reprimanded, as if it were his fault for getting sick. She stared straight ahead at the wall in front of them.

Vince smiled to himself. He couldn't remember ever being so pleased to listen to someone's grumbling. He held Sonny's head and pulled her close, cradling her to his shoulder. To his surprise, she relented as though her spine was made of melting wax.

'I'll get better soon,' he said. Then, Vince touched his knuckles to Sonny's cheek and almost burnt himself. 'Careful, feels like you're getting a fever yourself.'

Before he could even think of leaning in, her elbow whacked him in the face. 'Get out!'

He could feel a bruise starting to form on his cheek, the colour of a kiss. Vince kept his promise – he recovered quickly after that day. He did as Sonny's father instructed and turned over the soil, put down the grass seeds and kept the garden with always enough water to sip. Now Emma was allowed to play outside, and even the sun took a little longer to set.

Chapter 17

Getting to Gold

Spring was on its way, and Vince had anticipated its arrival before anyone else. At the corner of every street, and in the expression of every face, you could find something to praise. Girls let their hair out and kept the sun in the corner of their eyes like a childhood drawing. Boys buffed their cars to catch the light, and when they smiled they looked, if you'll believe it, briefly at peace with the world.

The season took a little longer to reach Sonny. It tapped on her window and invited her to come out to play, but she ignored its calls. Vince had imagined this weather would be prime trampolining time. When he was outside edging the lawn or putting down fertiliser, he often glanced over the fence, expecting to see her leaping body. He was faced with languid air; her absence marked every inch of the world. He heard her mother's screams; even louder, he heard Sonny's silence. She was stuck in the pinball machine of her home.

Vince stewed, waited for nightfall and reached for the walkie-talkie when the lights went out in the house next door.

'Hey, Sonny. Things not going too good at home?'

He lay in bed, waiting for a reply, wondering if she were asleep.

'No,' Sonny said, finally. Vince felt himself freeze at the wobbliness of her voice in that single syllable. 'Not too good.'

'What happened?'

'I don't know,' she said, trying to steady her breath. 'I don't know why she gets like this. I just forgot to fold the *fucking* clothes.'

'My poor Baby Blue.' He couldn't remember having ever folded an article of clothing in his entire life.

'I cried so much that I got a headache. And I feel so dehydrated.'

He made no reply.

'Vince?'

Sonny counted the forty-two seconds that passed. Then his voice returned.

'Hey.'

'Hello? Where'd you go?'

'Open your door.'

'Huh?'

'Your door, Sonny. Open it.'

Sonny crawled to the end of the bed and reached for the doorknob. Just outside, right in the middle of the threshold, was a ceramic mug. Without thinking, her eyes tricked her into seeing kiss-curls of steam rising from the rim. Would the aroma of cocoa pull her in for a warm hug? Would two melting marshmallows make gooey eyes at her? She could already taste the slow, dark decadence and feel the whipped-cream moustache that was to dangle above her smile.

As she inched closer to the mug and peered inside, her eyes were splashed with a cold, chemical blue. There was a metal spoon inside, and the liquid was still swirling in the cup from the competence of Vince's stirring.

'Why'd you give me Powerade?' Sonny asked, cracking up. 'Is this your idea of comfort food?'

'No, just thought you might've cried so hard that you've got to replenish your electrolytes now.'

Her stomach grumbled at the unavailability of hot chocolate. Her heart grinned at the warmth of Vince's gesture. 'Thank you.'

'Don't worry about it. Just leave it outside when you're done and I'll get it in the morning.'

She thought of Vince filling the cup with tap water and mixing in a heaped spoon of electric-blue powder to leave at her door. The two-ingredient recipe was simple enough. But as she took a gulp, Sonny finally understood how strange it felt to have somebody care for you, simply because they wanted to.

She pressed her lips to the walkie-talkie. 'Can we just run away together?'

Vince laughed. He knew she used the word *together* in the most practical sense – he was the only person she knew with a car. He knew how fickle she was too; how she could only resent her loved ones for so long. Still, it wouldn't hurt to imagine.

'Where could we go?' he thought aloud.

Thursday evening. With the sunset gently melting, the boys sat to smoke in the backyard. They had been discussing Cabramatta's most recent casualty. Last week, a gang of young men had stormed into the function hall of a Year 10 formal and dragged a kid down the staircase. Four shots to the face. Execution style. They threw his body out of a plate-glass window and left him there for all to see. It sent a clear message: skimming drug money carries a death sentence. While the others talked about the laws that governed the lawless, the imaginary lines between territories, Vince could only think of the blood-stained blazer the boy would never live to return to his father's wardrobe. The wood of the wardrobe, the wood of the coffin.

A soul was in transit somewhere, yet his friends still sat and talked. Vince watched his knuckles rise from their resting place.

'Bro,' Vince groaned, 'what are we fuckin' doin', bro?'

The boys looked at him, watched his eyes.

'Every day, it's just the same old shit,' he said. Alex, Tim Tam and Danny anticipated his rant in amusement. 'You on the street corner, you two at the station' – he left just a few seconds of silence: it glared at them cruelly, like a too-clear mirror; then he cut the string – 'me standing outside like a fuckin' prostitute.'

They laughed together as a way of holding their breath, as though death was only a hiccup away.

'The Year 8s are gonna do a bomb threat on the Girls' School tomorrow,' said Tim Tam with a gentle tap of his cigarette. The grey fell like a feather.

'Where'd you hear that?' Danny asked, dropping his cigarette to the ground and crushing it under his heel. He reached for another.

'My little cousin,' Tim Tam replied. 'Apparently some kid's got a three-month anniversary with his girl and he wants to take her out.'

The boys all grinned condescendingly at the thought of these younger boys, unversed in the intrigues of romance, going to such lengths to do something so sloppy. But Vince only smiled at himself.

'What a dickhead,' Alex sneered. 'If you're gonna jig then just jump out the window, man.'

'Fine for him but the girl's got strict parents,' Tim Tam said. The boys looked at him, doubtful of how strict parents could possibly be in Cabramatta. 'Her dad's a *bác sĩ*, bro.' The answer was 'doctor-strict'.

'Ahhh,' the other boys chorused in understanding.

'It's only three months anyway,' Alex said. 'Take her to eat a pork roll, bro, that's not even worth an anniversary.'

'This is why you've never had a girl, Alex.'

'And this is why you're always a broke cunt.'

'Hey, what time's the kid gonna do it?' Vince asked.

'Early. Think he said before recess.'

Friday morning. Outside the Girls' School, Vince walked beside the fence running along the train tracks and thought about how close the sky felt. Sweetness scented the air. He looked through the chain-link fence and found them at once; milk white, getting to gold when the sunshine hit right, wild and scattered around the embankment. So these were the flowers that Sonny so adored, the ones she walked beside each day he'd been away and perhaps stopped by, as he did now, to admire. Vince rolled his trousers up and fitted his fingers through the spaces of rusted metal. Barbed wire pricked and stabbed. The fence wobbled under his weight, but he thought kindly of gravity anyway, for it was fear of falling that had taught him how to climb.

Friday morning. The Boys' School's Year 7s were going on a five-day camping trip. Sonny helped Oscar pack his toothbrush, clothes and medication. She made sure to prepare his favourite food – fairy bread – for his bus ride. Sonny spread butter against slices of white bread, sprinkled hundreds and thousands on them and cut them into triangles, just the way he liked it.

'Will you and *ba* be okay at home?' Oscar asked, guilty for leaving them to deal with his mother on their own.

265

'We'll be fine, silly,' she replied, ruffling his hair. 'I'll protect *ba*. You have to go and have fun for the both of us!'

She stood at the front gate of the Boys' School and waved from the footpath as the dingy double-decker bus drove off. She knew it was only a matter of time before he'd realise, for the first time in his life, how wide the world stretched, how far away you could get from your family.

Recess. The jacaranda tree was concentrating on budding and the bubble gum flavoured Zooper Doopers were sticking to everyone's fingers. But if you didn't notice these things, you could tell the seasons were switching hands just by the conversations in the courtyard. The Lebanese girls sitting in the September sun were convincing each other that the colour of their eyes was honey, hazel, chestnut, chocolate, anything but brown, while the only blonde in the group was explaining that her eyes were only blue indoors, under halogen light.

'I've been feeling a little self-conscious recently,' said Najma, holding her right hand out and inspecting it.

'How come?' Sonny asked.

'I've been doing . . . *it* so much that I feel like my hand's gonna start bulking up.'

The girls laughed together at the idea of Najma with Sylvester Stallone's arm.

'So, yeah, I've been giving my left hand a go,' Najma said. 'I heard' – she stopped to laugh at herself – 'I heard it feels like a stranger if you use your other hand.'

'Why would you want it to feel like a *stranger*? Just a random creep off the street – that's who you fantasise about?'

'No, no, no!'

'I've tried that before,' Sonny said, reminiscing on the time Happy had bitten her and she had to have her sprightliest finger – the middle one – bandaged up for three weeks. 'It didn't feel like somebody else. I think, maybe doing *it* with your left hand uses a different part of your brain – the more creative side. Next thing you know you'll be jizzing watercolour paint.'

'We need a better word for *it* than "it".'

'A game of solitaire?'

'Fiddling with the female fiddle?'

The bell for the end of recess went, and its third chime was thundered over by the evacuation siren. What could it be this time? Had some bored student set something on fire? Could the sewerage system have exploded and flooded the toilets yet again? Was someone threatening to hold the students hostage in a siege? It seemed like every term needed at least one catastrophe to be complete. The girls were assembled in the courtyard, their names marked off the roll and told to make their way home. Sonny and Najma walked uneventfully towards the back gate, a calm which crumbled the moment they spotted Vince.

'Look, it's your guy!' Najma squealed.

Vincent Tran, leaning against a tree which was greater in height but not in beauty. Vincent Tran, beneath dappled shade with his hands stuffed in his pockets, so poised and perfect. Vincent Tran, dressed in his whitest singlet and finest microfibre pants, scuffing his shoes against the gravel beneath. This time, Sonny knew he was waiting for her. The world stood still with the certainty of this fact. Today was the 18th of September, the sky was blue, her best friend Najma had gotten so desperate for human intimacy that she'd tricked herself into believing her hand belonged to somebody else, and Vince was waiting for *her*.

She took a deep breath as she neared Vince – 'Three, two, one' – and stopped at the tree while Najma waved and continued walking. Vince had heard Sonny's whispered countdown and couldn't help chuckling under his breath.

'Hey, Vince.'

'Hey, Baby Blue.' They drank in the sight of one another. 'Nice weather today.'

'Yeah, it is.'

'Perfect for flower picking.'

'You couldn't afford a bouquet?'

It was twenty-seven degrees and the day felt the way a good mango tasted. Not just warm, mellow and slightly sticky; when you eat a mango, you taste all the light that ripened it and on a morning like this, you feel all the distance the sun travelled just to reach you.

'Oh god,' said Sonny, staring at the landscape in awe, already admitting defeat.

A bushwalking trail dipped and curled ahead of them. Lane Cove National Park. Sonny got out of the car first and stood before the entrance to do exaggerated stretches as Vince, she assumed, fumbled around in the car to look for his smokes. She emptied her backpack of its books and slung it over her shoulders, carrying only water and refreshments.

Passing a sign that said, 'Site of Fairyland Pleasure Grounds', she gave him a knowing look.

'*Pleasure* grounds?' she scoffed. 'Wow. Nice going, Vince. Real subtle.'

Though every tree was beginning to look just like every other tree, they still walked alongside the river in disbelief, sometimes blinking twice at the otherworldliness of this world. It was only eleven in the morning when Sonny became nervous about finding their way back.

'Are we lost?' she asked. 'Vince, we're in the middle of nowhere.'

He looked at her and grinned, his eyes reassuring.

'Or the middle of anywhere.'

'Okay, well, I think we should make our way back now. Before sunset,' Sonny joked. 'Don't use up our water supplies.'

Vince crouched down, took the pocket knife from his trousers and collected seeds. He slashed a few flowers at the stem. Sonny opened up her backpack and took out an empty container, which had been full of grapes in the morning.

'For your garden?' Sonny asked, crouching down and holding the box beside him.

'Yeah,' Vince replied. He smiled at her and dropped the flowers into the box. 'Thanks.'

'Your mum and Emma will love those.'

Sonny knew they both had to get home before dinner. And what about after dinner? What would their lives be like then? They couldn't lug the trees home or pour the river into a take-away container. There was nothing she could do to make the moment last as long as its memory.

Arriving at a place where dozens of red rowboats were lined up in the water, Vince reached into his pocket, handed money over to a man in the boat shed and grinned at Sonny. He unmoored the boat from the post himself and held onto it as she boarded.

They faced each other as they rowed up the river, but she did not look at him. He only saw the bridge of her nose, her eyebrow's abrupt ending, half of her melancholic smile. The happiness of this place was beginning to depress her.

'What's wrong?' Vince asked, watching her, thinking about how her blue-black hair resembled the crows back home. 'You look like you're thinking something.'

Sonny looked at him as though astonished that he was still here.

'I . . . I'm just thinking about how different things are at home,' she said. 'Now that I've felt this free, I don't know if I can ever go back.'

Some silence passed between them.

'God, you can even complain about having freedom. You're such a sook.'

She scowled at him vehemently.

'Maybe I am! Sorry I'm not as grown-up as you are. You've been everywhere, you've done everything. Do I like chopping people up? I don't know, I've never done it. Do I like snorting cocaine? I don't know, nobody's ever asked me if I wanted to try.'

'Hey, I've never done coke,' Vince protested.

'Oh, my sincerest apologies. I meant crystal meth.' They laughed. 'Sometimes, I think about what'll happen to me if I live like this for any longer. I feel like I'm losing myself.'

'We're sixteen, Sonny. We don't *got* much of ourselves to lose yet.'

This won a laugh from her, but when she looked away her eyes still seemed in a daze.

'I didn't bring you here just to show you how shit your life is.'

'I know. You needed help picking flowers.'

'No, Sonny, I brought you because,' he began, 'because I wanted you to see this. Like, really see it. The sun is out, and it's beautiful.' Vince turned his palms up, as if he could feel the light dripping on him, as if the atmosphere was made of muslin and there were holes in the handspun sky. 'The water's cool,' he said, reaching his long arm into the water and cupping it in his hand. He held it up to his face.

'Vince, you're not gonna drink that, are you?' Sonny said, at once smiling and wincing.

'The guy at the shed said it's fresh water,' he replied, lifting his hand to his lips and sipping it up.

'He just means it's not salty,' she cried. 'Vince, people probably pee in here.'

He scrunched his face up and flung the rest of the water back into the river. 'Okay, so that wasn't so fresh,' he said, and broke into laughter before continuing. 'But the air is fresh, and the sky is clear' – he looked at her, a look that pulled her in close and told her to put a bookmark beside his next words – 'and if we don't let ourselves forget any of it, we can come back whenever we want. Wherever we are.'

Vince sat his oars against the boat and looked at Sonny. He wanted to hold her but didn't know how. She was like a star of cotton that swirls around on windy days. Those things children catch, wish on and let go. No-one knows where they come from, or where they're going. But once you've got one in your palm, you can't think of a single thing left to long for.

He cleared his throat. Looked at the water for a moment, then back at her. 'You said you wanted to run away. Do you remember?'

'You're insane.'

'What?'

'We wouldn't survive a day out here. I mean, we don't know how to hunt for food, and I didn't bring my asthma puffer –'

He laughed in disbelief. The female mind was full of such forbidden fruit.

'Close your eyes.'

She looked at him distrustfully. Wondered what he could be thinking. Could the whole thing be just a prank?

'I'll close mine as well, look,' Vince said, shutting his eyes.

'Okay, they're closed.'

'Now, imagine you did run away. Maybe not today, maybe not tomorrow, maybe in ten or twenty years. Just forget for now about how you'd get there and focus on where you'd end up being. What's it look like?'

Sonny paused to breathe in. The air had an architectural beauty. 'Well, there's a house.'

'A house.'

'Yeah. Can it be near the beach?'

'Up to you, it's your imagination.'

'Okay, then it's right by the beach.'

'What else? You got a garden?'

'Of course!'

'What do you grow in it?'

'Fruits.'

'What kind of fruits?'

'I don't know – anything I have a craving for.'

'So, you just plant whatever you feel like eating that day?'

'Yep.'

'It takes like ten years for mangoes to grow. Longer for lychees.'

'Not in my imagination. You plant a seed at sun-up and it's ready for harvest in the afternoon.'

Vince let out a sigh. 'Fine, what else?'

'I've got my very own library, with a fireplace and a rocking chair.'

'Didn't know you were planning on being a grandma so soon.'

'Are you gonna let me finish?' said Sonny.

'Sorry.'

'Hmm ... there are huge windows that let in lots of sun. There's always something cooking on the stove and you can smell it wherever you are in the house. Oh, and a cardboard cubby house – like the ones we used to make – that I can crawl in to take naps throughout the day, whenever I feel like it.'

'What colour are the walls?'

'I'm still deciding.'

'What's the weather like?'

'Always warm.'

'Am I there?' Vince asked suddenly. He couldn't help but chuckle at her blushing silence. 'It doesn't matter if you say no – future me's already found the beachfront house with fruits growing suspiciously fast in the garden. I knock on the door but nobody answers – it looks like they're taking a nap – so I break in through the window . . .'

'Did you conduct a whole thought experiment just so you could rob my hypothetical house?'

'Close,' Vince said, laughing. 'I wanted to see what the future looked like for you.'

'Why?'

'Because as long as I can imagine it, I can meet you there. And if I can do that, then it's not just a place in our heads no more. It's . . . a promise.'

They opened their eyes, and it was as though they had woken up from the same dream, had all this time been sleepwalking towards the same morning. Vince reached into his pocket and pulled out the flowers from the embankment. Their petals were more than a little bruised, but this only made their sweetness melt more easily into the midday air. Sonny looked at the tiny grazes on his arms and instantly understood.

Vince broke a flower from the stem, twisted it between his fingers and placed it behind her ear. Like the bee does to the bloom, she gave him back to himself in a form that was easier to love.

*

At around four in the afternoon, Sonny and Vince arrived at their homes. They held the doorknobs reluctantly.

'Go in,' he urged with a smile.

She pushed the door open. Peered inside. Stepped back out and closed it behind her. With her hand still clutching the doorknob, she let out a sigh. 'When will the future come?'

She hadn't thought that Vince had heard her. But he must have been reading her lips. 'In a minute,' he said.

They laughed and let themselves in, then waited for the hours to pass until bedtime, until they could use the walkie-talkie. That night, Sonny claimed it had happened on the rowboat, when she opened her eyes and saw him sitting there. He argued that he knew even earlier, in the car on the way there, when she started singing along, out of tune, to an already dreadful 98 Degrees song, and he discovered that he didn't so much mind. In the end, Sonny and Vince decided it must have been while they were walking together in the middle of anywhere. How long had love been looking for them until they found each other?

'Before you, there was no-one.'

'No-one?' Vince asked, unconvinced.

'No-one! Well, I had a thing for my Chemistry teacher for a while, but he doesn't count. I even caught myself staring at manly-looking girls in class a few times.'

They had served her well but now she had to part with the butch teachers of the sport staffroom, the girls on the rugby team and Felix, the pixie-haired punk rocker.

'What?'

'It's over now. I can stop reassigning people's genders. And plotting to give all the girls in my school sex changes.'

His laughter almost broke the speaker.

'If I didn't have you, some girl would've probably been knocked out and woken up in a room with a cow penis attached by now.'

Chapter 18

The Wedding Portrait

The cuttings from Lane Cove were yet to sprout. Vince potted the freesias from the embankment and lined them against the windowsill, alive and well. When he began work in his backyard, he had to lock Emma inside to keep her from rolling around in the manure. She stood bow-legged behind the glass door in her baby walker, longing to know the taste of stems and petals.

Sonny would keep an eye on Vince from her trampoline, on his tattoo and his teasingly sweat-soaked singlet. When he kneeled down to water a bare root rose he'd set outside his mother's bedroom window, she wondered if the moth that was hovering over his shoulder might be a butterfly in plain clothes.

Oscar arrived home from camp on Wednesday afternoon. On the dinner table, he only gave one-word answers to his mother's questions about his trip. But he was not as sullen, or startled, as he was before he'd gone. He seemed sure of himself. It made

Sonny think of the first time she'd laid eyes on her little brother. He was so small, and he was born with a scowl, with his eyes tightly closed, his fingers clenching and unclenching, trying to determine whether he'd like to live in this world, as if he had a choice. And now, here he was, standing before her, thin but not quite malnourished, soon to be taller than her and taller than their father. Already beginning to have secrets of his own.

He only trusted his sister. When Sonny tucked him into bed that night, he told her all about the crackle of campfire, the wild games of Truth or Dare, the smell of eucalyptus leaves all around.

'Did you ever cry yourself to sleep?' she teased.

'Only the first night. Because I missed you.'

'Why not the second?'

'Because no-one forced me to drink any milk.'

Sonny felt as though she'd never really looked at him before. It struck her that she'd spent all her life trying to pry him open so she could protect all the parts inside, and only now was she beginning to see him in one piece. She couldn't help thinking about the rest of their lives, solitary and yet side by side, and when it would all begin. Sonny went to bed that night wondering about the day their mother would wake up to neither of them in the house. No matter how she dreaded it, she couldn't help but to dream of it.

One day, the afternoon light will leak into the bedroom, softened by the misted windows, and her mother will sleep in. She will not worry about preparing dinner, or mopping the house, or hanging the laundry. She will stay with her eyes closed, no longer willing to face morning on her own. When her back begins to ache from lying down for too long, she will know it is time to fold her sleep away. She will rise from the mess of bed linen and press the sheets flat with her palms, wishing wrinkles could be smoothed over as easily as creases in cotton. Outside the bedroom, she will find herself in the hallway mirror, ambushed by her own reflection. She has not plucked her grey hairs in a while now, and she is worried about the skin above her eyes beginning to droop.

She will, for the first time, know what it is like to wander around her house. She will peek into a room, hoping to find her children's bunk bed, muddled in all its glory, as though they'd woken up late for school and had no time to tidy. The beds will have been stripped bare. Hearing noises from outside, she will walk to the sliding door to the backyard and see the two of them through glass. They are on the trampoline, holding hands, their laughter a song from her own childhood. The clear sky will sketch an outline of their bodies. Make every strand of hair singular, every eyelash something to behold. She has never seen them this clearly. Just as she unlocks the door and calls out their names, the sun will flash, blind her for a moment, and turn the laughing children into silhouettes. She will squint, and they will be gone. It must have been a trick of the light.

The silence inside the house will not be reckoned with. She will stare at the family photos mounted onto the wall. Her children's faces have been etched into her memory with such force, the smallest details come to mind when she thinks of them – the dimple on both cheeks, the sunburnt upper lip, the brightness of eyes not hereditary. They were once her best kept secrets.

The wedding portrait will catch her off guard. The bride and groom don't see her; they are trapped in looks of love, a gooey and glutinous dessert. She will be careful with the image, take note of the delicate fringe which frames her face, her red and gold *áo dài*, her girlish smile. She holds a bouquet of bursting chrysanthemums and her husband holds her from behind, leaning his chin onto her shoulder, the vibrancy of his grin competing with that of the flowers. Their joy is so eager to evoke envy that it travels two decades into the future and glares up at her through the forgotten photograph. She will blink a lifetime away, a second time. She will look around, distrustfully, at the dream they have spent so long asleep in, at the framed photos of their accomplished children, his garden glimmering through the window, her cupboards filled with never-used china, and wonder where the two of them can possibly go from here.

The tumble of the tyres as his car delivers him home will pull her from her thoughts. Her heartbeat will catch in her throat as she listens to the key turning. She will run to the door and pull it open as he pushes, feeling the latch that longs to be caught and held by its mechanical lover. There he is. This time, like the first, she will be afraid even to blink. The light can sometimes withdraw if it finds you with your eyes closed.

Chapter 19

Endings, Beginnings and Fruit Market Leavings

Summer comes once more, and with it four kilos of bruised strawberries. On a sleepy afternoon, Sonny's parents arrive home with a trunk full of discounted groceries and marked leavings from the fruit market. Her mother turns on the gas stove outside with a *tick* and the blue flames shoot up, only to be crushed by the bottom of a pot. Half a kilo of sugar is poured in and the strawberries begin to simmer. Sonny is left to watch over; she runs to stir the cooking jam every so often, divided by her time on the trampoline. As the potful of bruises syrups into sweetness, she skims the foam gathering on its surface to eat. Even the strawberries wax sentimental on her tongue.

Vince stands outside in his garden. The cuttings from Lane Cove never made it through. But all around him, the ones from the embankment hold their faces up to the sun, seeming to see more of the sky, to breathe in the air around them. He thinks about their earlier life, behind that barbed-wire fence, and how we call things weeds when they flower in places we don't care to look. Hearing the groaning of tired springs, Vince gazes over the fence to find Sonny leaping from her trampoline. The crow-black hair catches the light. There she goes, the only girl he knows who can waltz with thin air. He stares, and stares, and cannot stop staring.

To think that anything that ever happened in the history of all history has led to this. What an enormous thought, and yet true of every moment. He takes a breath and keeps it in, thinks of this hour on its own and holds it, not like a fugitive but like a fruit. He feels its tenderness. Suffers with it. Knows it has been waiting to be held just like this, for longer than anyone has been alive.

Every metamorphosis has its melancholy. Every born blossom already feels itself beginning to be forgotten. But ask the tree how it gets through summer, autumn, winter, spring, and it will tell you about the ending of everything.

Epilogue:

At the time of publication, the following page was intended to be left blank in remembrance of a young boy's lost poem. The article had been declared missing since 4.08 pm on April 9th, 1994, shortly after the end of Mrs Bennett's English class that Tuesday. You may be surprised to discover, however, that the once empty page is empty no longer. The poem has since reappeared. At first almost invisibly, like a few specks of pillow dust or travelling pollen. And then as fine traces of graphite, like someone was trying to write something honestly but didn't want to cause the paper any pain. Finally, there was ink. Pale, pale lavender melting into the sepia tint of a grape skin, then deeper, and darker, until a semi-sparkling red. The concentrate of all those colours is how these words appear now. Black jellied stains, as indelible as the blood of a berry.

In fact, the words were still nervously getting ready to exist at the moment you were turning over to this page, as if summoned by magic.

Maybe the magic was you. Because you remember it, even if you weren't there.

I Will by Vincent Tran

I will be dawn
   I will be day
   I will be dusk
I will be dark

I will live longer than any sunflower
   I will make the stars gaze
   I will be louder than thunder
I will be the action that learns to speak

I will not be still in life
   I will struggle with serenity
   I will be more than my impression
I will be the painting, not the painter

I will be my self-portrait
   I will not believe the light's distortions
   I will be what I should see
I will be made in my own image

Acknowledgements

Ancestors. (Unreleased) *Flavourful Food and Transgenerational Trauma*.

Baldwin, J. (1964). Why I Stopped Hating Shakespeare. In R. Kenan (Ed.), *The Cross of Redemption: Uncollected Writings* (pp. 65–69). New York: Pantheon Books.

Bernard, S. (2018) *Paper Cuts: A Memoir*. London: Penguin Random House.

Bolanca, L. (2017) May you embark on your own epic narrative. *The Journal of Friendship*, *21*(3), 291–301.

Carrington, D. (Forthcoming) *Pluck the Living Flower*.

Chow, S. (Producer) & Chow, S. (Director). (1996). *The God of Cookery* [Motion Picture]. Hong Kong: The Star Overseas Ltd.

Curnow, M. (2019) *How to Stay Clear-Eyed in a World Out for Your Corneas*. Sydney: Penguin Random House.

Ellington, D. (1935). In a Sentimental Mood. On *Duke Ellington & John Coltrane*. Santa Monica, California: Impulse! Records.

Fante, J. (1999). *Wait Until Spring, Bandini*. Edinburgh: Rebel Inc.

Forster, E. M. (1971). *Maurice*. London: E. Arnold.

Gilbert, C. (2015) *Turning Into Dwelling: Poems*. Minneapolis: Graywolf Press.

Hafda, B. (2017*) Where all this rain came from*. Sydney: Story Factory.

Hodges, M. [milesXmiles]. (1 April, 2016). shoutout to Spring for being such a f*cking tease. [Tweet]. Retrieved from https://twitter.com/milesXmiles/status/715534882978529280

Keenan, C. (2017) *Lunch Hour Enlightenment*. Sydney: Story Factory.

Lyssa, A. (2017) *There's risk of the flow of the sentence feeling necessarily sticky because of the use of two adjacent clauses, both describing the 'trees' – one clause starting with 'that' and the other with 'which'. If you'd like to on Sunday we could talk about how you might change the syntax.* (pp. 32–34). Sydney: The Goodness of Her Heart Press.

Mangan, P. (2019) Now STEP AWAY from the page proofs! No more changes! *On the Virtue of Patience, of Which Patrick Has a Benedictine Amount. 14*(1), 32–90.

Oldfield, B. (2019) *The Nature of the Beast.* Sydney: Zeitgeist.

Pessoa, F., & Costa, M. J. (2010). *The Book of Disquiet.* London: Profile Books.

Pham, K. (1994) *The Best Sister in the World: An Autobiography.* Saigon: Can I Say Something? Press.

Pham, S. (2015) The Art of Telling Vietnamese Refugee Stories. *Refugee Transitions. 1*(30), 12–17.

Short, R. (2017) *Just FYI – lay is the past tense of lie.* Sydney: Story Factory.

Turner, A. (2011). Stuck on the Puzzle. On *Submarine* [MP3 file]. London: Domino Records.

Vo, A. K. (Photographer). (1970, 15 September). *Mobile Military Medical Clinic 9/1970* [digital image]. Retrieved from https://san-art.org/producer/vo-an-khanh/

Walcott, D. (1990) *Omeros.* New York: Farrar, Straus and Giroux.

Wittgenstein, L. (1922). *Tractatus Logico-Philosophicus.* London: Routledge & Kegan Paul.

Vivian Pham is a fiction writer, closet poet, amateur screenwriter, university student and hopeful dropout if any of the aforementioned ventures take flight. Her father was a boat refugee, and she grew up writing stories because she knew there was one stuck inside of him.

Her other literary influences include James Baldwin, Monty Python and early '90s Hong Kong cinema. She is currently completing a Bachelor of Arts with a major in Philosophy, but she will not be able to tell you the meaning of life until the relevant unit learning outcome is achieved in Semester 2.

When Vivian is not writing or trying to do a handstand, she is reading and replying to emails. You can write to her at longliveviv@outlook.com. (Please do – I hear writing can be quite a lonely profession.)